KT-211-740

SCORPIONS' NEST

KNOWSLEY LIBRARY SERVICE	
270950716	
Bertrams	01637720
CRI	
Hᴜ	10 - 1 . 13

A Selection of Recent Titles by M. J. Trow

The Inspector Lestrade Series

LESTRADE AND THE SAWDUST RING
LESTRADE AND THE MIRROR OF MURDER
LESTRADE AND THE KISS OF HORUS
LESTRADE AND THE DEVIL'S OWN

The Peter Maxwell Series

MAXWELL'S CHAIN
MAXWELL'S REVENGE
MAXWELL'S RETIREMENT
MAXWELL'S ISLAND

The Kit Marlowe Series

DARK ENTRY *
SILENT COURT *
WITCH HAMMER *
SCORPIONS' NEST *

* available from Severn House

SCORPIONS' NEST

M. J. Trow

CRÈME de la CRIME

This first world edition published 2013
in Great Britain and the USA by
Crème de la Crime, an imprint of
SEVERN HOUSE PUBLISHERS LTD of
19 Cedar Road, Sutton, Surrey, England, SM2 5DA.

Copyright © 2012 by M. J. Trow and Maryanne Coleman

All rights reserved.
The moral right of the author has been asserted.

British Library Cataloguing in Publication Data

Trow, M. J.
  Scorpions' nest.
  1. Marlowe, Christopher, 1564-1593–Fiction.
  2. Walsingham, Francis, Sir, 1530?-1590–Fiction.
  3. English College (Douai, France)–Fiction. 4. Great
  Britain–History–Elizabeth, 1558-1603–Fiction.
  5. Detective and mystery stories.
  I. Title
  823.9'2-dc23

ISBN-13: 978-1-78029-039-3 (cased)

Except where actual historical events and characters are being
described for the storyline of this novel, all situations in this
publication are fictitious and any resemblance to living persons
is purely coincidental.

All Severn House titles are printed on acid-free paper.

Severn House Publishers support the Forest Stewardship Council [FSC], the
leading international forest certification organisation. All our titles that are printed
on Greenpeace-approved FSC-certified paper carry the FSC logo.

Typeset by Palimpsest Book Production Ltd.,
Falkirk, Stirlingshire, Scotland.
Printed and bound in Great Britain by
MPG Books Ltd., Bodmin, Cornwall.

ONE

Dark is never totally dark. Even in the deepest cave the eyes staring into the blackness begin to see sparks and flashes which are not in front of the eyes but behind, inside the brain itself. In a room, thick curtains over the window notwithstanding, there is light enough to see by, if a man waits for long enough so that his eyes accustom themselves to the velvet dark. Shades of black are possible, as every artist knows, and it was by the shades of black that Kit Marlowe knew that someone had come into his room. He waited quietly, breathing shallowly through his mouth, trying to quieten even the beat of his heart. Kit Marlowe was a good listener.

The shape, black on black, edged round the room, laying gentle fingers on the edges of the furniture. Once, it stubbed its toe against a pile of books and Marlowe heard the indrawn breath as whoever was there waited to see if they fell and woke the dead. Marlowe shuffled in his sheets and made little drinking noises before settling back down to silence. It wouldn't do to lie too still; all sleepers made some kind of sound. After a pause that seemed to last an hour, the black shape moved again and this time reached the table, positioned in front of the window, to get the last of the light each evening and so save candle wax.

Marlowe lay back on his pillows, smiling in the darkness. He started to count slowly to himself. He didn't expect to get into double figures. 'One,' he breathed as the figure quietly lifted the lid of the ornate box on the table.

'Two.' There was a louder breath from the figure by the window. If an exhaled breath could be a question, then this was one.

'Three.' Marlowe could have spoken the word aloud, because the scream from near the window would have drowned him out. And if not the scream, then the snap of iron jaws closing just seconds before the scream would have been almost loud enough.

The dark figure ran the few steps to the door, but seemed to be crouching over as he ran, as a man might if he were cradling one hand in another as the pain shot up his arm like white hot lightning. Marlowe waited in the darkness for another moment, until he heard the door at the bottom of his staircase slam, reverberating on its hinges. Then he climbed from his bed and crossed to the window, pulling back the curtain. He peered down into the quadrangle just in time to see a figure disappear into a door opposite, making for the street. Smiling, he let the curtain fall and felt with practised fingers for the tinderbox on his table. Striking a spark, he lit a stub of candle and held it up, near his face. Then, he lifted the lid of the box.

In the flickering light of the candle, he looked down on what at first sight looked like two small hands, made of metal, folded in prayer. The middle fingers gleamed wetly, as though painted red. A nice little piece of machinery, part of the armoury of Nicholas Faunt and his kind, the men who listened at keyholes. It had been impressed upon Marlowe most firmly that this had not been tested in the field yet, that no one knew quite what damage it might be able to inflict on prying fingers. They should be pleased that he could now fill in this gap in their knowledge. When he next saw Robin Greene in the cloisters, the market or the Buttery, he could ask him what it felt like. He looked a little closer. No actual fingers, sadly, but plenty of blood. He checked the untouched papers. All was well. Perhaps the plagiarizing fool would learn his lesson this time and leave Marlowe's plays alone.

With a tight smile, he went back to his bed and slid between the sheets. Blowing his candle out, he turned over and was immediately dead to the world.

Dark is never totally dark. And the dark in Nicholas Faunt's bedchamber was less dark than it seemed, with small and cunning slits in the curtains letting through the faint grey of predawn to bounce off concealed mirrors to light a cranny here, a nook there. Faunt had wrapped himself in a fur, quieter in movement than leather, and had propped himself up against the bed head to wait. The night had been long and he had nearly nodded off a couple of times, but the holly leaf tied under his chin had given him its non-too-gentle warning each time and now the worst was past; the dawn was almost here. He was getting a little testy, though;

when he had settled down to watch and wait, he had not expected to be watching and waiting quite this long.

Suddenly, he pricked up his ears. The topmost stair was famous throughout the house as having a squeak to wake the dead, so all the housemaids knew to avoid it early in the morning. They didn't know that the third board along the gallery from the topmost stair was rigged to ring a tiny bell on Faunt's bedstead; they just thought it was a marvel that the master was always sitting up smiling, waiting for them to bring in the beer and heel of fresh-baked manchet bread with which he began his day. He had the bell in his hand now, silencing its tongue, but he felt the vibration and stiffened. Someone was creeping very, very slowly towards the door of his room. But how prepared were they for all of his little tricks?

He smiled wryly as he sensed rather than heard that the intruder had avoided the tiny caltraps he had scattered outside his door and made a mental note to sweep them up before dawn. They already had two servants laid up with pedal injuries and three would test housekeeping beyond endurance. He took in a deep breath and held it as the door edged open, just a tiny amount. He nodded when he realized that the heavy weight propped over the door – designed to alert rather than maim, though there was nothing wrong with maiming in Faunt's view – was lifted and removed by skilful fingers.

Then, suddenly, all Hell broke loose and he reached across and uncovered the window of the dark lantern beside the bed. In its flare, he saw a man pinned to the ground by a heavy net, anchored at two corners by boxes, attached to the floor by staples and to each other by a loosened tripwire, their lids open, and at the others by crossbow bolts, still quivering with the impact.

With the light, the man stopped struggling and turned beseeching eyes up to meet Faunt's. 'This is none too comfort-able, Nicholas,' he said. 'And how that left-hand bolt missed my head I'll never know. It parted my hair.'

Faunt was sitting at the end of the bed, feet folded in front of him, knees raised. He looked like a homicidal schoolboy. He gave a low chuckle. 'Thomas, Thomas, Thomas,' he said, shaking his head. 'If you were really burgling my house, I wouldn't care overmuch whether it took your head from your shoulders.'

The man under the net made a strangled noise of dissent and wriggled his shoulders. 'Let me out,' he said, then louder, 'let me out. You're scaring me, Nicholas. Let me out!'

Faunt jumped down and reached into first one box, then the other, releasing the net, then folded it back to release the struggling man. 'Stay still,' he enjoined him. 'You're all caught up somewhere. It's your dagger. Wait . . .' Faunt was vaguely surprised he was carrying one. He unravelled the net and the man was free.

Thomas Phelippes was not at all amused. He was not a man of action, as any casual observer could tell. He was slightly built and had something of a scholar's stoop. He wore his thirty-odd years lightly, but he was pale and didn't look like a man who saw much of the sun. He was a thinker, not a doer and Faunt's latest amusement, to get Phelippes to try out his newest ideas, did not strike him as at all funny.

'This won't do, Nicholas,' he said, standing up and tweaking his doublet back into some kind of comfort. 'I'm far too old for your little games.' He felt all rucked up in the unmentionables, but decided that adjustment could wait. 'Those caltraps could have maimed me.'

'Ah –' Faunt tapped Phelippes on the shoulder with an admonitory finger – 'you were too clever for me there, Thomas.' Faunt could patronize for England and win against all comers.

'And the weight over the door?'

'Again, what can I say? You mastered me once again.'

Phelippes harrumphed and metaphorically ruffled his feathers. He turned to the tangled mess behind him, the ruined floor, the place where his blood and brains might well have been. 'I doubt this will come in too useful, though,' he said. 'Too much damage, too easy to spot.'

'You didn't spot it, though, did you, Master Phelippes, eh? And you knew it was there.'

'In fairness, Nicholas, no, I did not. Since you had moved it full three cloth yards, I had no idea it was there.'

Faunt chuckled. 'It had to be a proper test, Thomas, or what would be the point? You did well, though I think you may be right; this is not an engine which will see much use in the normal way of things. Well done, though, well done.' He went over to the window and pulled back a draped curtain to let in the grey light of dawn. 'How late it is getting. I must clear the caltraps, before the kitchen sends up food to break my fast.'

As he spoke, the tiny bell rang and before the clapper was still, the scream of Faunt's third maimed maidservant echoed in from the gallery.

'Damn.'

Dark is not always dark. The two sets of breath from the bed made the only sound, but the faint light of the half moon and the stars came in through the uncurtained window and picked out the rise and fall of two breasts in perfect harmony. It gleamed on the pale ovals of four nails of fingers lightly curled into a palm, it glinted off two lips, damp with the pearl of sleep. It sprang from the tip of the upraised blade, it splintered in the spray of gushing blood. It shone into the mouth opened, screaming. It lit the buckles on the booted foot as it kicked back the door in its flight.

Dark is not always dark.

TWO

'Good morning, Betsy.' Kit Marlowe was in merry mood as he bounced up the last few steps into the Buttery at St John's College, ducking under the archway with its rose and portcullis, there just to remind everyone who was patron of the place these days. 'A fine morning, so late in the summer. It's lease has, after all, too short a date, wouldn't you say?'

Betsy was in a quandary. Kit Marlowe was the darling of every maid from scullery upwards throughout all the colleges in Cambridge, but their masters were not always so taken with his charms. Someone, a penny-pinching Bursar, had worked out how much he cost the university, breaking his fast and taking his luncheons and suppers wherever he thought fit and, by some quirk of possibly inaccurate mathematics, had brought forth a figure similar to the complete upkeep of the menagerie at the Tower. It was suggested gently by some kinder souls that surely even the mercurial Master Marlowe didn't eat as much as even one very small lion, but the damage was done. He was to be forbidden entry to any refectory but his own and, even there, he was to pay his reckoning at the end of every week, rather than never.

'Oh, Master Marlowe . . .' Betsy began, thinking hard but none too fast. 'You can't go in there, because . . .'

He stood, mellow sunlight filled with golden dust motes sparkling around the aureole of his hair. 'Because?' He cocked an eyebrow.

Betsy, caught on her back foot, could think of nothing. She shrugged. 'Fresh eggs today, Master Marlowe,' she said. 'Fresh sent in from Cherry Hinton. You'll get one if you're quick.'

Marlowe leant out of his sunbeam to put a friendly arm around the girl's shoulders. 'You look after me so well, Betsy,' he said, smiling. 'This is my very favourite place to eat in the whole university.' He paused, taking in the bright reds and blues of the stained glass and the fierce-looking Masters of generations gone by who frowned at him from their gilded frames. 'Possibly, in the whole world.'

Betsy grimaced, but happily and pushed him off. 'Go on with you, Master Marlowe,' she said, a laugh in her voice. 'But don't say I let you pass. I could lose my position if they find it was me.'

'My lips are sealed,' he said and turned to the door. 'Oh, one thing, though. Is Master Greene here yet?'

'I haven't seen him,' Betsy said. 'And glad not to have. Nasty, posturing thing he is.'

'He is, he is, indeed he is,' carolled Marlowe, swinging round the doorpost and into the hall. The fun was still to come, then.

Sir Francis Walsingham stood in the shadows of the awning that had been strung across the frontage of the merchant's house on the edge of St Giles' Fields. This ought to have been a great day for him but the boil on his neck was infected and bleeding and his whole body ached. The sun was shining on the iron helmets of Her Majesty's guard and the bells of the city were crying out their joy. Her Majesty's enemies would meet their God today. He had delivered the great Queen – not for the first time – and her people had turned out in their thousands to see the murdering bastards turned off.

All the way from Tower Hill they had been spat at and kicked as they struggled on their hurdles, the ropes that lashed them to the timbers cutting into their wrists and ankles. Each of the seven bore the marks of the Rackmaster. Chideock Tichborne was barely conscious; Henry Dunne couldn't see out of his right eye; every bone in the hand of the chameleon-like James Ballard was broken. Now they had reached the open space of St Giles, they were hauled up from the ground and their wrists tied behind their backs. The crowd surged forward, threatening to break the cordon of steel that the Lord Mayor had set up.

The bells were still pealing – Paul's, St Giles', St Magnus', St Mary's – drowning out the charges of conspiracy levelled against each of them by the Lieutenant of the Tower. The crowd had nothing but contempt for all of them, but there was only one they had come to see turned off. Anthony Babington took his place on the high scaffold first. The Rackmaster had knocked out three of his teeth and his once-handsome face was a mask of blood. The Queen for whom he was about to die had captivated him as a child when he had seen her walking with the Earl of Shrewsbury, a prisoner even then. He had not even known she was a queen, let alone the queen of a whole country, the Queen of Scots. She was a gentle-faced little woman, dressed in black, with crisp white at her throat. She had held out her little dog for him to stroke, had smiled her quiet smile and he had given his heart to her, in that childish, romantic way that some men have. Now he would give his head.

But giving his head was a euphemism Francis Walsingham had engineered. He watched from his secret corner, almost on a level with the scaffold as the executioner showed Babington the tools of his dubious trade, gleaming wickedly on a blanket of velvet. Sam Bull was hardly the most elegant gentleman on Walsingham's pay roll but he knew his job. His thick neck was covered in strips of black leather that hung from the hideous mask that covered his face. Both Bull and his master knew that the crowd's mood could turn in these moments on a groat and many was the common hangman chased out of town by an ungrateful mob bent on tearing him apart. To that end, the mask. To that end, the pay – half now, half when the job was done.

Babington scorned the services of the Puritan priest at his elbow. He would have made a speech to the crowd but, at a signal from Walsingham, the drums and tabors struck up and the man's last words were drowned out. Bull squinted across to the balcony where he knew Walsingham stood. He saw the huge ruff, the black robes, the cold, glittering eyes and he saw the man nod. The hangman grabbed Babington's hair and hauled him backwards, looping the hemp noose over his head in seconds and hauling on the rope.

Anthony Babington, gentleman, somebody's husband, some- body's son and graduate of Lincoln's Inn, was given a bird's eye view of the city as he twirled at the rope's end. As his eyes bulged and the veins stood out on his forehead, he saw the dead stone walls of the Tower that had been his recent home, the merchant ships riding at anchor on the Queen's wharves, the cluster of church steeples and the smoke rising from a thousand homes. As he twisted in a desperate attempt to take the appalling pain away from his throat and chest, he saw the ancient walls and the golden fields stretching away to the north, the harvest done. The sky was just darkening for him and his lungs were threatening to burst when Sam Bull cut the rope. Babington's feet hit the planks with a thud, followed by another as his body followed. The air rushed into his lungs as the hangman loosened the rope, screaming past his tortured throat in a sound audible across the crowd, a sound never to be forgotten by any man jack of them there that day. The crowd roared as he dragged the half-conscious conspirator across the scaffold floor and kicked his legs apart.

'Now!' he grunted to the four men, masked like him, standing at the gallows stairs. The drums thundered and the tabors rattled as each man knelt beside Babington, each taking hold of a fist or a foot nearest to where he knelt.

Bull looked across at Walsingham again. And again the Secretary nodded. The billhook rustled as it left the velvet and then it was slicing through the shirt and skin of Anthony Babington, biting deep into his sternum and into the soft and vital tissue below. Blood sprayed the hangman's hands and arms and dripped through the boards of the scaffold into the dark recess below. Soldiers stood here with halberds at the level, their spikes pointing outward at the crowd. Walsingham didn't want Anthony Babington to die a martyr or any misguided soul waiting below to catch the man's blood in a phial and add it to the superstitious claptrap of the Roman church.

By the time Babington's body had stopped twitching, the crowd had fallen silent. So had the drums and tabors. Only the wild bells still rang out, music to Walsingham's ears.

'One down, six to go,' a voice murmured in the ear of the Secretary.

Walsingham turned as best he could, given the pain he was in. He knew the voice and understood the intrusion. 'Not exactly, Nicholas,' he said.

Nicholas Faunt raised an eyebrow. He had wondered for a while whether he'd be able to get through the rank-smelling multitude in time to witness the passing of this present danger. But he was in time, especially as it was Sam Bull's next customer, the slippery Father Ballard, he'd come to see dispatched. Babington was a simplistic fool, a knight-errant born out of time.

Men had followed him because of his rank not because of his brain. Men like Ballard were a different proposition. If he hadn't known better, Faunt would have thought that Ballard served the Devil. He saw the disquiet on his master's face and took the slip of paper from his hand.

'What do you read there?' Walsingham asked.

Faunt looked at the document. 'Today's bill of entertainment,' he said. 'Babington, Ballard, Tichborne . . .' He was reading the list of the damned.

'Turn over,' Walsingham told him as he watched the four men throw Babington's ripped and mutilated body into a coffin, prior to its being quartered.

'Tomorrow's delights,' Faunt said. 'Habington, Tilney, Jones . . . I don't see . . .'

Walsingham fished inside his doublet and pulled out another piece of paper. This was parchment, good-quality vellum and on it were a series of ciphers and squiggles so small he could barely make them out in the shade of the awning.

'This is Phelippes' nonsense,' Faunt said, dismissing it. 'You know I can't make head nor tail of it, Sir Francis.'

Walsingham took it back from him. 'That's why we've got Phelippes. You have fourteen names on your paper,' he said, 'conspirators against Her Majesty, men guilty of treason to the crown. One of them has died today – six will follow later. Tomorrow, the next seven will join them. And we'll all sleep easier in our beds by cock-shut time.'

'Well, then . . .'

Walsingham turned to his man. 'Except we won't, Nicholas. We won't. This is one letter I didn't get Phelippes to forge.' He slipped the parchment away again. 'It's one we intercepted from the Queen of Scots and it mentions one name not on that list of yours.' He looked his man fully in the face, the eyes cold, the skin grey and drawn. 'Matthew Baxter, The fifteenth man. One of the fish has wriggled through the net.'

Faunt nodded grimly. 'I see,' he said. 'So you want me to . . .'

Walsingham turned back to the entertainment as Father James Ballard stood on the gallows with a rope around his neck and a prayer on his lips and the crowd was baying once again. 'I want you to find Kit Marlowe,' he said.

'Marlowe?' Faunt looked at the man he had served faithfully for more years than he cared to remember.

'You have someone else in mind?' Walsingham asked him.

'That depends what's involved.' Faunt scanned the baying crowd below, looking for any faces he knew.

Walsingham turned to face the projectioner, a man who might one day wear the chain of office that he himself wore. 'Nicholas,' he said softly, 'we are a conspirator short. I thought I made that clear.'

'Indeed, Sir Francis, but . . .'

'And where would a Catholic conspirator run, Nicholas, knowing the hounds of Hell were after him?'

'Anywhere out of England,' Faunt said. He knew as he said it that he had left the options rather wide. Walsingham was obviously looking for an answer smaller than the rest of the world.

'Oh, come, Master Faunt,' Walsingham tutted, smiling. 'I thought more highly of you. Where would a Catholic conspirator run who still wished to be of service to the Catholic cause? Where is the one place in the world where an English Papist can lose himself?'

Reality dawned on Faunt. 'The English College,' he said, a little too loudly perhaps and checked himself. 'The Rue de Venise.'

'The English College.' Walsingham nodded. 'Late of Douai, now in Rheims. A nest of scorpions devoted to the cause, the cradle of every Jesuit assassin we've found in this country these fifteen years.'

'But Marlowe?' Faunt came back at him. 'That fiasco with the Stadtholder . . .'

'William the Silent was a marked man, Nicholas, we both know that. He had death written all over him. Marlowe kept the man alive for months longer than I, for one, expected.'

Walsingham looked at Faunt, head cocked on one side, but carefully, to spare his neck. He could see his man was not convinced.

'And Marlowe is a new face on the road,' he continued. 'Dr Allen won't know him or what to make of him, and that gives Marlowe an edge . . . unless, of course, Nicholas, you'd care to go yourself?'

Nicholas Faunt had tangled with Dr William Allen, Master of the English College, before. He'd rather sup with the Devil. He favoured his paymaster with a small smile and a nod of acquiescence. 'Marlowe it is,' he said.

The noise of dozens of scholars and tutors breaking their fast had settled to a dull roar when Robert Greene slid into a seat at the end of one long table, worn smooth by the years. He held one hand protectively inside his jerkin and flinched if anyone came too near or made a sudden movement. He kept his eyes down on his plate and ate like an animal, nervously and urgently, afraid that at any moment a lion might leap out at it and grab it by the throat. A movement across the table made him glance up quickly, taking in the view from beneath his brow. It wasn't a lion, but it was the next best thing.

'Good morning, Robin,' Marlowe said with a bright smile. 'You're quiet this morning. Not feeling well?'

'I feel perfectly well, Dominus Marlowe, if you please.' A ghost of the old, confrontational Greene emerged from the shrinking shell. 'Why are you here? I understood you were to keep to your own college Buttery.' He paused for effect and then said loudly, 'That's Corpus Christi.'

Marlowe waved the suggestion off with a flourish of a hand. 'A serving suggestion merely, Robin. I'm here to see you, as a matter of fact, and I wasn't sure where else to find you. You are as slippery as an eel these days.' Greene didn't speak, but continued to peck away at his oatmeal. 'Busy writing, I expect,' Marlowe ventured. Greene shrugged, but with just one shoulder. 'Wonderful new play, I wouldn't be surprised.' Marlowe dipped his head to come into Greene's eyeline. 'I said, a new play, Robin? Is that why you are cradling your hand? Writer's palsy, perhaps?' He straightened up and looked around the room then cleared his throat. 'Is there a doctor in the house?' he called. 'Of medicine, that is. Dominus Greene has a painful hand here that needs attention.'

A few men rose to their feet, but uncertainly.

'He can pay a fee,' Marlowe added.

Ten more got up and there was a gentlemanly scuffle as they made their way to Greene's end of the table.

'I am quite well,' the erstwhile playwright snarled. 'Dominus

Marlowe will have his fun. Ha. Ha.' He glared at Marlowe, who smiled happily back.

'You clearly have a problem with that hand, Greene,' said the first fledgling doctor to reach him. 'Here. Let me see.' He grabbed Greene's elbow and pulled his hand from inside his jerkin. A crude bandage emerged like a genie from a bottle, blood soaking through the rough linen. 'Good God in Heaven, man,' the doctor exclaimed. 'This is no palsy. What have you done to yourself?'

Greene snatched his hand away from the man. 'I caught it in a door,' he said, tucking it away again. 'An accident.'

'Sharp edges you have on your doors, here,' Marlowe remarked. 'It pays to be careful in St John's College, I can see that.' He cocked his ear as a clock struck in the quad. 'Hark. Time I wasn't here. Aristotle awaits. Get well soon, Robin. I'm sure I will be seeing more of you, but perhaps if you wait for an invitation that would be best. I must be off to sharpen my door.'

The physician looked after him as he left. 'He's an odd one,' he said to Greene. 'Clever though. Have you read his Ovid?'

'Certainly not,' Greene snapped. 'And I am surprised you have, seeing that you are a student of medicine. I had always assumed such as you could not read.' And, pushing his plate savagely down the table, he strode out of the refectory.

Dr William Allen stood in the doorway high in the eaves of his home along the Rue de Venise. It was a Sunday and the bells of the cathedral were calling the faithful to prayer. But Allen would not be with them today. He crossed himself as he entered and waited until the shutters were thrown back and the windows opened. Sunlight fell sharp and unforgiving across the bed, showing the blood a dark crimson, pooling and still liquid on the floor.

The doctor was still shaking his head when he heard Gerald Skelton clearing his throat. It was always a sign the pompous idiot had a pronouncement to make and, normally, Allen didn't give him too much rein. This morning, however, was different.

'Well, Gerald?' Allen looked at the man. 'What do you make of it?'

'We need a physician, Master,' Skelton said. 'Canon law is my forte. I have no experience of . . . . this.'

'This' lay sprawled on the left side of the tester. It had once been Father Laurenticus, tutor in Greek at the University of Douai. Now it was a stiffened corpse with the head thrown back in a silent scream. Allen came as close as he had to and saw the nightshirt ripped and torn from half a dozen wounds across the chest and throat. The dead man's knuckles had locked around the coverlet and his sightless eyes stared at the crucifix high on the wall to the bed's head.

'No.' Allen shook his head. 'No physician. We both know that Father Laurenticus has met his Maker. I don't need a physician to tell us that.'

'They have ways, Master,' Skelton pointed out. 'Knowledge of the humours . . . Galen . . . I understand that there are more modern views.'

Allen bent over the body as far as his rigid old frame would allow. 'There is nothing modern about a dagger to the vitals, Gerald,' he said, softly. Then something, a flicker in the morning sun, caught his eye. Near the dead man, on the smooth, bloodless side of the bed, lay a ring. It was gold and carried an enamel device, small and exquisitely cut. Allen took it up and held it to the light where the gold gleamed like fire in his gaze. He reached down and took the cold hand of the dead man, wrenching it free from the covers and tried the ring on his smallest finger. It fitted perfectly.

Allen sighed and pocketed the trinket. 'That's why no physician,' he said. 'Whatever happened in this room, Father Laurenticus did not die alone. Or if he did, it was not long after someone had left him. Who found the body?'

'Er . . . a maidservant,' Skelton said, only now realizing what Allen meant. 'This is her floor.'

'Find her.' Allen turned away. 'Double whatever we pay her. Then put the fear of God into her, Bursar. If she breathes a word, Hell Fire – you know, pull out all the stops. I want her mute by Matins.'

Skelton nodded.

'And Gerald –' Allen turned back in the doorway – 'get this mess cleaned up. And do it yourself. As far as the College is concerned, Father Laurenticus died of apoplexy. Called by God.'

THREE

The carrack took him by the next tide out of Deptford, butting through the Black Deepes and out beyond the Essex marshes where curlews called in the mists of the morning. All day he faced the wind, his hair streaming, his cloak snapping like the shrouds behind and above. The little ship veered south in the Channel Roads, the gulls wheeling in its wake. As night fell they skirted the shallows by Ponthieu. The Master was an old hand and knew these winds and currents like he knew his Paternoster. France was the old enemy but France was now at war with itself and English ships came and went unhindered.

They rounded the sweep of the headland at the second dawn and sailed in under the battered old walls of Harfleur where King Harry of blessed memory had lopped the French lilies. The Seine lay dark and brooding as its banks narrowed and the fishing smacks bobbed at anchor by a thousand little jetties and moorings. By nightfall they had reached Rouen, journey's end, and he bade the Master farewell before setting foot on French soil. As he left the planking, he said goodbye to an old life. As he strode the quay, he began a new one.

Michael Johns was not feeling in a very chirpy mood. It was true that years of keeping his face set in a sober expression not really natural to it had made it rather difficult to tell how he was feeling, but it was not necessary to be too much of a scholar of the human condition to know that he was not happy. He stormed through Corpus Christi like an avenging angel, whipping the dust of early autumn into little eddies with his passing over the stones of the Court. He reached the door of the Master of the college and threw it open without his customary courteous tap. A man was sitting behind the desk, a slight but satisfied smile on his face. A manservant was standing by, swathed in an apron and holding a broom.

Johns met both men's gaze and then spoke to the servant. 'You. Get out.' He didn't raise his voice. It was just a remark.

With a doubtful look at the Master, the man bobbed slightly and
scurried from the room.

'Can I help you, Dominus Johns?' the Master said.

Johns looked at him for a long minute. He ignored the slur to
his status. How many times in the recent years past had he longed
for Dr Norgate to remember his name and those of just a few
scholars? Recently, if the old man could have remembered his
own name, it would have been a pleasure and a surprise. The
man sitting behind his desk might have all his faculties, but he
was Gabriel Harvey and that far outweighed any good points.

'Well? I am, as you can see, a busy man.'

Johns looked around the room. 'I can see you are. I am here
to . . .' He was staring into a corner, where various portraits
leaned against the wall. 'What's that?' He pointed. 'Over there.
What's that?'

Harvey didn't even bother to turn his head. 'Old portraits. I
bring in a new era, Johns. We don't want old faces reminding
us of the past, do we? This is the Year of Our Lord 1586. We
must move on.'

'Must we?' Johns said, pushing aside a wooden box and a
half-filled sack to get over to the pictures. He looked at the faces.
'William Norgate. Matthew Parker. And . . . I might have known
it. Christopher Marlowe.'

'Upstart popinjay,' Harvey said. 'How dare he have his portrait
painted? How dare Norgate hang it here?'

'It was painted for him by someone who loved him. The Master
hung it here because he liked the man's style. It reminded him
that we were all scholars once.' He narrowed his eyes at Harvey.
'Some better than others. It was a signal that anyone can aspire
to be anything they want.'

'What a very Christian outlook,' Harvey said, picking up his
quill, after he had quaffed his wine. 'But as I think I mentioned,
I am a busy man. Things have been allowed to slide. Have you
any idea how deep in debt the college is? As you go out, please
send my servant in, will you? He needs to take some things to
the bonfire. And don't you have some lecturing to do?'

'Surely you don't intend to burn the pictures?' Johns was
aghast.

'They make excellent kindling. I think it must be the oil in the paint, or perhaps the pitch in the varnish or whatever it is painters use. They go up in ten-foot flames with hardly a spark being applied.' He smiled at Johns. 'Pictures can be so inflammatory, can't they?'

Without a word, Johns picked up the portrait of Kit Marlowe and tucked it under one arm. He didn't look at the dark eyes flashing in oils, the forehead broad and bold, the hair flying, the velvet-and-silk doublet the university didn't allow any of its scholars to wear. And he didn't need to read the words on it again. He knew them by heart. *Quod me nutrit me destruit.* That which feeds me, destroys me. And Johns in one mood might have added 'Amen'. Then he slowly and deliberately upended the inkwell so that a thin stream of black poured onto the desk, the papers and Harvey's left hand.

The Master looked down at the wriggle of ink. '*Abdico,*' he read. 'παραιτομαι. *Rwy'n ymddiswyddo.*'

Johns gave a short, mirthless laugh. 'From your varied accents, I feel I perhaps must translate for you,' he said. 'I resign. I resign. I resign. Have it in any language you will.' He turned to leave and then stopped and spoke over his shoulder. 'Would you like me to tell your servant to bring some soap and hot water with him when he comes back in?'

He closed the door behind him sharply. As it closed, so Harvey's inkwell spun across the room, trailing the last of its contents, to crash against the wood. He had seen the devil in his chamber for one last time.

The river Vesle murmured in its banks as he crossed the little bridge. This was Rheims, the place of coronation of so many kings of France and the black bulk of the great Gothic cathedral loomed over the city now that night was falling. As the candles were lit in the high houses and the squatters' tents, knots of ragged children crowded around him, their hands outstretched for money or food, their trill voices babbling in the curious dialect of the Marne. One or two of them tried to touch his sword, his Colleyweston cloak, but a tap from his gloved hand or a flash from his dark eyes made them think again, to recoil until they felt a little braver.

He climbed the cobbled hill that wound below the old city

wall and saw in the flickering half-light the name he was looking for – the Rue de Venise. Instinctively he checked behind him and hauled his knapsack higher on his shoulder, releasing his sword arm as he vanished into the blackness, the dark that is never really dark. A cat scurried away from him, belly to the cobbles, tail trailing and a couple of drunks collided with him as he looked for the door he had come so far to find. They smelt of the cheap cider of Normandy and they bounced away from him with a mutter of oaths.

'I wouldn't go in there,' a soft voice said from the shadows. The dialect was heavy, but his French was up to it and he half turned at the wicket gate.

'Why ever not?' he asked.

A harlot stepped out into the half-light. It was difficult to tell her age under the hood she wore but there was no mistaking her calling. A thin chemise was tied at her breasts with a single bow, a bow that could be undone by a client in a second. She closed to him, taking in the long hair, the sensitive mouth, the smouldering eyes. 'Men die in there,' she told him.

He removed her fingers from the points of his doublet. 'Men die everywhere,' he told her with a smile. 'And that's not why I'm here.'

She looked at him, pouting, trying to weigh up the measure of this newcomer, the one who spoke awkward French with an accent she hadn't heard before. 'Know why I'm here?' she challenged him.

He smiled again. 'Of course,' he said, not taking his eyes off her as he rapped with his gloved fist on the studded door at his back. He cocked his head to listen to the bells clanging beyond the building's facade. 'That's Vespers,' he said. 'You're a lay sister come to pay your devotions.'

For a moment she just stared at him, then she threw back her head and shrieked with laughter. She rested her hands on her hips and let him see her breasts wobble. 'Yes,' she said, 'I'm a lay sister, all right. And talking of paying . . .'

The wicket in the great door squealed open and a little priest stood there, a skullcap on his head and a lantern in his hand. He took one look at the girl and scowled. 'Be off with you, Jezebel!' he snapped. 'Why don't you leave clean-living men alone?' She flicked her thumb off her front teeth at him, turned smartly and threw her cloak up to wave her naked backside at him. The little priest crossed himself and ushered the newcomer inside, slamming and bolting the wicket as they heard a string of blasphemies echoing along the Rue de Venise.

In the quiet of the courtyard where torches were already flickering against ancient stones, the priest looked up at the stranger. 'You *are* a clean-living man?' he checked.

'They don't come any cleaner,' the newcomer said. 'This *is* the English College?'

'It is.' The old man lapsed into English, clearly not his native tongue, but he sensed the traveller would welcome it. 'I am Brother Tobias. You are . . .?'

'Robert Greene,' the young man told him. 'From Cambridge. And I have need of a priest.'

Brother Tobias squinted in the lantern light. There was something about this man that unnerved him. He was armed to the teeth for one thing, with sword and dagger and dressed like the roisterers of the town Tobias would usually cross the street to avoid. There was a coldness about him, a chill that was beyond the gentle breeze of the Michaelmas night. If this man needed a priest, he would rather not be the priest in question. There were bigger fish in the collegiate pond and he led Greene across the moonlit quadrangle in search of one.

The chapel they entered was glittering with the candles of the Mass. At every pew, in every niche, monks and lay brethren knelt in silent prayer, shoulder to shoulder with scholars. One or two of the sleeve badges the Englishman recognized. Here was a Flanders guildsman, there a Dutch apothecary and, facing their kneeling forms and surveying them all with a stern eye, sat a man whose face he knew, a man he had travelled long to see.

He waited with Father Tobias until the Vespers prayers were over, then lolled against a wall rich with tapestries until the Master of the College came his way.

'Master,' Tobias whispered to him. 'This is Robert Greene, of the University of Cambridge.' He spoke Latin, but the scholar followed every word.

'Dominus Greene.' The Master nodded. 'We are honoured. I am . . .'

'I know who you are,' the newcomer interrupted. 'You are Dr William Allen, Regius Professor of Divinity at the University of Douai and Master of the English College.'

'What brings you from Cambridge, Dominus Greene?' Allen asked him. 'Is it such a Godless place now?'

The Cambridge man risked a short, sharp laugh in that hallowed hall and instantly regretted it as several disapproving heads bobbed up from their devotions and stared at him.

'Will you hear my confession, Master?' he asked.

'*Volo*,' Allen answered and led the way to the little oak cubicles beyond a rich velvet curtain.

'Bless me, Father, for I have sinned,' the Englishman intoned, adjusting his rapier as he sat.

'When did you last confess your sins, my son?' Allen asked, kissing the crucifix that dangled from his neck. Both men were whispering in English now.

'Some time ago, Father,' he told him. 'Before I left London.'

'Go on.'

There was a pause and Allen glanced sideways through the lattice as he saw the newcomer struggle for his words.

'I killed a man.'

Allen crossed himself. There was always a darkness hovering over the English College but these days it seemed likely to engulf them all. 'Tell me,' he said softly.

The newcomer leaned forwards and sideways so that only Allen – and God – could catch his words. 'His name was Christopher Marlowe,' he muttered. 'A playwright of sorts and scribbler of obscene poetry.'

'Is that why you killed him?' Allen asked.

'No,' Greene said. 'I killed him because he was an atheist.'

Allen's eyes widened and he crossed himself again, clutching convulsively at the crucifix. 'Mother of God,' he whispered.

'Amen to that,' Greene mumbled.

'This . . . Marlowe . . .' Allen had to know more, 'was a member of Cambridge University?'

'A graduate of Corpus Christi,' Greene told him, 'destined, like all of us, for the church.'

'Ah,' said Allen, well aware of the critical state of things in England, 'but which church?'

'I had assumed,' the Englishman answered, 'Mother church, the only true church. As it turns out, he was not even a Protestant.'

'I hear there is a new college in Cambridge now –' Allen was testing the waters – 'bound to the Puritan persuasion. Magdalene?'

'Emmanuel,' Greene corrected him, shaking his head.

Allen smiled. 'Founded by Dr Willoughby, I understand.'

'Sir Walter Mildmay,' the stranger said, putting him right again. Allen's dark eyes flashed and his furrowed face was serious again. 'What evidence did you have of this man's atheism?'

There was a silence.

'Dominus Greene?' Allen prompted him.

'He was in his cups one night,' the scholar told him. 'At the aptly named Devil, an inn he frequented. I hope you will believe me, Master, when I say I hardly ever go to such places . . .'

Allen waived this particular confession aside.

'Marlowe was roaring drunk, spouting rubbish about Moses being nothing but a conjuror and . . . Father, forgive me, but . . . he said that Christ and John the Baptist were bedfellows. Sodomites together.'

Through the grille, Allen's sharp intake of breath echoed round the little box and he went even greyer, his eyes dead, his skin like parchment.

'I couldn't just stand by and listen to such filth,' the scholar went on. 'I challenged Marlowe and he insisted we go outside.'

'To continue your debate?' Allen asked.

The curls shook in the dimness. 'To kill me,' he said. 'The man was as devious with his dagger as with his tongue. He went for me in the dark and I had no choice.'

'Did he die on the spot?' Allen asked.

'Screaming foul oaths as the breath left his body,' his murderer remembered.

'There was no time for Absolution? The last rites?'

A dry sob shook the man beyond the grille. 'I tried. But he was gone.' He sat bolt upright as the door of his cell was wrenched open and Dr Allen stood there, grim-faced and trembling. 'Bless me, Father . . .' the stranger began, astonished. The confession was unfinished.

Allen made the sign of the cross over him. 'No need, my boy,' he said. 'You have done God's work.' He laid a fatherly hand on the man's shoulder. 'You are surely one of the mysterious ways in which He moves. What will you do now?'

'Dance at the rope's end if I ever set foot in England again,' he said with a chuckle.

Slowly, Allen smiled. 'Well then,' he said, 'you must stay here as long as you like. We have need of such men. And –' he half turned on the cold stone of the chancel floor – 'welcome to the English College, Dominus Greene.'

Francis Walsingham looked from the portrait to the glass and slowly shook his head. Was it only two years ago he had sat for that fussy, fastidious Dutchman? Surely, his nose had never been *quite* that bulbous? And what was with that huge ruff? He'd never worn one that big in his life. The sallowness was right, though, and getting worse, the looking glass told him. He bridled every time the Queen patted his cheek and called him her Moor. And she did it every time. It was just her way, he knew that; she would have no master. Even so, it was irritating. No man would dare do that. He was Sir Francis Walsingham, for God's sake, the Queen's Secretary and if there was peace in the realm and the Queen slept easy in her bed, that was because of him.

'Master Faunt, sir,' came his manservant's voice from behind him, and he let the velvet curtain fall over the painting. He saw the blur that was his reflection glide like a ghost from the glass and Nicholas Faunt was surprised that he had a reflection at all.

'Nicholas.' The spymaster nodded to his projectioner. 'What news?'

'On the Rialto, Sir Francis, or elsewhere?'

Walsingham looked at him stony-faced. 'I have a man on the Rialto,' he reminded him, 'and it isn't you. Marlowe.'

'Should –' Faunt looked out of Walsingham's window to catch the position of the sun – 'by now be well on his way down the Rue de Venise.'

'Lost your timepiece, Nicholas?' Walsingham asked archly. Everybody knew about Faunt's timepiece because he mentioned it whenever he felt the need to upstage anybody.

'Oh, I never carry it in the London streets, sir.' Faunt smiled. 'Too many foins around. I'm fast, but some of those people have fingers like butterflies' wings. I wouldn't feel it go.'

Walsingham crossed to his sideboard and poured a goblet of Rhennish for each of them. He sipped from one then handed it to Faunt. The man had been too long on the road. He trusted no one, not even the Queen's spymaster. Was this what the world of Gloriana did to men like Faunt, that they feared their shadows?

'I've heard from Aldred,' Walsingham said, taking up the other goblet.

'Oh?' There was a name Faunt hadn't heard in a while.

'He thinks there's evil afoot in the English College.'

'Long may it flourish.' Faunt raised his goblet in salutation.

'Evil that may rebound on us,' Walsingham told him. 'He thinks we need a code-breaker.'

Faunt frowned, closing to his man. 'In the field? A code-breaker? Is that wise?'

Walsingham chuckled. 'If you and I dealt in wisdom, Nicholas, Her Majesty would be rotting in her grave by now, her throat slit and her heart sent as a present to Philip of Spain. There are times –' and he turned away – 'when wisdom flies out of the window.' He turned back to his projectioner. 'Times when we have to send Thomas Phelippes.'

Faunt's jaw dropped despite himself. 'Sir Francis, you can't be serious. Phelippes at the English College? They'll eat him alive.'

'No.' Walsingham was firm. 'There is no need for him to set foot inside the English College. He has Aldred and he has Marlowe to watch his back. He can stay in the town; give him some money so he can pass as a gentleman. Not too much –' he raised a finger – 'but enough.' He put the goblet down. 'See to it, will you, Nicholas?' He eased the ruff away from his swollen, purple-skinned neck where the boil had burst yet again. 'I'm not up to the whining of friend Phelippes today.'

Michael Johns was not in his element. Cloistered Cambridge had been his world for so long that he had almost forgotten what it was like to be elsewhere. When other professors went home to their families in the holidays that were no longer holy, he stayed in his rooms, reading esoteric documents, sometimes happily puzzling over a single word or phrase for hours at a time. On market days, when the clucking of chickens and the hissing of geese rose from Petty Cury, he stayed indoors, avoiding the crowds. And now here he was, struggling against a mass of people which seemed to fill the street from edge to edge, from end to end. A Londoner would say that it was a fairly quiet day on Cheapside but Johns was definitely beginning to regret his decision to follow Kit Marlowe to the capital. A huge woman with shoulders like a dray horse threw a loaf at him. He thought he had caught it, but it landed on the greasy cobbles anyway and he bent to pick it up.

'I wouldn't do that, mate,' a Cockney voice croaked in his ear. 'Not round 'ere. Your purse is the least you'll lose. Know what I mean?'

The professor straightened, passed the loaf to the large woman who shrugged, gave it a cursory wipe on her apron and put it back on her stall, well to the front to make sure it sold before the greasy sludge from the street soaked in and made it soggy.

Johns walked on, smiling wryly to think that he had not planned anything beyond his arrival. Somehow he had just imagined that he would stable his horse, turn a corner and bump straight into Marlowe, walking with that confident stride, hair flowing, eyes bright with watching the world go by. As he had seen him a hundred times along the High Yard and over Magdalene Bridge.

But it had taken him half a day just to find a stable that would take his mount and the cost of a week's livery had made him swallow hard. He hadn't allowed for the cost of living in London, either. All around him the street sellers of Cheapside bawled their wares. Cheese was *how* much? Milk? They had to be joking. Honey? Forget it. He hoped the streets around the corner were paved with gold; there would be no future for him here unless he could prise up a flagstone to use as currency. But his main concern was that he didn't know a soul and that he would die, unknown. Everywhere were faces, hard and greedy, cold eyes and cold hearts. His imagination began to take wing, as it does when people are alone and more than a little scared. He would contract some hideous disease from one of these filthy, stinking city dwellers. He would crawl off to a garret alive with fleas and lice and bugs. He would die unshriven. His body would lie unburied, food for vermin. He . . .

'Michael Johns, by all that's Holy! What are you doing here?'

Johns shook his head. He was hearing things now. The hideous disease could not be far away. Thomas Phelippes stepped out of the press of people and grabbed his old friend by the arm. 'Michael. Michael Johns. What are you doing in London? Have I been away from university so long that I have forgotten when the terms begin and end?' This seemed a little precise for a hallucination. Johns looked up and his face split in a smile. 'Thomas! You haven't changed a bit. I am so glad to see you.' He grabbed his old friend and hugged him to him. He had never been known to be demonstrative and Phelippes, though not famed for being much of a people person, saw that Johns was definitely a man on the edge.

'My house is quite nearby in Leadenhall Street. It's just around the corner, really. Shall we go there and talk about old times? I've got a jug of claret with your name on it. Where are you staying?'

Johns shrugged. 'Nowhere. I'm not even sure I could find my way back to where I left my horse. London is so . . .' he searched for a word, looking at the rickety houses pointing to the sky and settled on 'big.'

Phelippes clapped him on the back. 'It's a village still in some ways. It has still a lot of growing to do. Church property up for grabs, everywhere you look. But you're lucky you caught me.' A shadow passed over his face. 'I have been ordered to France.'

'Ordered?' Johns was confused. 'Who by?'

'It's a very long story,' Phelippes said, 'and in truth I shouldn't tell you the half of it.' He checked behind him that none of the street vendors was listening too closely. 'But we are friends from many years back and you don't know any intelligencers or projectioners or any of that mad crew, so I will tell you what I know.'

'Intelligencers?' Johns repeated. 'Projectioners?' His old friend was speaking a foreign language, right here in the streets of the Queen's capital. But he caught the man's look and he caught the man's mood and assured him, 'It will be like whispering your knowledge down a hole in the ground,' he said. 'Like King Midas' barber did.'

'That isn't a good analogy,' Phelippes pointed out, dredging out his Classical memories. 'Didn't the reeds tell everyone about the ass' ears?'

'Hmm,' Johns said, smiling. 'Perhaps not a good choice of story on my part. Well, let's just say I am a good listener.'

They turned up Cheapside skirting Old Jewry and Phelippes led the way down a twisting lane, which led through Leadenhall to his house, leaning at a crazy angle against its neighbour. While they walked, both men's minds were whirring with plans. They would both need to be cunning to get what they wanted, but they both had a knack with words. It would just be a matter of whether the better man would win.

Robert Greene put his head round the door of the Master of Corpus Christi, face already set in an expression of sycophantic approval, his eyebrows almost hidden in his hair, his mouth a rictus smile. He was glad he had prepared himself. He had rather liked the old, fusty look of Norgate's study on the one occasion he had been in it. The very cobwebs on this side of Cambridge had a gravitas of their own. Now it was bright and plain, with hardly any comfort left. The fine paintings were gone from the walls, the thick, dusty curtains from the windows. The desk was scrubbed and the chairs were wooden with no cushions to make a visitor want to stay.

'Gabriel,' he exclaimed. 'I just love what you've done in here. Very . . . now.'

Harvey looked around, smug and pleased. 'I rather like it,' he said. 'Too much clinging to the past has gone on in this room. I shall be taking Corpus Christi into the next century whether it likes it or not.' He paused. 'Did you speak?' he asked, a little waspishly.

'I just said "*Deo volens*",' Greene explained.

'Why?'

'Well, you said you were going to take the college into the next century. I just said . . . God willing.'

Harvey had had enough of people translating for him. Did they take him for some kind of idiot? First Johns and now Greene; it was really too bad. Did they not realize he was Master-designate of this college? True, old Norgate wasn't actually in his coffin, but he hadn't discernibly moved for three days, so it couldn't be long. 'I know what it means,' he spat. 'I just was wondering why you said it.'

Greene was discomfited. He and Harvey had always seen pretty much eye to eye and suddenly they were arguing. He couldn't work out where the conversation, short though it was, had gone so wrong. He shrugged.

'In my experience,' Harvey said, his voice low and even. If an adder could speak, it would have sounded more friendly and reasonable. 'In my experience, people only say "God willing" if they think an outcome unlikely. Do you think it is unlikely, Dominus Greene?'

'Dominus Greene? Robin, surely?' Greene felt the earth move beneath his feet.

'I think not,' Harvey said, closing his mouth with a snap. 'I must be careful with whom I mix now I am Master of Corpus Christi.'

Greene wondered whether it was only his imagination or whether Harvey really did change his voice to a more sonorous tone every time he used the phrase.

'We've been friends for . . .'

Harvey smiled a wintry smile. 'Acquaintances, surely?' he said and sat down at his empty desk. 'You must excuse me, Dominus Greene,' he said, not looking up. 'As you can see, I have much to do.'

Greene, who had come to ask his friend if he could search Marlowe's rooms now he seemed to have disappeared, decided now was not the time. He looked at the top of his erstwhile friend's head, wondering how long he could keep up the pretence of reading the top of a desk without so much as a scrap of paper on it. Then, suddenly, he felt the anger surging up through him to erupt out of his mouth.

'Gabriel?'

The man looked up but didn't speak.

'I hate what you've done to this room. It has no gravitas, no weight of years. When you are as nebulous and pointless as you are, Gabriel, you need the borrowed trappings of men greater than you. You have thrown it away. You are –' as his anger waned, so did his vocabulary – 'a boil on the arse of humankind. You . . . you . . .'

Harvey folded his arms and waited while the would-be playwright and poet searched for a deathless phrase. After a minute or so of watching Greene struggle he spoke. 'Please close the door on your way out, Greene. And perhaps I should warn you that when you have hauled your sorry, plagiaristic, thieving self through the gates of this college, I will take steps to see that you never enter it again. The Proctors will have their instructions. Good day.' And he bent his head to the contemplation of his empty desk again, while the motes of dust, which were all that remained of Norgate and his kind, slowly settled in the corners to be forgotten.

FOUR

Christopher Marlowe was settling in to his unexpectedly pleasant room, unpacking his travelling bag and putting out his few possessions. He had not been able to resist bringing paper and ink but had left the manuscript of his latest play stashed safely behind the wainscoting back at Corpus Christi. Tamburlaine, Zenocrate and the pampered jades of Asia could rest easy there. He knew that should he ever need the manuscript and be unable to go back, Michael Johns could always retrieve it for him. He still had nightmares about his Dido and had become rather more careful about his work, as Robert Greene could no doubt attest. Marlowe could not resist a wry smile whenever he thought of the overdressed hack, his hand all bound up in linen.

The room, as well as being spacious and light, was also almost impossibly clean. There seemed to be no sign of the normal wear and tear of a recent inhabitant and yet he was sure that the English College was not so well off for rooms that this one had been empty for long. He sniffed. Rosemary; that was no great surprise, most laundresses added a sprig of rosemary to the press. He sniffed again. There was a strange smell, slightly acrid but not unpleasant, of a plant, green but sharp. He knew it and would remember it in a minute. Along with the herb smells there was a strong smell of wood shavings, as though someone had been sawing in the room, doing carpentry of some kind. But he could see no new furniture or repairs, just this overwhelming sense of clean.

Mare's tails! That was what he could smell. He clicked his fingers as the words came to him. The plant his mother would use to scrub the plates and any stains she might have in the kitchen. She scrubbed the big table down once a week with mare's tails, telling the children to watch out, the crushed stalks could cut their fingers. His sister had got a cut once, he remembered, from just touching the table before his mother sluiced it down. He looked round the room and then dropped to his knees and reached gingerly into a corner with one finger. Yes, there was definitely a sharpness in the dust pushed against the wall. He got up and walked to the window, pulling a small lens out of his waistband. Yes, there were tiny fragments, sharp and fine as fairy glass twinkling on the skin. Someone had scrubbed this floor to within an inch of its life. That also explained the smell of wood; the old surface patina of many feet had been removed in places and the new wood, exposed after so long, was giving off a last breath of sap.

There was one last thing he had to check. He went to the foot of the bed and reached down to where the sheet was tucked under the feather mattress. He unloosed a fold and buried his face in it, inhaling. The smell was faint and underneath the rosemary and the lye but it was unmistakable. Although the linen would have been rinsed and rinsed then rinsed again any housewife would admit it was a little while before the smell of human urine would completely fade from bleached linen. It wasn't strong enough to be noticeable, but a sensitive nose could sniff it out.

Marlowe tucked the sheet back in and wandered to the window, standing away from the glass so that he could see and not be seen. Down in the street, he could see the good burghers of Rheims scurrying to and fro like everybody else, in search of a sou. His friend from earlier, the lay sister of last night's Vespers, was pacing her beat from corner to corner. She was even prettier in the day than in the night. But did she never sleep? He got the distinct impression that he saw the same face more often than he should in the people passing beneath the window, but he wasn't sure. He hadn't travelled widely but he had noticed when in the Low Countries that there did seem to be a face of the place. It was true in Cambridge as well, a certain fenny pinched look around the eyes and nose. Perhaps that was all he was seeing here – a face of the Marne; the look of the Catholic League. He glanced round the room again, then shrugged. If there was any more for this room to tell him, it would tell him in its own good time.

Gerald Skelton was used to being at everyone's beck and call. He didn't feel comfortable with nothing to do and his next lecture wasn't until the afternoon, so he stood at the window, tapping one finger on the sill and whistling through his teeth. His was a well-oiled machine and his team of clerks were meticulous with the paperwork. William Allen sat at his desk, a quill in his hand and a tortured expression on his face.

'Gerald,' he said at last. 'Could you either stop that infernal whistling or the tapping? In fact, I would deem it a personal favour if you would stop doing both.'

Skelton didn't turn round, but he was silent. Only someone with the razor-sharp hearing of the Master of the English College could have heard the tiny hum from the man's throat, the hum of a tone-deaf bee down a mine.

'And the humming. In fact, all small and irritating noises, if you would be so good.' A small drop of ink fell noiselessly from the tip of his quill, sending minute splashes over the work in hand. Allen was a patient man, by and large, but he had been writing this particular piece of prose for some time and it was important to be accurate. His writing was tiny, neat and even the splashes offended his sense of neatness and what was right. 'Gerald,' he said, reaching for the sand to try and minimize the damage. 'Please. Could you go elsewhere? Or, perhaps, as I must now wait until this ink is dry to see if I can rescue this document, perhaps you would like to tell me what the matter is?'

Skelton didn't turn, but in the blessed silence Allen could almost hear the turning of his brain.

'Well?' The Master put down his pen and leaned forward on his desk, his hands calmly folded in front of him, his expression patient.

In a fractured, clumsy bound, Skelton was across the room and in the chair facing the desk. 'It's that new man. Greene. I don't like him.'

'No? I find him quite an attractive kind of personality. Many depths, I believe, which we can plumb before he leaves us.'

'Bad things live in the depths,' Skelton said. 'Sea monsters.' He sketched something ghastly and tentacled with manic hands. 'Creatures of the pit.' His eyes burned and he leaned forward. 'Why did he come here, all unannounced? Why have we never heard of him? Our world is a small one; we should have heard of him. Most of our guests come with letters of introduction.'

'Perhaps he has only recently decided that he wants to walk

our path,' Allen said, soothingly. 'It isn't for everyone. And he is very young.'

'And you have put him in Father Laurenticus' room. Is that wise?'

'It's the only one we have. If Father Laurenticus had not . . . died –' there was the smallest moue of distaste in the word, which described better than any medical treatise what the maid had found that day, what Allen and Skelton had seen – 'we would have had to put him in the dormitory and something tells me that Dominus Greene is not a dormitory sort of man.'

'But what if he finds . . . anything.' Skelton had only to close his eyes to be back in that room, that blood-soaked bed, the sprays on the curtains, windows and wall.

'The room has been thoroughly scrubbed,' Allen said. 'Do try to calm down, Gerald. You are supposed to be our Bursar, looking after us, making sure the English College runs smoothly. If we start to rush about just because someone is killed . . .'

Skelton was speechless. 'Someone is killed?' he said, trying to keep his voice down. 'Someone is killed, Master? It isn't as if this is the first incident of . . .'

'Murder,' the Master supplied blandly.

'Yes. Of that.'

'Is there another instance? Do tell me what.' Allen was carefully wiping his quill-nib.

'Master! You can't have forgotten the hanging?'

The Master flung a dismissive hand towards the man. 'A student was trying to climb out of the window, hell bent on pleasure and quite literally so as it turned out. That was scarcely murder. You might say it was God's judgement.'

'But, Master—'

A rap on the door made Skelton turn as if the door were the gate of Hell and Satan himself was knocking.

'Come in,' the Master said, putting a quietening hand up to Skelton, who shrank into his chair.

The door opened just a little and a cheery face peeped round. Its owner was either very small or was crouching as the top of the unruly hair was only just over five foot from the floor.

'Ah, Master Aldred!' cried the Master of the English College.

'Come in, come in. Dr Skelton was just going, were you not, Gerald?'

Skelton got up sulkily and edged past the little man in the doorway without speaking. Bursar of the English College he may have been but what Master Aldred had to sell only the Master handled.

'Gerald is feeling unwell,' Allen said with a smile. Solomon Aldred put down the bag he was carrying with a satisfying clink. 'Now, what have you for me today?'

The vintner liked to arrive in the mid-morning, spend time sampling his wares with his old friend the Master, popping in to genuflect with a solemn face and supple knees at Sext and then partake of the top table's luncheon before making his excuses before there was more praying at None. Today, though, was different. He slipped a particularly fine brandy to Brother Tobias and they downed a few before the old man told him of the newest arrivals. There was a surly fellow from London who kept to himself in his room over the bakehouse. There was the gentleman from somewhere in the north if Brother Tobias was any judge, who went by the name of Salter and there was a Cambridge scholar called Greene, who had asked to see a priest urgently. Things must be bad indeed in England, Tobias nodded, anything but soberly after his third glass, if the current flood of the Old Faithful was anything to go by. The College was running out of space to put them all.

Aldred padded around the cloisters where earnest young priests sat gilding their vellum as though there were no such thing as a printing press. He caught sight of the surly fellow from London. He knew him by his clothes – rough fustian no Frenchman would be seen dead in and he smiled at him as he brushed past.

'And now the Western wind bloweth sore,' he said softly.

The Londoner scowled at him. 'What?'

'That is in his chief sovereignty,' Aldred assured him.

The Londoner stopped walking, careful to keep the little man in full view. 'I don't know where you've escaped from, sirrah,' he said. He took in the man's bag with a quick glance. 'But whatever you're selling, I have more than a sufficiency.' And he was gone.

It took Aldred longer than he expected to find the northerner called Salter and he only knew him because of the song he sang to his lute and he recognized the flat vowels of the Ouse. The vintner tried again. He applauded the man's playing politely.

'And now the Western wind bloweth sore,' he said, beaming. 'That is in his chief sovereignty.'

Salter looked at him, frowning, then struck a slight discord on the lute. 'No.' He shook his head. 'I don't know it. Perhaps if you could hum me a few bars, I could pick it up.'

Aldred smiled, bowed and wandered away. Life was too short to talk to musicians. In desperation, he scampered up the stairs by the chapel, ducking under the beams where the organ pipes wheezed and blew. He knew this short-cut of old and soon he was out in the fresh air again, watching the sun glow on the old stone. He saw his last target lounging against a cloister pillar, arms folded, jaw set. In front of him, in the corner of the quad-rangle, three monks knelt before a crucifix set into the wall. Their robes were hauled down around their waists and they were slapping knotted ropes across their backs, adding little sprays of blood to the cuts and old scars already there. Each of them was deathly pale, but no sound escaped from their gritted teeth and the flagellation had got into a ghastly rhythm.

Aldred barely noticed this. It was a daily practice in the English College, as regular as Sext or None. He smiled at the watcher by the cloisters. 'And now the Western wind bloweth sore,' he said, looking up to the sky, because all Englishmen talked about the weather, pretty much all the time. 'That is in his chief sovereignty.' He grinned sheepishly at the other man, expecting another inane rebuff.

Instead, he heard, 'Beating the withered leaf from the tree. Sit we down here under the hill.' The voice was not over the top, it was not quite an actor's voice but it certainly made a better job of the lines than Aldred had heard before. The Cambridge man looked down at the vintner and continued. 'Or, since we're a little short of hills, how about over there?'

Aldred sighed. Even for a visit to the English College, he'd downed rather more than was strictly good for him today and he was beginning to wonder whether it was the thickness of his tongue that was letting him down.

'Marlowe?' he hissed, scuttling alongside the man's longer stride.
'Greene,' Marlowe corrected him. 'Robert Greene. Corpus
Christi College.'

'Ah, of course,' the merchant said with a bob. 'Solomon Aldred;
my card.'

He passed Marlowe a crumpled piece of parchment. It read
'Vintner to the English College. Minimum orders only.'
Marlowe slipped it into his left cuff. 'When the strain gets too
much and I have a need of a skinful, rest assured, Master Aldred,
I'll be in touch.'

Aldred dropped heavily onto the cold stone bench in the
cloister's dead corner. From any angle here, the pair could keep
an eye on anyone getting too close and could change their conversation accordingly.

'Overrated, don't you think?' Marlowe asked.

'What is?' Solomon was unpacking his samples again.

'Spenser.'

'Er . . .'

Marlowe looked at the little soak. What was Walsingham
thinking? This place was too crucial to trust it to a man who
took his cover too seriously. 'The code,' Marlowe reminded him.
'The western wind, the withered leaf. Edmund Spenser.'

'Is it?' Aldred grinned. 'Well, well. To business, Master Greene.
Tipple?' He held up a rather pleasing claret.

Marlowe shook his head.

'You're looking for someone.' Aldred shrugged and swigged
in one fluid movement.

Marlowe nodded. So far, so correct.

'We've no idea when he arrived,' Aldred told him.

'Are you sure he's here at all?' Marlowe asked.

'Oh, yes. He was shadowed from Deptford, on board *The Lady
Liberty* on the tenth. He met someone – and don't ask me who
– at Rouen. I'm afraid we lost him for a day or two, but found
him again on his way here.'

'Who is he?'

'No idea.' The vintner swigged again.

Marlowe held Aldred's drinking hand, forcing the glass from
his lips so that it clinked loudly on the stone. 'What do you
mean, you've no idea?' he hissed.

Aldred forced his eyes to focus. 'Tell me,' he said. 'Why are you here, exactly? Why has Sir Francis Walsingham sent you here? Have you come to kill him?'

'If I have to,' said Marlowe. 'A man who plotted with Babington isn't likely to undergo a change of heart and throw himself on the mercy of the Queen of England, when all is said and done.'

'Agreed.' Aldred nodded. 'Have you done this before?' He found himself looking the man up and down, assessing his likely strength and speed.

'Have you?' Marlowe countered.

Aldred ignored him. 'Look, it's one thing to sit in Whitehall or Placentia with the spymaster, drinking his rather excellent Bordeaux and putting the Papist world to rights. It's a bit different out here, I can tell you. Watching your back morning, noon and night, going to endless bloody masses, speaking French. You don't know the half of it.'

'I don't need to know the half of it,' Marlowe told him flatly, 'I just need to know who I'm looking for.'

Aldred sighed. If he'd hoped for a kindred spirit or even a sympathetic ear from Walsingham's new man, he wasn't going to find it in Kit Marlowe. 'Your Babington plotter is either a Londoner whose name I don't know – big fellow, lodges over the bakery. *Or* he's a singing idiot called Salter, from Yorkshire. What's his real name, the one you're after?'

'Matthew Baxter,' Marlowe told him, 'and he's not from London or Yorkshire.'

Aldred shook his head, grinning, and risked another sip. 'Don't you just love this business?' he asked. He cleared his throat as a lay brother ambled past, smiling and nodding at them both. 'Any way,' he muttered to Marlowe as soon as the coast was clear. 'There are complications.'

'Oh?'

'How are you at –' he closed in to his man – 'unexplained deaths?'

Marlowe shrugged. 'I've seen a few,' he said.

Aldred looked to right and left again, just in case the walls indeed had ears. Satisfied that they didn't, he murmured, 'Three months ago, a scholar fell out of a window. To be precise, that one up there.' He nodded to the roof and Marlowe followed his gaze.

'Singularly careless of him,' he said.

'Absolutely,' Aldred said, nodding. 'To the point of physically impossible.'

'And "accident" is the official College line? The verdict of them all?'

Aldred chuckled. 'Not exactly,' he said. 'You'll learn, Marlowe, that this place is a nest of scorpions. Don't turn your back on anybody.'

'I never do,' Marlowe assured him.

'The accident verdict first appeared the next day, courtesy of Dr Allen in one of his interminable sermons. Father Laurenticus had other ideas.'

'Laurenticus?'

'You're in his room. At least, according to Brother Tobias, you are.'

'Tobias is your eyes and ears?' Marlowe asked. It was as well to know who was who in this place.

'Four of them, anyway,' Aldred told him. 'It's damned useful with a cover like mine. *Vino, veritas* and all that. The stuff loosens tongues better than any of Master Topcliffe's infernal gadgets in the Tower. And the best thing is, hardly anybody remembers what they've told me.'

'This scholar,' Marlowe reminded the vintner, steering his mind back onto the subject. 'What do we know about him?'

'Nothing.'

'Nothing?' Marlowe's eyebrows were nearly in his hair with surprise. 'You've let me down, Master Aldred. Tell me –' and he lowered his voice still further – 'you *are* a spy, aren't you?'

'More of a facilitator, really,' Aldred said modestly. 'I would never venture to claim I was an intelligencer, still less a projectioner. A humble vintner, with a twist.'

'But even a humble vintner must know something. This is a small place. People talk.'

'Oh, there's always tittle tattle in the town,' the vintner told him. 'The boy was a secret alchemist. He was in league with Satan. They even said –' and he paused to check behind him and to both sides once more – 'they even said he was an illegitimate son of Pope Sixtus.'

Marlowe let out a slow whistle through his teeth. 'Be still, my beating heart,' he said.

'Ah, you can mock,' Aldred said, 'but I tell you, Marlowe, there's something unnatural about this place. Apart from the fact that it's full of Papist fanatics who have all sworn to slit the throat of the Queen of England, of course.'

'Do we know the scholar's name?'

'Charles, is all I know. From Westley Waterless. You might know it.'

'I do indeed,' Marlowe said with a nod. 'God-awful place in the fens. I ride through it on my way to Cambridge. What was he doing here?'

'Same as everybody else,' Aldred said. 'Plotting the return of the Catholic faith to England. If you mean how did he get here from Cambridge and what particular demons drove him, I haven't the faintest idea.'

Marlowe looked up again to the sharp slope of the roof and smiled broadly as two brothers walked past, deep in liturgical conversation. 'So,' he said, marshalling his thoughts, 'Charles of Westley Waterless jumps – or was pushed – from that casement. He would have hit the roof . . . about there . . . bounced or rolled down, probably hitting that gargoyle and landing . . . there, in the quad.'

'At least two blows –' Aldred was following the man's thinking – 'perhaps to the head.'

'Did you see the body?' Marlowe asked.

'No,' Aldred told him. 'By the time my weekly visit was due, Scholar Charles was with his Maker. Or at least in the vault. Want to see him?'

'What?'

'Hm, intriguing, isn't it? And not for the faint hearted. Every scholar of the College who passes over is placed in the cata-combs, a little south west of where we're sitting now. It's a little tradition they had when the College was at Douai. It took Allen months to find a suitable building here, with deep enough foundations. The rumour is that he had to pay a small fortune. He brought all the bodies with him, or at least the most recent. Something to do with keeping the Papal flame. It's beyond me.'

'How do I get there?'

'You don't.' Aldred wafted the last of the brandy under his

nose. 'Members of the College only. I only know *of* it. I've never been there.'

'Aren't I a member of the College?' Marlowe asked, a little indignantly.

Aldred guffawed, then stifled the noise with a swig. 'Let me see. You've probably told Allen a cock-and-bull story about why you're here and you kneel down inside while they spout the bell, book and candle nonsense and you think you're a member of the College?' Aldred looked hard at the man. 'You really haven't done this before, have you? Allen didn't come down with the last manna from heaven, boy,' he said. 'He was dodging Lutherans and Calvinists while you were still in your hanging sleeves. He'll be checking out your story.'

'I know,' Marlowe said.

'And he'll test you. Not once. But again and again. Count on it.'

'I will,' Marlowe assured him.

'Well, sir . . .' Aldred was suddenly on his feet and Marlowe looked across to his right to see Gerald Skelton and the Master walking in their direction. 'If I can't tempt you with the finest claret south of the Seine, I'll trouble you no further.'

'We are not famed for our wines in Cambridge, vintner,' Marlowe said with a frown, 'but I know a good one doesn't usually taste *of* the Seine,' and he pointed ostentatiously to the bottles Aldred was stuffing back into his bag. Doctors Allen and Skelton walked past in a waft of incense and a flap of black wool. When they were far enough away, Marlowe caught up with the retreating Aldred. 'You said death*s*. Unexplained death*s*. Plural.'

'Did I?' Aldred smiled. 'Oh, yes. So I did. One more, anyway.'

'Who?' Marlowe asked him.

'Oh, didn't I tell you? Father Laurenticus. You're sleeping in his bed.'

The little room under the tiles was never brightly lit. In the depths of winter, with the sun low in the sky, a fragile grey beam sometimes just managed to percolate through the cobwebby skylight and touch a corner of the ceiling. In early autumn, the sunshine was just a golden glow reflected into the room from some distant cupola. But even that was not brightening the room today. The

thin curtain was drawn across the window and the huddled shape
on the bed had, in any event, its face turned to the wall.

The door latch rose slowly, with just a faint click to alert
anyone who cared that there was someone creeping into the room.
In the gloom, the thin figure wrapped in a cloak could have been
a boy, woman or child. It sat on the bed, and gently stroked the
shoulder of the huddling body, not speaking, just rubbing up,
down, round; up, down, round to the time of the beat of a broken
heart. After a while, the intruder heaved a sigh, then spoke.

'Sylvie.' The stroking became a gentle shake, still loving, but
firm. 'Sylvie, sit up now and speak to me. You have been like
this for far too long.' The figure muttered and shook its shoulder
like a petulant child. 'That's no good, Sylvie. You'll die if you
don't eat and drink and *don't* say you don't care. Of course
you care. Come on now, sit up.'

The girl got off the bed and reached up to draw back the
frowsty curtain. The sunlight bouncing off happier roofs glowed
into the room. The golden motes danced in it like faeries.

'Come, now, Sylvie. The afternoon is at its height. It is so
beautiful out there.'

There was still no movement from the bed and the girl lost
her temper and stamped her foot.

'I can't go on like this any longer, Sylvie. I am working day
and night to try and make enough money for both of us. I fell
asleep under poor old Beausales the baker last night. He didn't
seem to mind. I'm not sure he even noticed, to be honest, but
he is a simple soul.' She sighed. 'Not everyone would be so
understanding, Sylvie. He paid me and gave me a loaf of bread.
Some men would beat a girl who did that to them. Beausales,
he knows he is hung like a mule. Other men are not so confident
in their prowess.' She kicked the bed and screamed. 'Sylvie!'

Slowly, the girl on the bed sat up and turned round to lean
her back to the wall. She was wearing a short chemise and sat
with her knees akimbo, leaving nothing to anyone's imagination.
Her friend slapped her thigh.

'Stop it, Sylvie. Where is your modesty? If you won't take your
wares out on the street to earn some bread, don't display yourself
to me.'

Sylvie shrugged and put her knees together, hugging them to

her flat chest. She turned wide eyes up to her friend. 'Mireille,' she said, in a voice harsh from crying, 'I don't care what you or anyone else sees. I will walk down the street dressed as I am. I am no one without him to love me.'

Mireille spun on her heel across the room and threw herself down onto the bed against the opposite wall. 'Have you gone simple, Sylvie?' she asked in disgust. 'What makes you think he loved you? You know what we are; no one loves us if we don't love ourselves.'

The girl's mouth turned down at the corners and then her bottom lip began to tremble. A tear rolled fatly from each eye. 'He did love me.'

'You gave him for nothing what other men pay for,' Mireille screamed in her face. 'Of course he loved you. Who wouldn't? Everyone loves a bargain.'

Before either girl knew what was happening, Sylvie flew across the room like a tigress, nails out for Mireille's face. But the older girl was too quick for her and she grabbed her slender wrists. She pushed them both off the bed and twisted the girl's arms behind her back, holding her hands effortlessly in one of her own. She reached for a broken shard of mirror from the top of a battered press and held it up so their faint reflections looked back at them.

'What do you see, Sylvie?' she asked, savagely.

The girl tried a smile. 'Sylvie and Mireille,' she said, in an ingratiating voice.

'Yes, Sylvie and Mireille. Mireille with the big tits and arse, Mireille, all woman, the woman who shows her backside to men at the English School door. And Sylvie. Flat chested as a boy. Sylvie who goes for free into the bed of a wicked priest who wants a boy in his bed but doesn't want to be damned. So, he goes for Sylvie, the lesser sin.'

The girl pulled away and sank to the floor. 'No,' she sobbed into her friend's skirts. 'No. He loved me. And now he's dead.'

Mireille put a gentle hand down and stroked her hair. 'Yes,' she murmured. 'Yes, indeed. We can argue for ever whether he loved you. But that he is dead is without question. I wonder if we will ever know why.'

FIVE

'*Benedictus, benedicat.*'

'Amen.'

Members of the English College, Master, professors, scholars, lay brothers and guests brought up their heads from their devotions and jostled with each other briefly as they took their places on the benches before their long tables. A long line of popes glowered down at them from the portraits on the walls and a chanting priest began reciting in perfect pitch and indifferent Latin in the corner. He needn't have bothered, because once grace was over, it was every man for himself on the long tables. Marlowe had experienced this mad free for all before, as a crop-headed sizar at Corpus Christi. He remembered how it was then, running up and down the Court, desperately trying to keep warm in the biting Cambridge winds, longing to hear the clang of the bell that called the scholars to dinner.

But now he was on the top table, four along from the Master. His hair lay on his shoulders and his shoulders were clad in velvet. He had no satchel bulging with his Lucan and Aristotle, just a purse comfortably portly with Walsingham's money. And he had a dagger in its sheath in the small of his back. He noted that while the scholars in front of him crammed bread and cheese into their mouths and washed it down with water, the bowl in front of him was brimful with a rich stew with a mouth-watering aroma.

'It's called ragout,' a voice muttered to his left. His neighbour was unlike the others at the top table. In fact he looked just like the rest of the lads in their grey fustian and with their cropped hair.

'Robert Greene.' Marlowe extended a hand to him before sampling the excellent wine. Master Aldred had outdone himself.

'Edmund Brooke,' the lad said, shaking the man's hand. '*Secundus convictus.*'

'Ah.' Marlowe smiled.

'I know what you're thinking,' Brooke said, tucking into the stew with gusto. 'Why is a poll man sitting at the Master's table?'

Marlowe leaned towards him, 'Got something on him?' he whispered, with a dark smile.

Brooke looked aghast. 'It's my turn,' he explained. 'Every night, the Master chooses one of the scholars to dine with him. It's done on a strictly rotational basis.' He closed his eyes as his stew-laden bread went down. 'I've been waiting a hundred and sixteen days for this.'

Marlowe chuckled. 'Otherwise it's bread and cheese, eh?' he asked. Brooke nodded, loosening up as the unaccustomed combination of good food and wine found their mark. 'What brings you to the College, Master Greene?'

'The same as everybody.' Marlowe carefully inspected the contents of his spoon. Most of it he recognized. 'To serve his Holiness in any way I can.'

'How are things at home?' the boy asked, a stranger now to his own land.

'Where is home, exactly?' Marlowe asked. He smiled as the Master caught his eye and raised his glass, twinkling in the light of what seemed a thousand candles.

'Berkhamstead,' Brooke said. 'It's in Hertfordshire. Though I barely remember it. My parents left when the Jezebel of England became Queen.'

Marlowe sighed. 'I wish mine had.'

'Where are you from, Master Greene?'

'Cambridge,' Marlowe told him. It was only a half-lie. 'Westley Waterless. You wouldn't know it, of course. Horrible little place in the fens.'

'I couldn't help noticing . . .' Brooke paused now that the stew had taken the edge off his hunger. 'You're armed.' He nodded at the cold hilt of Marlowe's dagger.

'Most men are,' he told him, 'beyond the confines of this place. And perhaps even here.'

'Oh, no.' Brooke shook his head, taking a huge swig of the wine. Marlowe ignored the hovering servant and took the silver ewer, topping up the scholar's glass, 'No. No one goes armed here. By order of the Master. Only guests like you.'

'Are there many guests like me?' Marlowe asked. It was a more loaded question than the boy knew.

'A constant stream,' Brooke said, 'whenever that Godless Church of England persecutes our people. But it won't be long now.'

'What won't?' Marlowe held his wine up to the light as if the talk he was making was the smallest thing in the world. Hundreds of tiny candles seemed to dance in its depths and he seemed to be doing nothing more important than counting them as they winked and sparked.

Brooke looked a little taken aback. 'Until we make our great return, of course. Oh, I'm not privy to such discussions but there are moves afoot. The Duke of Guise, they say, is ready with twenty thousand men to invade England. The Duke of Parma has more. *And* he's the best soldier in Europe.'

'So I've heard,' Marlowe said.

'And that's not all . . .'

But Brooke's sentence was cut short by the dinner guest on Marlowe's right.

He leaned around Marlowe, with a deprecatory gesture and said sharply '*Κρατμστε το στόμα σας κλειστσ, λαουτξκοζ!*'

Marlowe's Greek, thanks to the unstinting efforts of Doctors Johns and Lyler was excellent and it was difficult to look uncomprehending. He took a large mouthful of stew and smiled brightly at each man. The scholar had been told to shut up in no uncertain terms and that road looked closed. The boy had turned pale and watched as the steward took both his plate and his glass away.

Marlowe saw that a hand was being held out, he assumed in friendship, although the recent exchange made him feel that this was by no means genuine. 'Thomas Shaw,' the man said, 'I'm the College Librarian.' The man was huge, utterly the wrong build for a man closeted away with books. He looked as though one touch of his ham-like hand would cause the more fragile tomes to disintegrate to powder.

'Robert Greene.' Marlowe took the proffered hand and shook it.

'Ah, the Cambridge man. How does the Master's table compare with your old college fare?'

'It outshines it –' Marlowe raised his glass – 'as day is to night.'

A huge platter of pickled vegetables appeared at Marlowe's right shoulder. He didn't recognize much of the contents, although Nat Sawyer of Lord Strange's Men would have made much comedic play with the large white one in the middle. Shaw sensed his difficulty. 'Artichokes –' he pointed – 'cauliflower. The big one in the middle is chicory. It doesn't matter which you choose. They all have a kick like a mule. We had to stop them sending in the horseradish; poor old Father Bernard almost died one night when he absent-mindedly took a large bite. God knows what cook soaks it all in. But, as long as you are reasonably circumspect, I guarantee you'll like it.'

Marlowe sampled some on his spoon. The librarian was right; it was a taste explosion, although it did burn rather on the way down. However, he could appreciate the skill that must have gone into its preparation.

'Which college?' Shaw asked, helping himself to twice the amount Marlowe had. 'In Cambridge, I mean.'

'Corpus Christi,' he told him.

'Ah, the Parker Library.' Shaw beamed.

'You know it?' Marlowe topped up the man's glass from the decanter to his left.

'Sadly, no,' Shaw said, 'but I know of it. I'm an Oxford man myself; Merton. I'm ashamed to say we had nothing like Parker's books. Tell me, is it true that the fellows of Gonville and Caius go to Corpus Christi every year to check if the old boy's books are still there?'

'They do,' Marlowe told him. 'At the Library Feast in August. Archbishop Parker's birthday.'

'I don't suppose you knew Parker personally? I mean, you'd be too young.'

'He died when I was nine, I believe. But I can see his portrait in Hall now. A kind face, I always thought.'

'I've heard him described as the Pope of Lambeth,' Shaw said with a chuckle. 'Odd, that, in an Archbishop of Canterbury of a bastard church.'

Marlowe tapped the side of his nose. 'Man on the inside,' he lied.

'Really?' Shaw's eyes widened. 'I had no idea.'

'I must say,' Marlowe said, topping up his own glass, 'you live in some style here. May I see your library?'

'Whenever you like,' Shaw said. 'It's across the gallery from here. After Compline, I'd be delighted to show you.'

'Thank you.' Marlowe clicked his glass against the librarian's, sealing the deal. 'I'm in Father Laurenticus' room.'

'Are you?' There was hardly a pause before Shaw's answer.

'I understand he died.' Marlowe picked at the plate of candied orange rind placed between them.

'He did.' Shaw nodded, suddenly sober, suddenly withdrawn. 'Sad. Very sad.'

'An elderly gentleman?'

'No, indeed.' Shaw sighed. 'In his prime, in fact.'

'Really?' Marlowe flicked the napkin off his left shoulder and wiped his mouth. 'What was the cause, I wonder?'

Shaw looked at the man, this dark newcomer with the bright doublet, the easy manner and, he suspected, an excellent command of Ancient Greek. 'He stopped breathing, Dominus Greene,' he said, 'as one day we all must.' He crossed himself and pushed back his chair. 'But not, yet, Oh Lord, not yet.'

Marlowe crossed himself also, the movement still feeling clumsy after many years disuse. 'Amen,' he murmured, and picked up another fragment of candied peel. 'Amen to that.'

But Kit Marlowe did not go to Shaw's library after Compline. Instead, he stayed over the cheeseboard to survey the ground, test the waters, whatever analogy he had once wrestled with in the Discourses at Cambridge. Shaw he'd met and Father Tobias. The Master and his shadow, Skelton, seemed beyond his reach tonight, hemmed in as they were by serious-looking priests with earnest faces. The lad, Brooke, had vanished into the crowd of scholars and Marlowe shook his head to realize that, from his high vantage point of top table and twenty-two summers, all scholars were beginning to look alike.

'Robert Greene.' He shook the hand of a roisterer, dressed not unlike himself, who had slid along the bench to sit by him.

'Peregrine Salter,' the man said, smiling. 'I haven't seen you before, Master Greene.' Unless Marlowe missed his guess, this was Aldred's lute-playing Yorkshireman.

'Newly arrived,' Marlowe said, beaming. 'You?'

'I've been here a couple of weeks,' Salter told him. 'It's good to be among friends, isn't it?'

'Oh, indubitably.' Marlowe nodded, surrounded, as he was, by enemies. 'You've heard the news, I suppose, from London, I mean?'

Salter paused with his wine glass in hand. 'No. What news?'

'The Queen . . .'

'The Jezebel?' Salter was all ears.

'No.' Marlowe frowned. '*The* Queen. Of Scots.'

'Master Greene . . .' Salter sighed. 'I am not ashamed to admit, in this august company, that I am of the old religion. I am a Catholic.' He suddenly stood a head taller. 'But I am also an Englishman. Religion and politics do not go hand in hand with me, sir. I would sooner cut off my right hand than see that Frenchwoman on the throne of England.'

There was only one man breathing in the darkness of the vault. The darkness that wasn't totally dark. A solitary candle with a red glass around it quivered in the draught from the world above. It had taken Marlowe over an hour to find this place and he'd had to dodge the faithful attending vigil in the incense-laden chapel overhead. The faint scent of amber and frankincense clung to his clothing; in his case, the odour of the unsanctified. There were niches at intervals in the recessed archways where the spiders crawled in their twilight world. The dead watched him through sightless eyes, hunched on the iron pegs that held their bones. Each corpse wore a simple robe with a cheap crucifix around the neck. On the longest dead, the robes were rags, crisp with age in this airless tomb and the bones glowed an eerie white. He made his way, feeling each one, to the far wall. Here the bodies were fresher, flesh on the bones still filling out the clothes. He struck his tinder flint and lit his candle, holding it up to each face. A cadaver seemed to be mocking him, the jaw hanging open in a hollow laugh, the eyes dark, dry and sunk back into the sockets, the skin brown as vellum and just as dry. The nearest body to the door on this wall of the catacombs had been a young man. His hair was plastered on the left side with dark brown flakes Marlowe knew was blood. He felt through the black robe, patting the chest under the crucifix. One arm, the left, appeared to be broken. It hung lower than the right and as he squeezed the soapy flesh he felt the bones move under his fingers. A broken arm and a blow to the head. As if the man had fallen from a great height. This must be Charles of Westley Waterless, dead these three weeks. But as Marlowe's candle crept higher in the faint breeze, he knew it was neither of these wounds that had killed him. The boy's eyes were hollows, the pupils all but gone and a thick layer of brick dust coated his hair and eyelashes. His tongue, black and purple, protruded through his teeth and his head jutted awkwardly to one side. This poor shattered thing had not been buried here with all the panoply of death which the Catholic Church had in its armoury. This body had been carried down here, probably on a hurdle, and propped unceremoniously up in this niche until time disarticulated the bones so that they could be shovelled up and put higher up in the smaller niches in the wall, where he would be forgotten. A weeping mother in Westley Waterless would remember him, then she would die and he would be no more. Just a whispering ghost across the fenlands.

Marlowe peeled back the robe's hood and saw the tell-tale mark of a hanging. There was a dark purple line across the throat and up to the ear on the left side. Gently, he patted the dead boy's cheek and the head lolled to the left with a click.

'Who's there?' he heard a voice call. He snuffed out his candle and stood stock still in the darkness. He blessed his velvet clothes, silent as the grave without a rustle to betray him. The call came again, first in Latin, then in Greek, then in French. For a split second, Marlowe toyed with trying to pass himself off as one of the dead, the company of the catacombs all around him. Immediately, he knew how hopeless it was. He was too bright of eye, too quick of breath. And his clothes were wrong. The flicker of a candle was moving towards him in the vault, someone coming in a hurry on padding footfalls.

He felt for the dagger hilt at his back. He would have achieved nothing if he had to leave the English College like this, a fugitive on the run from the place that was a refuge for fugitives. On the other hand, he had no excuse, no reason to be here in the dark with the dead. '*I lost my way*' sounded hopelessly inadequate even as the words formed in his mind.

The candlelight flickered once in his direction, then doubled back on itself and a black figure was crossing to the far arm of the vault's cross. Marlowe saw his chance and ran for the stone steps that led to the light. He didn't look back and didn't stop running until he had reached the room that had once belonged to a dead man.

In the middle of the night, Marlowe lay back on the fat feather mattress which had once borne the imprint of Father Laurenticus. He breathed in gently, trying to detect any hint of death in the bed, but there was nothing; just the faint memory of the bleaching and scrubbing. He didn't quite know why he thought the bed was the scene of the man's death. He had had no clue as to what had happened. For all he knew, the man had dropped dead in the street; but if that was the case, why was this room so very, very clean? He was tired, the meal had been heavy and the wine generous, even for his strong head, but every time he closed his eyes, he saw the rotting dead in line abreast and every time he breathed in, there was the faint sweet odour of incense and corruption in his nostrils. He tossed and turned and decided to try to wait for the dawn, if sleep would not come. The clocks of Rheims chimed the hours, quarters, halves and it seemed every minute in between. None of them seemed to agree and their constant tintinnabulation didn't help his attempts to sleep. In the end, he bowed to the inevitable, got up quietly, dressed and slipped out of the College, by the wicket gate that led to the East. A walk in the predawn light might clear his mind enough to let him catch some sleep. He had had some of his best nights wrapped up in a cloak propped up against a tree somewhere with a mighty line thundering in his head, so he went in search of a quiet, grassy corner.

He finally found a welcoming tree, with roots straggling above ground almost making a chair for the wandering insomniac, growing on the bank of the Vesle as it meandered through the town. He wrapped his cloak over his head and round his body, then curled himself into the welcoming arms of the tree. He tuned his hearing to the rattle of the water over the stones and was just drifting off to sleep at last when he heard a sound which had him awake again at once. It was a slither of silk and a gentle breath and it was very close to his left ear. He was too wrapped up to reach his dagger from where he sat but before he could jump up, a hand was on his chest and a quiet voice spoke.

'Haven't I seen you somewhere before?'

He turned his head and found himself almost nose to nose with the lady of uncertain virtue, the self-proclaimed lay sister who had accosted him outside the English College on his arrival.

'Yes,' she said, 'I have. You're at that English College, the one on Venise Street.' She subsided in a cloud of cheap perfume at his side and leaned against him. 'Are you feeling more friendly now?'

'I'm always friendly,' Marlowe pointed out reasonably, 'except to those who give me cause.'

'But not *friendly*,' she said. 'Not friendly for my purposes.'

'No,' he admitted. 'Not that kind of friendly.'

She examined his face by the light of the growing dawn. 'You're a handsome one, though, aren't you?' She squeezed his thigh, just above the knee. 'Fit and strong.'

'Thank you,' he said, politely. He had never been one to judge ladies who earned their living by their best features. This one seemed more intelligent than most and she was certainly pretty enough. But it had always been his belief that anything that could in the best of circumstances be had for free, should not be sold. 'I just . . . don't.'

She tossed her head. 'Ha! English College. What will we do with you, eh?' She settled herself more comfortably and he was glad of the warmth of her down one side. The year was a little old for sleeping out, especially near the cool of running water. 'As it happens,' she said, 'I'm not sorry. I have been on my . . . feet for days and nights now, without pause. My friend who works shifts with me has been ill.'

Marlowe tensed to move away. 'Ill?' He hadn't heard of any pestilence in the town, but it paid to be careful.

'No, no.' She put a hand on his arm. 'Nothing a man could catch. She has been in her bed with melancholy. Her man has died.'

Marlowe was confused. Had he misjudged this girl? Sleep was beginning to dull his brain and he said nothing.

She gave a harsh laugh. 'Because we sell what we have doesn't mean we don't have those who love us,' she said, curtly. 'In these times, we are not all harlots by nature. Sylvie is one who is not. She wants a man, a house, some babies, roses round the door. I pray to the Holy Mother that one day she will have them all. But for now, she has tied her wagon to the wrong star.'

'He couldn't help dying, poor man,' Marlowe said. Sympathy would cost him nothing and although her perfume wasn't subtle, it was better than the lingering stench of decay. And anyway, he liked her panache.

'None of us can help that, when our time has come,' she said, and he felt rather than saw her sketch the sign of the cross on her breast. 'This one, though, he could probably have helped having his throat cut from ear to ear.'

Marlowe pricked up his ears. He had no idea how many throats were cut on an average day in Rheims, but his guess would be not many. He also had no reason to suppose she spoke of Father Laurenticus, but his instincts were awakened, nonetheless. He kept his head and tried to keep the interest from his voice. 'That must have been terrible for her. Did she witness it?'

The girl sighed wetly in his ear. 'She was at home, covered in blood when I came in that night. I was early, because I had had a . . . shall we say a generous man.'

'You stole his purse.'

'If you say so.' She dug him in the ribs with a hard finger. 'I only work to live. If I make more than I might expect, I don't spend more time on my back than I must. So, I was early, so we came in almost together. She was undressing in the room we share and trying to wipe away the blood. She was covered in it, drenched. It was clotting in her hair. Her shift was stuck to her body with it. I have never seen such a horrible sight. At first, I thought the blood must be hers and I couldn't work out how she could still live.' She was facing forward, watching the silver lights of dawn on the water. She had begun her story, she was unburdening herself for the first time and nothing but her own death now would stop her.

'She was breathing so strangely, with drawn-in gasps and sobs like a person on their deathbed. It took me an hour to get her clean and then another to calm her down. She had been with her man in his bed, curled in his arms.' She paused and looked at Marlowe. 'You may not believe what I tell you now and I don't believe it myself, not completely. But Sylvie thinks it is true, and it keeps her as sane as she will ever be again, so I will tell it as I heard it.'

'The best way,' he assured her and she settled back to her tale.

'I have to ask you to believe that this man loved her. It is the only reason she kept going back to him, because it wasn't easy. She loved him, there is no doubt. She had been seeing him for months. He had hired her first, on a street corner, like any man would. Sylvie is a pretty little thing, boyish, not like me. Men like to look after her, she has always had . . . shall we call them regular friends. She doesn't often have to go looking, but this time, she did and she met this man. He took her against a tree to begin with but then he smuggled her into where he lived.'

'The English College,' Marlowe said, softly and almost to himself.

She stiffened. 'Have you heard this from someone else?' she hissed.

'No,' he assured her. 'It was a lucky guess.'

She settled down again and carried on her story. 'In that case, I won't need to tell you how difficult it was for her to see him. And what it was doing for our earnings, because he wasn't rich enough to pay for her time. She was spending all night with him and then all day with other men. She was almost dead on her feet.'

'As well as . . .' Marlowe couldn't think of a polite word for what he was thinking. And what he was thinking was only a rough guess.

'Yes. That too.' The sharp finger dug into his ribs again. 'You are a bright scholar, Monsieur Whoever You Are.'

'Greene.' The name had become automatic.

'Monsieur Greene. Yes, she was not giving good value to the paying customers, that is true. This man of hers . . .'

'Father Laurenticus.'

'Was that his name? She never told me. Well, he was quite active, from all accounts. She would regale me . . . but enough of that. One night, she went to him as always and by some miracle he let her sleep. She woke up when she heard a noise, a grunt, she says and a deep sigh. The door was closing and this Father Laurenticus was lying dead beside her, or dying perhaps I should say, with his blood arcing from his throat with the rhythm of his heart. She leaped up and ran. She ran past his murderer, who was on the landing, cleaning his knife against his thigh, as calm as you please.'

Now Marlowe really was interested. 'Did she see the man clearly?'

'No. He had a habit pulled over his face. Black. He made a grab for her, but she wriggled free. She hasn't left the room since until today.'

Marlowe sat up, unwinding himself from his cloak. 'Did he see her face? She could be in danger.'

'She says he didn't. And we are always in danger, Monsieur Greene. We are used to it.'

'Can you get her away somewhere?'

'No.' The answer was flat. 'She has nowhere to go and neither have I.' Again, the finger poked him in the ribs. 'You must find the killer for us, Monsieur Greene, and keep us safe that way.'

Marlowe stood up, brushing moss from the tree from his breeches. 'I'll try my best,' he said, and meant it. 'Meanwhile, I may need to see you again. Where can I find you?'

She waved an arm. 'Around. About.'

'What's your name, then? So I can leave messages for you if I need to.'

'Mireille. But, why not pay me and then we can make a regular appointment?'

'I have no money,' Marlowe lied. 'I come from the English College, remember.'

She laughed. 'You tell me that, wearing those clothes. That doublet of yours would keep me in bread and cheese for a year and more. Besides, everyone in town knows where the money is around here. The vintner, Aldred, is kept in funds by their business alone. No, if you are too mean to pay me, Monsieur Greene, you must find me where you can. Good night,' she said, and she walked away into the pearly morning.

Suddenly, Marlowe felt desperately sleepy. He went back to the room he would never feel at home in now and dropped fully clothed onto the bed and slept until almost noon, the clanging bells of Prime and Terce that called the faithful to prayer just a distant rumour in his head.

SIX

The amber sun of the autumn had climbed high by the time Marlowe found Solomon Aldred's wine shop in the shadow of the tanneries. It was a smell the projectioner knew well, reminding him of his Canterbury home and the calling of his father, tapping studs into the soles of the shoes he sold to the gentry. Most people gagged at the stench from the curing hides and recoiled at the carcasses rotting along the Vesle, but Marlowe had grown up with all that and he hardly noticed it.

He ducked under the low portal and groped his way to a bar laden with bottles wrapped in straw.

'*Bonjour, Monsieur,*' a female voice called. '*Ça va?*'

'Do you speak English, *madame*?' He wasn't in the mood to banter in French this morning and besides, the French of the Marne region was particularly unpleasant. It sounded not unlike a cat coughing up a hairball down a well.

'Ah, you're from the English College.' The owner of the voice emerged from the shadows. 'Solomon!' Her shriek could have shattered the bottles around her. It certainly gave Marlowe, hung over from drink and lack of sleep, a feeling that someone was dragging their nails down the slate that was surely embedded in his skull. She was a very large woman, perhaps forty, wearing the apron and cap of the vintner's guild. Such a thing could never be allowed in England; perhaps she was an honorary member. She glanced back into the bowels of the building, then beamed at Marlowe and disappeared again. There was the sound of an argument, brief, vituperative and hysterical from a passageway further off and then suddenly she was back.

'Solomon will be with you presently,' she said, taking a rag stopper out of a bottle and sniffing the contents. 'He's in the Jacques. Ah, here you are.' The little vintner appeared at her elbow and stood no higher than her shoulder. She looked down at him. 'I hope you've washed your hands,' she said with a frown.

Aldred grinned at Marlowe. 'It's something we vintners have

to do,' he said to explain the odd question, 'and yes, I have, Veronique, thank you, *ma chérie*. Now, bugger off and leave the gentlemen to talk.' Veronique snorted and bustled away as Aldred slapped her disappearing backside.

'Mrs Aldred?' Marlowe asked politely.

'Good God, no.' Aldred led the man to a low table lit by the window that looked out onto the street. 'The last I heard of Mrs Aldred she was living with a fish-curer in Lowestoft. You married, Marlowe? Er . . . Greene?'

Marlowe smiled. 'Never had the time.'

'Lucky man,' Aldred said. 'Claret?' he reached for a bottle.

'It's a little early for me,' Marlowe told him. 'And, incidentally, don't Frenchmen drink beer?'

Aldred looked horrified. 'Wash your mouth out,' he said. 'Rheims is the heart of the area where they make a wine called champagne. You get cider further north and west, but *beer*?' The vintner shook his head. 'You'd need to go to Alsace to get that. And believe me, you don't want to go to Alsace.'

'I went to the crypt last night,' Marlowe said, bringing the man to the point of his visit.

'Did you?' Aldred paused momentarily as the wine hit his tonsils. 'And?'

'And I wasn't ready for Charles of Westley Waterless' neck.'

'Neck?' The vintner was totally lost.

'It was broken,' Marlowe told him. 'The man had clearly been hanged.'

'Good God.' Aldred drained his glass in one swift jerk of head and hand. 'I was reliably informed he fell from a window.'

Marlowe looked at the man. 'You *are* an intelligencer, Master Aldred?' he asked and not for the first time. 'Walsingham's man in Rheims? It's just that you seem more of a . . . well, may I be frank? Wine merchant.'

Aldred bridled. 'How dare you?' he hissed and poured another glass. 'The whole essence of intelligence work is blending, Marlowe. You must know that. Everyone in Rheims knows I'm an Englishman, I make no secret of that. But they also know I deal in wines . . .'

There was a sudden explosion, like a musket's wheel crashing in the confined space of the vinter's. Marlowe threw himself sideways, his back to the wall, his dagger glinting in his hand. 'Jesus!' he hissed.

'A useful name to conjure with around here,' Aldred said. He hadn't moved. 'It's all right. It's the sparkling wine. It does that sometimes. Care to try some?'

Marlowe sat upright again, sheathed his weapon and straightened his doublet. 'Not if it's laced with gunpowder,' he said. 'You didn't know Charles was hanged?'

'No. Now look here, Marlowe, I warned you about this. The English College is a scorpions' nest, remember. I have to tread warily. Softly, softly, catchee Jesuit. I wouldn't be much use to Walsingham if my cover were blown. If I pried too deeply in the College's doings, they'd get suspicious. Clam up. That wouldn't suit Walsingham either.'

'Tell me about Laurenticus,' Marlowe said. 'And get it right.'

'Laurenticus?' Aldred nodded. 'Real name, David Vervain, from the south somewhere, the Languedoc, if memory serves.'

'What was he doing in the English College?'

'Oh, they're a pretty cosmopolitan bunch; haven't you noticed? Allen's willing to accept anybody as long as they're prepared to piss over Puritans. They are Walloons, Italians, Germans, Spaniards. Oh, and Frenchmen.'

'Like Laurenticus.'

'Yes. He was a Greek tutor at the university of Douai. When the locals kicked the English out of Douai, Laurenticus came with them. Don't ask me why.'

'When was this?' Marlowe asked.

'Er . . . let's see, 1578, give or take.'

'How did he die?' Marlowe asked. 'You said his death was unexplained.'

'Apoplexy,' Aldred said.

Marlowe blinked. 'That sounds quite explained to me,' he said.

'No, no.' Aldred shook his head. 'That was the official line. Allen's version. But . . . didn't you see his body? In the catacombs, I mean?'

'No,' Marlowe said. 'I was interrupted.'

'By whom?'

Marlowe shrugged. 'I didn't see his face. They have some sort of chantry priest down there, I suppose.'

'Possibly,' Aldred said, nodding.

'Whatever the cause,' Marlowe told him, 'it involved blood.'

'Really? How do you know?'

'His room for one thing,' Marlowe said. 'It's been scrubbed to within an inch of its life. Herbs scattered everywhere. New sheets. New bedding.' Something told him not to mention what he'd heard from Mireille only hours ago. 'How easy is it to get in and out of the College? After dark, say.'

'You're thinking Laurenticus was murdered by an outsider?'

'Not necessarily,' Marlowe said, sighing. 'But I believe the man was not always alone in his bed.'

'Really?' Aldred's eyes widened. 'Do tell.'

Marlowe chuckled. An intelligencer who could gossip for England was perhaps after all what Walsingham was paying for; perhaps Aldred just needed practice at sorting the wheat from the chaff, sheep from goats. 'What do we know about Dr Allen?' he asked.

'Got friends in high places, that one,' Aldred ruminated. 'Apart from God, I mean. His patron is the Duc de Guise and he's bankrolled directly from the Vatican. That makes him pretty much unassailable in this part of France. He's an Oxford man, but we mustn't hold that against him, must we?'

Marlowe smiled.

'Spends most of his time sending Papists back to England. Walsingham believes there are about forty of them at any given time.'

'And you monitor their leaving? Keep Walsingham informed?'

'I do my humble best,' Aldred said. 'Of course, Allen's been a target himself in the past.'

'Has he now?'

'Stands to reason,' Aldred told him. 'After the Pope, he's the biggest antichrist on Walsingham's list. I know of at least one attempt to poison him.'

'Do tell.' Marlowe gently mimicked the man.

'A Welshman called Ceurig. Before my time here the English College was more the Welsh College, in fact, while they were still at Douai. The rector was Moris Clynog and the poor bastard spent most of his time sorting out punch-ups between the English and Welsh scholars. Allen's banned them now, of course.'

'Punch-ups?' Marlowe asked.

'Welshmen,' Aldred said. 'They hanged Ceurig at Douai.'

'And did this Ceurig work for Walsingham?'

'I always supposed so,' Aldred said. 'But now . . . I don't know.'

'Those deaths . . .' Marlowe was thinking aloud. 'Charles and Laurenticus. They couldn't be Walsingham's work, could they?'

'Without telling me?' Aldred was outraged. 'No. Impossible. Unless Sir Francis is even more devious than I take him to be. The papers would tell us more, probably.'

'Papers?'

'Didn't I mention the papers?'

Marlowe eased the bottle from Aldred's grasp and poured himself a stiff one. 'Perhaps you could now.' He was patience itself, but he could see the end of his tether from where he sat.

'Right. Well . . . when I visited the College shortly after Laurenticus . . . died, they gave me a whole pile of papers of his; cleaning out the room, you know.'

'Why?'

'To tidy it up for the next occupant, I would imagine. You, in short.'

'No, I mean, why would they give his papers to you?'

'Packaging. For transporting bottles to our richest clients, we wrap them in parchment. Best vellum for the Archbishop. I'm always scrounging the stuff.'

'So . . . what's your point?'

'It may be nothing, of course.'

'What may be nothing?' Marlowe looked at him through narrowed eyes. His tether was nearer now and closing.

'Well, I'd only sent a couple of bottles out when a college servant turned up, all hot and bothered. He'd run all the way from the Rue de Venise.'

'What for?'

'To get the papers back.'

'Did he say why?'

'Apparently, Father Laurenticus had willed them to the library. They needed them back to bind and add to the collection.'

'So, what did you do?'

'Well, I gave them back to him. I didn't really see that I had much choice.'

'Did you read them?'

'Well . . .'

'Well, Master Aldred?' The end of Marlowe's tether was within an arm's reach and it wasn't going to be pretty when it was finally in his grasp.

'I must admit I didn't read any of the stuff the servant took back, but I did glance at a sheet I wrapped a very good Bordeaux in.'

'And?'

'I couldn't read it at all. It was no language I have ever seen. I believe it was a code. Very small, spidery writing. It could have been nothing at all of course, but it preyed on my mind so I got a message to Walsingham. I asked him for a code-breaker. It could be important.'

'It could indeed,' Marlowe agreed. 'Who is Walsingham sending, do you know?'

'No idea. Thomas Phelippes is his best man. Got a mind like a razor. But he's not a field agent. Never been known to leave England. Doesn't like leaving London very much. I just hope it's not one of the Giffords.'

'Giffords?'

'Projectioner brothers. You know how Walsingham likes to keep his little business in the family. Either of them would be useless – too loose-lipped, too unobservant. They get things wrong.'

'No!' Marlowe feigned horror. 'Please tell me it isn't so. Where did you send the code paper?'

'Er . . . why?'

'I'm going to assume that Dr Allen has long since consigned the bulk of Laurenticus' documents to the flames. But there might just be an outside chance the one you saw has survived. Where did it go?'

Aldred sighed and crossed to a far corner. He hauled down a heavy, leather-bound ledger. 'Take your pick,' he said, tapping a page covered in his untidy scrawl.

Marlowe ran a quick finger down the page. 'There are twenty-three names on this list, Master vintner,' he said as he bent to read them. 'The wine business must be burgeoning.'

'It is, actually. I really don't know why I risk my neck for Walsingham's pittance.'

'Neither do I,' said Marlowe.

'Actually, it's not as bad as all that. Look at the dates. It has to be one of the last four. But . . . you're not going to try to find it, surely? The odds of it still being in one piece must be huge – and anyway, how odd it would look. "Excuse me, I wonder if I could have a look at your wine wrappings?" They'd see through you in seconds. My business would be in tatters.'

'They might see through me, they might at that,' Marlowe said, tearing the bottom of the page from the ledger. 'But, unlike you, Master Aldred, I don't have a second income. Sir Francis' pay is all I get. And again unlike you, I believe in working for it. I'll see myself out.'

The Feast of Michael and All Angels was celebrated with a vengeance in Rheims. While the entire body of town clergy, from the Archbishop to the humblest clerk thronged the narrow, twisting streets on their way to give thanks at the cathedral, everybody else saw it as yet another excuse not to work but to hold another street party.

Marlowe bought a cheap chain of office at a second-hand stall along the Rue Rouge and pushed his way through the illegal boules matches that endangered the unwary ankle, the dancers and the acrobats, to a shady corner in the angle of the wall that rejoiced in the name of the Dancing Chicken. The place was packed, tipplers spilling out onto the cobbles as they laughed and joked. No one seemed to be drinking smoke here, so Marlowe sensed the craze in London had not yet spread east. They were drinking everything else, however, including something glutinous that was taking the polish off the tables and it was not yet Sext back in the English College.

A lady of the night who was not Mireille winked at him, but when she saw his chain of office thought better of it and settled on a particularly stupid-looking country bumpkin in town for the festivities. The aroma of roasting suckling pig reached Marlowe's nostrils as he waved at the genial host, busy taking money hand over fist on one of the busiest days of his year. Marlowe whispered something in the confused man's ear and led him, protesting, away from the bustle and noise, to a trap door that led down into darkness. They might as well have been going down to Hell.

'I didn't catch your name,' the landlord said as they got to the bottom step and he snapped a tinder flint and set it to a candle in a waxy sconce on the wall.

'Baillet,' Marlowe told him. 'Comptroller of Wines.'

'For which district?' the landlord frowned at the medallion Marlowe flashed at him in the half light.

'*This* one,' said Marlowe, as though to the village idiot.

'You're not from round here.' The landlord was not convinced.

'Of course not,' Marlowe said. 'What would be the point? You know how this works, surely? Monsieur . . . er . . .?'

'Detrail,' the landlord said. 'How what works?'

Marlowe shook his head sadly, tutting. 'It pains me to admit it, Monsieur Detrail –' he was praying his French participles were holding up – 'on this saint's day of all days . . .'

'I've got a licence, you know,' Detrail was anxious to assure him, 'from the Archbishop himself.'

'No, no.' Marlowe raised his hand to calm the man. 'You miss my point. On this most holy of days, it is my miserable duty to inform you that there has, of late, been a certain . . . shall we say, malfeasance . . . in the Department of the Comptroller of Wines.'

'Tell me it isn't so!' said Detrail flatly, watching Marlowe as he used the landlord's lantern to check the neatly laid bottles of wine in his cellar.

'That's why they've appointed me,' Marlowe said with the minimum of lip movement. If you're going to be a conspirator, it's important to make sure that the person you're talking to is willing to join you. Detrail seemed to have the necessary credentials. 'The last Comptroller . . .'

'Lafontine.'

'The same.' Marlowe nodded. 'On the take.'

'Tell me about it,' grunted Detrail.

'To that end, *moi* –' Marlowe stressed the word – 'an out of towner, so to speak. No preformed . . . shall we say, bad habits.'

'Look . . .' Detrail held Marlowe's arm as he continued his search. 'I hope you're not implying any impropriety on my part . . .'

'My dear fellow.' Marlowe stopped and held the lantern under the man's nose so that he took a step back. 'Certainly not. No, we're interested in a man called Solomon Aldred. Know him?'

'I might.' Detrail was still being careful.

'Englishman, isn't he?' Marlowe hit just the right note of contempt.

'Yes, he is.' Detrail began to warm to this man. He hadn't been truly happy when the English College moved in, lock, stock and barrel, a few years back. The bastards were taking over the place. *And* they never left tips.

'Can you show me his latest consignment?' Marlowe asked.

'Why, yes,' Detrail said, leading the man by the arm. 'Over here.'

Marlowe looked at the bottles. All of them were wrapped in paper. 'Which are the newest?' he asked.

'Can't you tell?' Detrail frowned. What sort of Comptroller of Wines were they sending these days?

'I had hoped for your cooperation, Monsieur,' he said. 'Do you know how many hostelries I have to check today?' He looked at the man, a strange expression on his face. 'You *are* cooperating?' he asked.

'The last two rows,' Detrail told him sulkily.

'And since the Feast of the Blessed Virgin's Birth?'

'Um . . .' Detrail ran his finger over the bottles. 'Those five.'

'Have you sold any?'

'Not yet,' the landlord said. 'Of course, it will be a different story come cock-shut time tonight. I don't ever remember it so busy. Which is by way of reminding you politely, Monsieur Comptroller, that I must get back upstairs. So –' he pulled a plug-remover from his apron pocket, –'want to try some?'

'No, thank you. It's the packaging I'm interested in.'

'The packaging?' Detrail was incredulous.

'You don't think we Comptrollers of Wines just go round the country getting pissed, do you, Monsieur Detrail? We can't afford to get drunk, any more than a landlord can. It's a fine art, I can tell you, Wine Comptrolling. I served a seven-year apprenticeship in bottle labelling alone.'

Detrail, who had not spent a sober day for more than fifteen years, looked abashed but stood his ground, plug-remover still held aloft.

'Well, off you bugger, then.' Marlowe shooed the landlord away. 'I know how busy you are and I can manage. Just leave the lantern.'

'Er . . .'

The door at the head of the stairs crashed open and a frantic female voice called down. 'Bertrand, what the bloody Hell are you doing? It's a madhouse up here.'

'Madame Detrail?' Marlowe asked.

'Uh,' the landlord grunted. 'You've met her, have you? I'd better get back. Will you be all right?'

'Of course.' Marlowe smiled, promising himself he'd have to plant a grateful kiss on the cheek of Madame Detrail on his way out.

Nothing. The papers wrapped around Aldred's bottles were indeed from the English College but they were rough plans for a new fountain to be built in the grounds and had no obvious link with Father Laurenticus at all. He thanked a harassed-looking Detrail on his way out, assured him that all was in order, took one look at Madame Detrail and decided not to kiss her after all, before vanishing into the jostling crowd.

Proctor Lomas was on day duty. It wasn't his favourite time to work, as it meant spending time with Mistress Lomas at home. The many little Lomases also made his life difficult and it seemed to him that each and every one could measure their existence back to a stint on day duty. His wife was no beauty, sad to say, but she had always been a dutiful wife, he couldn't fault her that way. He sighed and scanned the faces of the scholars as they streamed past him on their way into college after their noon-time break. Wait a minute; that face didn't belong and not only did it not belong in that crowd, it actually *did* belong to Robert Greene.

As a rule, Lomas, like all his proctorial kind, had no jurisdiction over the graduates, who were a law unto themselves. Neither had he any jurisdiction over scholars of other colleges. But Gabriel Harvey had taken the time to send a special message to the Lodge, with a very specific description of Greene at the bottom, with strict instructions to prevent him by any means at the Proctors' disposal, stopping only short of the man's actual death, to enter the College precincts. There was anyway an ancient rule that prevented graduates of one College entering another, but this was largely ignored, though Lomas tried to keep it when he had the time. An edict from the Master Designate was a different matter though, and he stepped forward.

'Dominus Greene!' Lomas lent his not inconsiderable lung power to the general hullabaloo. To do the man credit, he didn't even flinch. 'Dominus Greene,' Lomas shouted again, even louder. 'I must have a word with you, sir, if I may.'

Greene still carried on, wedged in the press of scholars.

Lomas could see he had no option and stepped into the throng which parted, out of sheer habit, to let him through. 'Dominus Greene,' he said, hauling his quarry to one side. 'I have instructions not to let you through.'

Greene looked at Lomas blankly. 'I haf no iddya wot you mee-an,' he said, in a hopeless parody of a scholar of vaguely foreign extraction. Greene had travelled in Europe but he'd never done much there other than shout loudly in English. Had any of the locals shouted back at him, he would have been appalled. For this reason, his accent was modelled on a Spanish potman in the Eagle and Child, whom Lomas actually knew quite well.

The Proctor was pulling him towards the gate of the college as he spoke, more in anger than in sorrow. 'I'm sorry that you take me for a fool, Dominus Greene,' he said, through clenched teeth, 'I would have saved you the ignominy of this, but you give me no choice,' and, turning him round on the last word, planted his large, flat Proctor's foot on the graduate's backside and propelled him into the street. It had not been Lomas' intention that Greene should fall flat in a puddle at the feet of some sizars of St John's, whose lives Greene did his best to make miserable. But sometimes the Lord gives these little pleasures by the way and the Proctor returned to his post a happier man.

'Are you . . . all right with this, Michael?' Thomas Phelippes' voice sounded oddly muffled in the darkness of the bedchamber.

'Yes,' Johns said, at his elbow, a little surprised at the question. 'Why wouldn't I be?'

'Well,' the code-breaker said, 'I mean . . . sharing a bed. I haven't done this since my university days.'

'*My* university days have only just ended,' Johns reminded him. 'And such was the popularity of Corpus Christi I didn't actually have my own bedroom until . . . what? Six years ago, I suppose. You don't snore, do you?'

'I don't know,' Phelippes muttered. He had never had a chance to find anyone who would be able to tell him. All the way from Deptford Walsingham's code-breaker had felt awkward about all this. Give him a twist of lemon, a roll of parchment, a scattering of ciphers, numbers, letters and there was no one in Gloriana's realm to touch him. But here, in an alien land . . . and a *Papist* land, too. Nicholas Faunt had said it was vital. Solomon Aldred had discovered something at the English College. A code. He could make neither head nor tail of it. Faunt had asked him to send it but the intelligencer-turned-wine-merchant had had to admit he didn't actually have it any more. Not on his person. Not per se. So if the mountain could not go to Mahound, Mahound must make his way through France's mountains to Rheims.

Not that Faunt had been at all helpful. He had given Phelippes an alias – Thomas Webb, a collector of *objets d'art* for the Earl of Southampton, on a buying trip across Europe. But as to lethal gadgets balanced on door-tops, drinks and food laced with poisons, dagger-carrying ruffians on the road, Faunt had not said a word. And now Phelippes had compounded the problem by dragging Johns along as his eyes, his ears and, if needs be, his strong-arm man. All in all, it wasn't the most sensible of choices. Johns was an academic through and through. He never carried a weapon, not of any kind and he looked as though a strong wind would blow him over. Phelippes hoped, but not with much conviction, that he might turn out to be one of those wiry types, who looked weak but had enormous strength when pushed. Now was perhaps not the time to risk squeezing one of his biceps.

'Michael?'

Johns sighed. 'Yes, Thomas.' He had the patience of any one of the saints to whom he no longer prayed, but the last few days – and more especially, nights – had become a bit of a trial. He had come to realize that the happy-go-lucky lad who had struggled through Aristotle and Ramus with him in the Schools had changed. He was introverted, given to sudden bursts of verbal diarrhoea and he seemed afraid of his shadow.

'I haven't been honest with you,' the code-breaker said.

'If you're going to talk cryptically about intelligencers and projectioners again, it'll be my turn to start snoring loudly.'

'You can't just ignore it, Michael,' Phelippes snapped. 'Wrapped in swaddling bands in Cambridge, you've no idea. This is the real world. It's not about syntax and Dialectics and Discourses. You know there's a full-blown war coming, don't you?'

Johns took the slur on the chin and twisted round to punch his meagre pillow into something more comfortable. Propping himself up, he resigned himself to a long night. 'All right,' he said. 'Time for honesty. Your turn.'

There was a pause while Phelippes fiddled with the hem of the sheet. He played for time, tweaking the covers straight and smoothing the worn coverlet. Eventually, he found his words. 'I can't tell you,' he said.

The next thing he knew, John's pillow was bouncing off his face, threatening to knock him out of bed. Perhaps Phelippes had miscalculated John's right arm.

'Then go to sleep!' the ex-Corpus man shouted. He suddenly remembered where they were, in a flea-ridden inn on the arse of humanity somewhere near the Seine. The walls were thin and he wasn't comfortable speaking English. He lapsed into Greek. 'Unless of course, you want to hear my confession – and not in any Papist way, I assure you.'

'Confess what?' Phelippes meekly passed Johns' pillow back to him.

'The real reason I came along with you,' Johns said quietly, settling back and interlocking his fingers across his chest.

'I thought it was for old times' sake.' Phelippes said.

'It's because I'm terrified,' he told him.

Phelippes was amazed. He had never thought of himself as someone who could help a terrified person. In fact, he spent most of the time being pretty terrified himself, of shadows, odd sounds, people he knew, people he didn't know, his servants, Walsingham, Faunt . . . the list was endless. He was beginning to find himself being rather frightened by everyday objects such as bread and coal scuttles, but he had that more or less under control most of the time. Walsingham and Faunt he knew were reasonable fears, but the rest were surely not normal. Especially the bread thing. So he lifted himself up on one elbow and peered in the dark at the man who was looking to him for protection from whatever scared him.

'What are you terrified of?' he asked. He hoped Johns would say 'Bread' but he thought that was perhaps just his own special nightmare.

'The world,' Johns whispered. 'You were right, Thomas. The swaddling bands of Cambridge as you put it. That old midwife life has just cut me free of them. I don't remember how that really felt, to know the draughts creeping along your skin, to feel the hot blast of a fire, the ice of a morning wash, a rough towel over your face. But I'm facing it again. All of it, just like the first time.'

He turned to his old friend in the stillness of their room, hearing the straw crackle in the mattress, the string creak under the mattress, the floorboards shift under the bed.

'That's why I came. To have someone with me I can trust. I've used you.'

Phelippes laughed, a short and brittle snort really. 'No more,' he said, 'than I've used you. Greek, Hebrew, Latin, French, Italian, Spanish, German, Walloon and Persian. I speak them all. Or rather, I read them, write them, decipher them, work them out. Remember what happened at Rouen the other day?'

Johns did. 'You didn't hear the dock-keeper,' he said.

'Oh, I heard him all right. And I knew exactly what to say in reply. It's just that when I opened my mouth, nothing came out. You did my talking for me.'

'It was my pleasure.' Johns smiled into the darkness.

'Michael . . .' Phelippes was sitting up, hugging his knees. 'I work for the Queen's spymaster, Francis Walsingham.'

'I think I knew that,' Johns said.

'And we are going to the English College, the scorpions' nest itself. I wish I could tell you more, but I can't. Look, if you want to go back, back to England, back to Cambridge, I will understand. Honestly, I will.'

'The English College . . .' Johns rolled the name around his tongue. 'Dr William Allen, isn't it? The antichrist?'

Phelippes said nothing, but nodded his head. In the dark, Johns felt the motion transmitted through the bedclothes, and assumed assent.

For a while the two men kept a thoughtful silence, then Johns sighed and said, 'I admit that when we set off on our little adventure, I wasn't quite expecting the Holy Inquisition.'

'No,' muttered Phelippes, lying back down and pulling the bedclothes around his ears, 'no one ever does.'

SEVEN

A chill October wind rippled the surface of the lake below the chateau. Christopher Marlowe checked the purse at his hip to make sure he still had the ring there, the one he'd appropriated from Gerald Skelton's study. The pale sun shone on the whitewashed circular towers and glinted on the fleurs-de-lys wrought in gold-flecked iron above the roof. No one challenged him at the gate and he trotted on his hired horse into a wide courtyard, strewn with straw and chickens. Clearly the Sieur de Fleury had known better times. Marlowe knew the name. One of the man's ancestors had died at Agincourt, trampled in the mud of that wet October day and it looked from the state of this place that the family fortunes had died with him. Marlowe had made enquiries around the town. Anne de Fleury was a passionate Frenchman and a Papist through and through but he was old and had quarrelled with his sons so that whenever the family met they squabbled incessantly over inheritance. Was it that, Marlowe wondered, that meant the man went in fear of his life? Perhaps not, but it was a useful thing to know.

And suddenly, he also knew why no one had challenged him at the gate. Armed men were creeping out of the shadows of the stalls that lined the courtyard. He heard the gate slam shut and lock behind him and he steadied his horse, stroking the animal's neck and whispering to it in his best French. A dozen pikes prickled all around him and Marlowe held up Skelton's ring so that it flashed in the cloud-shrouded sun.

'I have a message from Dr Allen,' Marlowe said, 'from the English College.'

One of the pikemen spat volubly but a sharp voice barked a reprimand. A fierce old warrior in obsolete armour came waddling out of a darkened archway. He wore a tabard with the arms of Fleury embroidered on it, but the colours were pale and some of the intricate needlework was unravelling, trailing cobwebs of old glory in the eddying air of his movement.

'What have I to do with the English College?' the old man wanted to know. His face was almost purple and his beard snow white, along with the remnants of the hair he still had on his head.

'You are the Sieur de Fleury?' Marlowe didn't trust himself completely with another country's heraldry and it was as well to be sure.

The old man folded his arms with a rattle of metal. 'I am Anne de Fleury,' he said as the pikemen drew back to let him approach. 'Who wants to know?'

'I am Robert Greene,' Marlowe lied again, 'and I have news for your ears only, my lord.'

The old knight looked at the man. He was well mounted, dressed in the English fashion, but flashily, like a roisterer. He invited Marlowe to dismount and one of the pikemen took his horse. Another whisked the dagger from the small of his back and a third patted the sleeves of his doublet and the bulges of his Venetians. He even peered into the tops of Marlowe's buskins and shook his head at his master.

'Show me that,' Fleury snapped, pointing to the ring.

Marlowe passed it over. The old man squinted at it. His eyes weren't what they had been but he wasn't letting his people know just how bad they were. Even so he recognized the cross maline of the English College and threw it back to Marlowe.

'What's this all about, Greene?' Fleury asked.

'For your ears only, my lord,' Marlowe reminded him.

The old man beckoned him forward and a pikeman raised his weapon. 'Stand to!' Fleury barked. 'I thank you, gentlemen, for your diligence.' He took Marlowe's dagger from the flunkey who held it and waved it in the stranger's face. 'But I was at Calais that great day we took it back from you English. My artillery crossed the frozen marshes and blasted seven kinds of shit out of your garrison there.' He winked at Marlowe and said, 'I haven't lost my touch.'

Marlowe had talked to men from the Calais garrison when he was a boy. He thought it would be impolite to remind the Sieur de Fleury that the French had outnumbered the English nearly fourteen to one. *And* all that was nearly thirty years ago.

'Well, boy?' the old knight squinted up into Marlowe's face. 'What is for my ears only?'

'May I see your wine cellar, my lord? You may care to have your steward present.'

'My wine cellar?' Fleury frowned. 'Very well. Seurat!' he shouted at a flunkey wearing his livery. 'Keys, please. Wine cellar.'

The man Seurat hefted a solid-looking bunch of keys from a belt at his waist and slotted one into position in a studded door under the shade of a roofed awning. The cellar was hardly that, but it sloped away under the courtyard wall and there were enough bottles to survive the siege of Troy. If the old knight wasn't spending much on his fortifications, he was more than making up for it with his wine bill. The steward fumbled with a tinderbox and lit a large candle.

'Why are we here?' Fleury asked.

'Where is the latest consignment from Solomon Aldred?' Marlowe asked.

'Over here.' The steward took them all to a far corner.

'When did these arrive?' Marlowe asked.

'Last week. Thursday, I believe.'

'Ten bottles?' Marlowe needed to be sure. There was no room for error because he knew he couldn't possibly pull this stunt again.

'That's right. Anything . . . wrong with them?' The steward might just as well have said 'Are they stiff with poison? Have people died in their hundreds by drinking this wine of the devil?' But he was a professional. He tried to keep cool. 'Have there been any . . . incidents?'

Marlowe smiled at him, but there was no comfort in what was really just a grimace. 'When you serve a bottle to my Lord Fleury –' Marlowe stood between them – 'how do you bring it to his hall?'

'I don't,' the steward said, looking down his nose as only a Frenchman can, 'I have people.'

'These people,' Marlowe said, lowering his voice and clutching the steward's sleeve. 'Are they . . . well?'

'What?' the steward frowned, stepping back a pace.

'For God's sake, man!' The old knight exploded, turning ever more purple in the candle's flickering light. 'What are you talking about?'

Marlowe turned to the man and said quietly, so close to his ear that the old warrior could feel the breath warm on his neck. 'Do you have enemies, my lord? Those who might wish you ill?'

The old man blinked, twitching his moustache. 'Seurat, leave us, will you?'

'My lord . . .?'

'That will be all, sir,' Fleury snapped. 'Double up, dammit.'

The steward bowed and, leaving the candle with Marlowe, bowed his way out of the room.

'Well –' the knight leaned back against the nearest wall – 'that one for a start. Hates my guts.'

'Anyone else?'

'Two of my three sons,' the old man said. 'Possibly all three. It's no use pretending. I was never much of a father, but at the time I thought I'd given them everything.'

'Ah, filial ingratitude.' Marlowe shook his head.

'What has this to do with Solomon Aldred's wine?' Fleury asked.

'Possibly nothing,' Marlowe said, 'but we've had . . . hmm, let's call it intelligence . . . at the English College. Someone is poisoning wine and sending lethal bottles to certain key people in Rheims. Dr Allen, the Archbishop. And you.'

'Aldred's a poisoner?' Fleury was astonished. He'd always found the man rather good company, once he was able to put to one side the fact that he was an Englishman.

'No, no.' Marlowe was quick to correct him. 'Someone has used Master Aldred's services to commit murder, or attempt to, at least. Aldred himself is not involved.'

'Poisoned wine, eh?' Fleury was taking it all in. 'Wait a minute, you say Dr Allen has received some? The Archbishop?'

Marlowe nodded grimly.

'Then it can't be my boys.' Fleury was secretly relieved. 'They're only on nodding terms with His Grace and they don't know Allen at all.'

'Amen,' said Marlowe. 'The diabolical thing, my lord, is that the poison isn't in the wine itself.'

'Not?' Fleury frowned. 'Then, how . . .?'

'That's why I asked your steward how he delivered it to your table.'

'In the wrapping, as it comes in from Aldred's shop,' the old knight told him.

'Mother of God!' Marlowe crossed himself, thinking briefly how this action was getting to be frighteningly natural to him these days.

'What?' Fleury did likewise, a knee-jerk reaction.

Marlowe closed to him and lowered his voice. He suspected the old man was at least partially deaf, but it didn't seem quite right to yell if he was meant to be working secretly. He tried to pitch it right, so that he could still hear. 'The poison is in the wrapping, my lord,' he said, enunciating crisply. 'Anyone who touches it is dead within the hour. Earlier if they put their fingers near their mouths in that time.'

'Mother of God indeed!' Fleury repeated and sketched another cross.

'My lord, I would not want your health risked any more than necessary. May I check the wrappings on these bottles?'

'Is that not very dangerous?' Fleury asked, backing away.

'Indeed, but I have a natural immunity to the poison.'

'You do? How so?'

Marlowe looked at him with narrowed eyes in the candlelit gloom. 'All men from where I was brought up as a boy have it. It is something in the water, I have always been led to believe.' He hoped his French was up to the explanation. 'I shall still take precautions.' Marlowe unhooked his gloves from his belt and drew them on with much solemnity. 'I suggest that you stand well back. It has been known that the fumes alone, when the wrapping is disturbed . . .'

Fleury backed away. 'Um . . . look here, Greene. I don't want to break your concentration, you know. Probably a bit of a tricky exercise, this checking and what not. I'll just sit outside, shall I? No need for both of us to . . .?' He looked hopefully at Marlowe, who nodded enthusiastically.

'My lord,' he said, bowing slightly, 'I wouldn't have it any other way.' And he waited until the old man was through the door before turning back to the rack of wine.

Nothing. There had been nothing in the wrappings of Aldred's bottles at the Dancing Chicken and there was nothing now. Just a selection of some of the more salacious verses from Leviticus, copied over and over in an indifferent hand, as if to improve the calligraphy. And not even, Marlowe guessed, in Father Laurenticus' hand. Was he risking life and limb on a wild-goose chase? Assuring the Sieur de Fleury that his wine cellar was safe, he spurred his horse under the low archway and galloped Hell for leather back to town.

The Compline bell was sounding as Christopher Marlowe ducked under the archway that led to the Archbishop's private cellar. Behind him rose the colossal Gothic masterpiece that was Rheims cathedral and the saints of old Christendom, cold in their chiselled stone, watched him go. At the main door he had been stopped by a verger who told him the church was about to start divine service. Marlowe was very welcome to join them, but if he had just come to marvel at the architectural splendour of the place, that would be three sous, please, and could he call back. Marlowe declined both, explaining that he had urgent business on behalf of the Archbishop's vintner and Compline or not, the mercantile bureaucracy of France could not wait. There had been a grave error. The wrappings on Solomon Aldred's recent consignment were not finest vellum. They must be replaced, at no cost to His Grace, of course. And Master Aldred would be pleased to send the next crate free of charge.

A choirboy led Marlowe through a labyrinth of stone paths, through wicket gates without number. The lad's surplice billowed out behind him like a race-built galleon under full sail. Not long ago, this could have been Marlowe himself, hurrying to the cathedral at Canterbury under the shadow of the Dark Entry on his way from school. He smiled to himself at the water that had flowed under the bridge since then, by way of the Stour, the Cam, the Thames and Seine and now the Vesle; water that ran dark and deadly; water in which bodies floated.

The boy showed him into yet another cellar and he told his story to yet another cellar-keeper. The monk seemed easier to hoodwink that either the landlord Detrail or the steward Seurat and Marlowe was soon reading the wine wrappings by a flickering candle. The sixth bottle made his heart thump, but his face didn't move. Small, spidery letters, in blocks. They didn't seem to form

words but were simply a jumble of squiggles. A Mohammedan
would take them for gibberish, but Mohammedans didn't work
for Francis Walsingham and Marlowe recognized their importance
at once. He shook his head, tutting, collected up the sheets and
stuffed them into his doublet. Bottles seven and eight were
wrapped in St Paul's letter to the Ephesians and he made a great
show of feeling the parchment between his fingers, sniffing the
dry ink as if to make doubly sure.

'Thank God,' he muttered to the cellarer monk. 'Only one
bottle contaminated. I cannot apologize enough. I will be back
by Matins with Master Aldred's free crate *and* the correct
wrapping for bottle six.' He caught the bemused look on the
cellarer's face. 'Look, I feel very bad about this,' Marlowe
said, preparing to leave. 'Is there a priest free? For confession,
I mean?'

'Will I do?'

Marlowe turned at the stentorian voice behind him. Framed
in the archway with the torches of the cathedral precinct behind
him stood Dr Allen. Marlowe felt himself transported back to
his boyhood for the second time in half an hour and had to fight
down an urge to lick his palm and flatten his unruly hair.

'Master.' Marlowe was wrong-footed again but his face didn't
betray the fact.

'Dominus Greene.' Allen walked towards him. 'I thought I
saw you on your way here. The lad who brought you confirmed it
for me. An Englishman, in the habit of a roisterer, armed
and looking for the wine cellar of the Archbishop of Rheims. And
at a time when every other member of the English College
except my good self is at their devotions. Nothing odd in that,
is there?'

'Merely helping out a friend,' Marlowe explained.

'Oh?' Allen's raised eyebrow said it all. 'How so?'

'Solomon Aldred,' Marlowe said. 'The vintner. He fears he
may have sent His Grace the wrong consignment.'

'And has he?'

'All is well,' Marlowe assured him.

'Good of you to be so concerned about Master Aldred,' Allen
said. 'I hadn't the two of you down for friends.'

'I admit,' Marlowe said, 'I didn't care for the man when I first met him. But he grows on you. I was coming to the cathedral anyway . . .'

'You were?' Allen asked. 'Why?'

'It isn't often you see one rose window as lovely as in this cathedral, but to have two is almost too much. I heard that at this time of the year and at this time of day the light strikes through them just right. What fairer monument to the glory of God? I had never seen it from the inside.'

'And you still haven't,' Allen observed. 'Nor will you from down here in the cellars. Shall we?'

'Delighted,' Marlowe said and thanked the cellarer for his understanding before walking with the black-robed Master towards another Catholic Mass. His heart was still in his mouth but the documents he had sought for so long were at least safe, for the moment, in his doublet. He mumbled the Latin chant alongside Allen as the candles flickered and threw their long shadows on the soaring pillars. And the rose windows were undeniably beautiful, so his story held up on that score. But Allen needed watching. Used as Marlowe was to the unworldly Dr Norgate, a Master who was in charge of his faculties in more than one way was something of a novelty.

It was late by the time Kit Marlowe and Solomon Aldred trudged home along the Rue des Capucins that Wednesday. The town Watch nodded at the little Englishman who had become such a fixture in the city over the recent months. They didn't nod at Marlowe. But they watched him nonetheless; there was something in the way he carried himself, saw everything, remained silent while Aldred jabbered on in his incomprehensible babble. Marlowe was one to watch for all eternity.

Around the corner of the old convent of St Remi, Marlowe spoke for the first time. 'You know we are not alone, Master Aldred?' It was whispered out of the corner of his mouth in the way he had first learned as a choral scholar, chatting in the sermon, but had honed to perfection in two years of playing Francis Walsingham's games.

'Two of them.' The vintner nodded without changing his tone, turning or breaking his stride. 'By the trees. How long, would you say?'

'Since we came through the Mars Gate, I think.'

'That would be my guess. Let's see what they do if we split up. Do you know the Palace of Tau?'

'You could hardly miss it,' Marlowe pointed out, mildly. Even if it had not been rubbing shoulders with Notre Dame, it would have stood out in any city.

'Well, yes.' Aldred had become a local through and through and could not help condescending just a little to the newcomer. 'Go there, the best route is past my house, I think, from here. Then if you double back on yourself, you can end up back at my house. Hide and wait for me in that little archway across the road. I'll go in the opposite direction from here, to the river and then double back through some little lanes I know. Wait for me for as long as it takes; my route will be longer than yours and more dangerous.' He paused and looked Marlowe in the face, seeming to learn each feature. 'Take care of yourself, Master Greene. We're all on dangerous ground, wherever we are.' He spoke in Greek, not well but with feeling. It paid to be on the safe side.

The pair separated, Aldred clattering with his brass-bound pattens on the cobbles, sending the odd spark across the stone. Marlowe slipped silently into the darkness, avoiding the moon and the occasional guttering torch-flame at street corners. He couldn't see his shadows now and concluded they must have both gone after Aldred. Feeling a twinge of guilt, he increased his pace. Solomon Aldred was a field agent of repute, a project-ioner par excellence and if it sometimes seemed that he had gone a little native, a little too absorbed in the day-to-day business of vintning, it had not slowed him up too much. Besides which, he was *very* short and therefore likely to be able to hide in places where the normal-sized followers couldn't go.

It was only as he was reaching Aldred's front door that Marlowe paused. He squeezed himself into the shadows on the opposite side of the street and watched for a while, letting his eyes settle into using the available light. Was it a trick of the dark, or was the door ajar? There were no lights in the building and even if Aldred had somehow got back first, he couldn't see him leaving the door open even for a moment, given the circumstances.

He slid his dagger from its sheath nestled in the small of his back and slipped across the street, watching like a cat for small movements in the shadows. There was nobody. No footfalls, no drunken curses, farts or shouts to mask a secret foe's approach. It was the open door that bothered him more than his shadows now. Aldred would have snuffed the candle as he left, but he would also have closed the door; if he wasn't thinking like a projectioner, he would have been thinking like a vintner and a bottle stolen was a bottle that would make him no profit.

Marlowe pushed the door open with his foot, gently, so that the hinges didn't creak. The waft of old wine hit him like a wall and he saw a head bob up, black and hatless, against the far window. It flashed for a second only but it was enough and Marlowe drove his left elbow hard against the open door. It thudded on something solid behind it and the groan of pain and the grunt of an exhaled breath told him he'd guessed right. It was a reception committee. He spun round the door and hauled the groaning figure in front of him, jerking the man's arm painfully up behind his back and holding his blade across his throat.

'You, by the window,' he shouted in French. 'Identify yourself!'

'Friend!' came the nearly hysterical reply.

'What the Hell's going on?' It was Solomon Aldred's voice, calling through the doorway from the street. 'Marlowe, is that you?' There was the whisper of a flint being struck and candle light warmed the room. In front of the window, standing behind a stack of wine crates, stood a scholarly-looking man with a wheel-lock pistol in his hand.

'Kit Marlowe,' Aldred said, crossing the room and removing the gun from the other man's fist, 'meet Thomas Phelippes, who should not, I might add, be allowed to play with things like this.' He waved the pistol rather aimlessly in the air and everyone ducked slightly, by instinct. Aldred half turned and looked towards Marlowe, still tensed behind his captive. 'I must admit that I don't know the gentleman whose throat you were about to slit.'

Marlowe spun the man round so that he was facing him.

'Hello, Kit,' he said.

Marlowe stood there, gaping like an idiot. Then he recovered himself and, with an expansive gesture, introduced the man to

Aldred. 'Master Aldred,' he said, 'please meet Professor Michael Johns, of Cambridge University.'

'*Late* of Cambridge University,' Johns corrected him, adjusting his clothing after his mild rough housing.

'Ah,' Aldred said calmly, lighting more candles. 'If you two are going to have a little reunion, do it in your own time. We have more pressing business. Marlowe, the door, if you please. You might have to give it a shove; it tends to jump its hinges when roughly handled. We don't want half of Rheims knowing all about the Queen's business.'

Robert Greene had dressed and prepared with care. He had learned a lot since his last encounter with Marlowe and his little box of tricks and he was armed with a chisel, a clamp and his right hand was squeezed into a gauntlet he had prised from a tomb in St Mary's on his way from his rooms to Corpus Christi. He had learned his lesson with the Proctors and had watched carefully to find their Achilles' heel. They were always on their guard, but they were slightly less wary at shift change and it was then that he had managed to get through the gate. He was wearing a fustian gown, to blend both with the mass of scholars and the dark and he felt that he would succeed this time in finding Marlowe's manuscript, wherever it might be hidden.

In a scurrying half crouch, he had made it in the twilight to the doorway that led to Marlowe's stair and was now crouched beneath a straggling rosemary bush which leaned damply on the wall. He had been quite comfortable for the first hour, as the final scholars had come and gone, in chatting groups or alone. He had leant his back against the wall and braced his knees to take his weight and had at first happily thought he could stay like that all night if need be. Then he had felt a strange sensation across his face and in brushing off the source of it had crushed a large and juicy spider against his upper lip. He had jumped with the horror of it and had not been without cramping pains here or there since. The rosemary smell, which had been so enticing to begin with, now began to cloy and with the smell of the dead arachnid overlaid on it, was beginning to turn his stomach more than somewhat. Finally, he knew his moment had come.

He edged out from behind his rosemary bush, swathed in

cobwebs, crusted with stone flaking from the old wall and as stiff as a board. He walked on unsteady legs, the calves aching from what seemed like hours in the same, unnatural position. Leaning on the wall and the door jamb for support he insinuated himself into the dark of the small lobby at the foot of the stair and stood for a while in the shadows, catching his breath and calming himself down. He breathed in and out slowly through his nose, counting each breath to make them even. He had found that he needed to calm himself down like this more and more lately, as the obsession with finding Marlowe's manuscript had grown and grown, excluding all else, including his own weak muse.

He had reached a count of eight on the exhaled breath when a voice quietly spoke in his ear.

'Dominus Greene,' said Proctor Lomas in the happy tone of a man once more on night duty. 'I believe that I have already told you that you are not allowed on College premises.' He grabbed at the man's fustian robe at the shoulder, preparing to haul him away, but was left with just the fabric dangling in his huge fist. He looked down, puzzled, at the inert body of Robert Greene, fainted dead away at his feet. He was sorry that the whole thing had been so easy and, sighing, picked the St John's man up as though he were a child and flung him over his shoulder.

Reaching the gate, he was about to fling the scholar down on the cobbles, but a rare spark of humanity stayed his hand. Instead, he leant him against the wall, with his legs outstretched and the gown over his head. Anonymity thus preserved, Robert Greene twitched and slept his way through the remainder of the night, his hand cold inside its iron glove, clutching and swatting at phantom spiders, grown as big as Kit Marlowe, and just as tricky.

EIGHT

Aldred had reached down four glasses by instinct and was prying the stopper from a bottle of wine before the men had found seats on crates and sacks in his shop. He explained in a low voice that the 'little' woman was not a heavy sleeper and she would be rather raucous in her discontent should they wake her. She slept in a truckle bed in the room at the back and so the shop was by far the safest place for their talk, if they wanted to avoid a broom across their backs. Marlowe, who had met the lady and Phelippes and Johns, both equipped with good imaginations, complied happily and soon they were assembled in the light from the candles round the room.

After the excitement of their meeting, the men were all a little uncertain how to begin. Johns was the first to speak.

'You have a nice shop here, Master Aldred,' he said, in a conversational tone. 'Does it do well?'

'It's a living,' Aldred said, shrugging a shoulder. 'I have some very loyal customers.'

Marlowe looked around the circle and his heart sank. This should have been a meeting of Francis Walsingham's top men, but instead the group seemed to consist of a vintner, a lecturer, a strange academic and a playwright. Perhaps Walsingham and Faunt knew what they were doing, but if so, he wasn't quite sure what that might be. He coughed discreetly and brought the meeting to something resembling order.

'Would it perhaps be better if we bent our minds to what we are here for, instead of pleasantries?' he asked.

Aldred drew himself up a notch. 'As the senior man here,' he said, testily, 'I think I should direct this meeting.'

'You may be older, Aldred,' Phelippes said, 'but I am the expert called in specially. This should be my meeting.'

'Do you know anything about Rheims?' Aldred said, sweet reason overlaying the venom.

'Do you?' Phelippes asked. 'We may be strangers here, but

we found your house straight away, while you two were playing hide and seek. We didn't need much skill to break in.'

'I just leaned against the door,' Johns said, proudly, smiling round the group. 'It gave way.'

'It does that,' Aldred said. 'It was just a lucky push. So, as I was saying . . .'

'As *I* was saying—' Phelippes broke in before being interrupted himself.

'What in the name of Sant' Remi and all the Saints in Heaven,' came a screech from the back room, 'is going on out there? Solomon, have you taken leave of your senses? You know I need my beauty sleep. Be quiet, or you will feel my broom across your backs!'

The men fell silent. Aldred looked round beseechingly and then called, 'Sorry, my little turtle dove. I just have a friend or two out here for a chat. I'll be coming in to bed soon, precious heart.' He frantically tapped his finger on his lips, praying for silence.

'Madame Aldred?' Phelippes mouthed.

'No!' Aldred rasped. 'No, by no means.' The vintner wasn't going into the explanations again.

The voice from the back room changed its tone. It was as though a tiger was purring like a pet kitten. 'Solly,' it called huskily, 'why don't you come in here now?'

Aldred looked like a rabbit caught by a stoat. He cleared his throat. 'I have friends here,' he called back. 'And I don't think it's Friday, is it?'

'Let's pretend it's Friday,' the woman shouted. 'And your friends can wait. It isn't as if you will be long.'

In the mellow candlelight, Aldred's blush almost went unnoticed. The other three looked at the ceiling, through the dark window, at their own fingernails, anywhere but at the little vintner. He swallowed hard and called, sweetly, 'But beloved . . .'

'Get in here, Solomon Aldred,' boomed the voice. 'Don't make me come and get you.'

Aldred looked frantically from man to man, but none of them spoke. Then Marlowe took pity on him, in a way. 'Please, Solomon,' he said, 'don't mind us. Go and pretend it is Friday. I will explain what we have discovered to Master Phelippes. It doesn't need us both.'

'No, but I . . .'

'No, no,' Phelippes said, standing and helping Aldred to his feet. 'Off you go. We'll see you in an hour or so, will we?'

'More like a minute,' rumbled the voice from beyond the door. There was a creak and a rustle as Aldred's enormous inamorata prepared to join them in the shop.

Aldred looked at the door, then at the men seated around the candle and, with a whimper, went to his doom.

In the silence that followed his departure, the three men looked at each other, then Johns ventured, 'That was unusual. But of course, I am not generally cognizant of the life of a projectioner.'

'No,' Phelippes said. 'Even for a projectioner that was a little unusual. I'm not sure about you two, but I would be more comfortable discussing our business elsewhere.'

Distressing noises had begun to emanate from the back room and the others, with a quick nod, jumped up and made for the door, Johns taking the trouble to blow out the candle. The last man out pulled the door shut behind him.

The three men – the two projectioners and the professor – had walked a little way down the road before Marlowe began to laugh. By the time they reached Phelippes and Johns' lodgings they were as helpless as any drunkards and they had to pause for a while outside to compose themselves.

'It's a while since I had a laugh like that,' Marlowe said. 'The English College is not somewhere where laughter is welcome, particularly.'

'Corpus Christi is the same,' Johns said. 'Now Norgate is gone and Harvey is running the place . . .'

'Norgate is gone?' Marlowe broke in. 'Dead?'

'As good as. He tried to convene a meeting to convict his housekeeper of heresy some weeks ago. It was the last straw.'

'He has always been a little eccentric,' Marlowe mused. 'And his housekeeper is a very frightening woman, as I recall.'

'The meeting was called in retrospect,' Johns said. 'He had already tied her to a stake in the quad and tried to set fire to her. Heaven only knows what would have happened if the wood had not been damp.'

'Ah. I see your problem. But Harvey? How was that allowed

to happen? Surely, Dr Copcott . . .?' Marlowe suddenly realized something and the knowledge ran down his spine like iced water. 'Is Greene still hanging around?'

'I understand they have fallen out. I left Cambridge as soon as I tendered my resignation –' he held up a hand for silence as Marlowe opened his mouth – 'but the rumours had already begun.'

'You have described a hot friend cooling, Professor Johns,' Marlowe said. 'I am glad to hear it, though. Greene wants something I have hidden in my room.'

'It won't be your room by now, if I know Gabriel Harvey,' Johns said.

'That won't matter. It is hidden well enough to wait for me until I get back.'

'Which will be never if we stand around out here much longer,' Phelippes said. 'I will have caught the sweating sickness from the cold and you will never solve your code or whatever it is Aldred found.'

'Shhh,' Marlowe warned. 'There are ears everywhere, Master Phelippes. It doesn't matter what language you speak, there is someone who can understand it. You can't trust Latin at all, almost everyone has a little, from their church services. Greek is better, but even then you can't be sure.'

'Hebrew?' Johns ventured.

'Better still, but I'm not sure I could follow it,' Marlowe said.

'Shame on you,' Johns said. 'What about Walloon? Portuguese?'

'I think the best plan is to just say nothing in the open, Doctor,' Marlowe said. 'We want no misunderstanding.'

'So we can go inside, then?' Phelippes said, crossly, slapping his arms to try to get warm.

'That sounds an ideal plan,' Marlowe said. 'Lead the way. I need to discuss a little job I want you to do for me, Master Phelippes.'

Two men wandered the edge of the moat of Fotheringay Castle that Thursday. A weak sun gilded the old stones and the only sound was the splash of a trout leaping for the last gnats skimming low over the water. Lord Burghley's hair and beard had whitened over the last year and he needed more light these days to cope with the scrawled state letters everybody from the Queen to the scullery-maid bombarded him with. The cane he had once snapped upright at each step was now a crutch, a third and essential leg and his progress over the Northamptonshire grass was slow.

Francis Walsingham was edgy. The pain from his boil was gone but the lancing had been horrific and he had taken to his bed for three days to get over it. Burghley was his mentor, as wise as an owl and just as silent in his decisions. Owls hunted by night and their strikes were swift and deadly. Any Catholic vole bustling on its way to a Mass was fair game to Lord Burghley. The old man had weathered more storms than Job but the greatest rose up before him now, in the calm of a Midlands evening, with the trout leaping and the cold and calculating Secretary at his elbow.

'What did you think of her performance today, Francis?' Burghley asked. 'Our Queen of Scots?'

'Better than I expected, my lord,' Walsingham said, staring straight ahead. 'The stick was good.' He could have kicked himself for that, but it was out now in the air and he could not retract it.

Burghley snorted. 'She has rheumatism, apparently,' he said, limping on. 'Chartley was damp.'

Walsingham smiled. 'Not as damp as Fotheringay, I'll wager.'

'I'd forgotten her eyes,' Burghley said, growing poetic. 'The richest hazel. I'm not surprised that men are captivated by her.'

'I'll overlook that treason, my lord,' the spymaster said with a wry smile, 'bearing in mind the business we're about.'

'What are we about, Francis?' the Secretary asked. 'I sometimes wonder.'

'She's put on weight at Chartley,' Walsingham observed. 'Full and fat, you might say.'

'Not too fat for the axe, I'll warrant.' Burghley looked grim. 'Oh, Mother of God, no.'

Walsingham followed the old man's gaze to where a Privy Councillor was hurrying across the grass tufts towards them, striding on his dancer's legs with ease. 'The Queen's bellwether,' he muttered. He didn't like Sir Christopher Hatton and here at Fotheringay he liked him less and less every day.

'My lord.' Hatton doffed his hat in a courtly flourish to

Burghley and nodded curtly to Walsingham. Burghley sighed. Christopher Hatton had the political grasp of Burghley's donkey at Hatfield, but he was a formidable jouster, that most pointless and suicidal of sports and his galliard had captivated the Queen.

'Vice Chamberlain,' Burghley acknowledged him, laying stress, as he always did, on the first word.

'May I have a word, sir?' Hatton asked, his still-golden curls glowing in the fading evening light. He glanced at Walsingham. 'Alone.'

Burghley walked on, shuffling next to the Vice Chamberlain's great and easy strides. 'Anything you have to say is fit for the ears of Sir Francis. We are all members of the same Privy Council, when all is said and done.'

'But all was not said and done today, my lord, was it?'

Burghley stopped and frowned up at the man. He was still a popinjay, in his colleyweston cloak and roisterer's swagger. How such a man could have graduated from the Inner Temple was beyond Burghley's comprehension. 'Meaning?' the old man snapped.

Hatton was temporarily at a loss for words. 'The trial, my lord,' he said, 'of the Queen of Scots.' He looked at the Secretary of State, then at the spymaster and saw nothing but emptiness. 'Did you or did you not, gentlemen,' he asked, hands on hips, 'sit in that hall today and witness what I witnessed?'

'We did,' said Walsingham, sensing that Burghley was walking on again and had no intention of engaging this oaf in legal fisticuffs.

'Where were the jury? Her Majesty's counsel? Those letters the prosecution hinges on – where are they? Where are the witnesses in her defence?'

'Most of them are propping up London Bridge's spikes,' Walsingham told him, 'at least their heads are. Nether limbs you will find displayed in the Catholic parts of this great realm of ours.'

'The secretaries.' Hatton wouldn't give an inch. 'Er . . . Nan and Curle. Why were they not called? The Queen demanded it.'

'We have their written statements,' Burghley muttered, not bothering to look Hatton in the face. 'Let that be enough.'

'By God, it isn't enough!' the Vice Chamberlain roared, blocking Burghley's path.

Walsingham edged between them. 'I remember another court room,' he said softly. 'The trial of Father Ballard. You were impressive then. How did it go? I was particularly struck by it. You asked Ballard "Is this your religio Catholica?" and before the old Papist could answer, you hit him with "No, rather it is Diabolica". That was very good.'

'Don't patronize me, Walsingham,' Hatton sneered. 'I'm a better lawyer than you.'

Burghley snorted.

'I saw no justice today,' Hatton said, keeping his voice level with an audible effort. 'If we are to try the Queen—'

'Justice!' Burghley spat, spinning the man round. 'Hatton, do you love your Queen?'

'Of course.' the Vice Chamberlain stood half a head taller as if to prove it.

'Roughly from behind, we hear,' Walsingham muttered and in an instant Hatton's rapier tip was tickling his throat. Burghley surprised himself by being able to move so fast and his cane batted the blade aside, causing only superficial damage to the spymaster's ruff. His cold grey eyes bored into the Vice Chamberlain's. 'We know you are loyal, Christopher,' he said. 'And we know you would lay down your life for Her Majesty. We also know that you are an honest man. So . . .' he felt the tension slip and put a gentle hand on the courtier's padded shoulder, 'no, there was no justice today. Every man in that court speaks for the Queen of England. And the only way to see the Queen of England live is to see the Queen of Scots dead. Walsingham here would do it with poison. Isn't that right, Francis?'

Walsingham slipped his hand into his doublet and produced a little phial of dark glass which he waved slowly in the air.

'But it's important we put on a show,' Burghley explained as though to the village idiot, 'so that the world cannot point a finger at our Queen and call her a murderess. When the time comes she will put her signature and seal to an official document. And she will be condemning a traitor, one who has sworn to depose Elizabeth and have her head. Can you doubt it?'

'Will they call her less of a murderess,' Hatton asked, 'if she signs Mary's death warrant? Won't she always have blood on her hands? I want no part in it.'

Walsingham had already seen the riders galloping full tilt across the angle of the October fields, black silhouettes against the purpling sky. 'I don't think you have a choice, Sir Christopher,' he said. 'I don't think any of us do.'

The riders hauled their reins in and the officer at their head, wearing the Queen's livery under his cloak, swung from the saddle, bowing low and handing a letter to Burghley.

'From the Queen?' Burghley asked the messenger.

'From Her Majesty, my lord,' the man confirmed. 'From Nonsuch.'

The Secretary of State threw his stick to Walsingham and broke the royal seal. He squinted to read the clerk's scribbled hand and checked the elaborate swirls of the signature carefully. 'Gentlemen,' he growled. 'She's stopped it.'

'What?' Walsingham and Hatton chorused.

'The trial of the Queen of Scots will reconvene in London, ten days from now.'

As the horsemen turned their animals away, Walsingham watched them go and muttered to himself, 'Why can't she, just for once, let us get on with our jobs?'

Michael Johns couldn't sleep. He thought it would be easier, now they had moved out of the noisy inn to the relative peace of Solomon Aldred's best bedroom. He had taken a while to get over the embarrassment of sleeping above Aldred and his frightening lady, but at last he had stopped listening for noises he could only imagine and he found the bed, though still half full of Thomas Phelippes, comfortable. But his head was spinning with so much information he couldn't make sense of it all. He had been learning things, difficult things, since before he was five years old. He still had the scars on his back given to him by his father for failing to master the fourth declension just after his fourth birthday. But in all his years of learning, information had come at him in a steady stream, each piece clicking neatly into the matrix of its fellows to make a wall he could trust, a wall he could hide behind in safety.

But since he had left Cambridge, and especially since he had come to Rheims, information had broken over his head like a torrent and putting it into any kind of order was coming hard.

His wall had broken down under the flood and he had nowhere to hide. He had loved Kit Marlowe since he first saw him, a scholar all eyes and hair standing in the crowd of his peers what seemed like a lifetime ago. And now here he was, a projectioner, a man with secrets, paying the piper, calling the tune.

Johns let his head fall back on the pillow with a sigh. If he woke Thomas Phelippes he wouldn't be sorry; he needed to talk. He knew Phelippes was a code-breaker. He knew he was here in Rheims against his better judgement, against his wishes. And, if the fragment of code Marlowe had passed over the night before was any guide, he was here fruitlessly. As soon as the two men had looked at it, in the wavering candlelight in their shared room, Phelippes had admitted defeat at once. The type of code had been simple enough; it was a substitution, for certain. But without the original book it came from, it would never be broken. It was as simple as that. Even taking the books that Johns himself owned – more than most men, but still pitifully few – it would take a lifetime to find the page. And if the original was in a library somewhere, or even an original piece, written for the purpose and committed to memory, it was truly an impossible task.

Phelippes was all for going home. Marlowe agreed with him, with such alacrity that Johns had spun his head to look him in the face. In the eyes there was the look of the devil he had seen so often before, the shadow of Machiavel. He felt he should warn Phelippes, but then shrugged and decided to watch where the play might go. Marlowe encouraged him, even to the extent of asking where his pack was stowed, so that they could begin to gather his things together for the journey. Phelippes, all innocence, went so far as to thank Marlowe for his kindness. Then, like a viper, the projectioner had struck.

'Will you be going home, Master Phelippes?' Marlowe had asked.

Johns had stifled a smile. Here it comes, he had thought, the coup de grace.

'Of course.' Phelippes had been puzzled. 'Where else would I go?'

Marlowe had raised a shoulder and an eyebrow and favoured Johns with a knowing smile. 'I just thought that you might want to stay away from where Sir Francis Walsingham and Nicholas

Faunt can easily find you,' he said, smoothly. 'They can be . . .
well, they don't always seem to understand how hard it can be
in the field.'

Phelippes had leant forward into the candlelight to look into
Marlowe's eyes, but only concern for a new friend was shining
there. And so, Johns and Phelippes still shared their rustling bed,
waiting to be told what to do, where to go and when. He smiled
and turned his head to the window and his heart skipped a beat.

Outlined against the grey of the casement, was a head, cowled
in what could have been a monk's habit, or simply a loose hood.
He closed his eyes in disbelief. How could anyone have got into
the room so silently? For a moment, he hoped it might be
Marlowe, but in a second he could see this man was bigger, much
broader in the shoulder and taller, probably by half a span. He
held his breath, watching, praying that Phelippes wouldn't give
vent to one of his frightening snores or, worse, one of his ripping
farts that Johns had been too embarrassed in the morning to
mention. Breathing through his nose he made no sound, but trying
to burrow lower into a straw palliasse proved to be louder than
he had expected and the figure at the window turned.

Johns stayed as still as he dared. He closed his eyes, so the
intruder couldn't see the faint light shining on them, but then he
couldn't tell whether the man was approaching or had kept his
place at the window. He was so frightened he just wanted to
scream and shout out loud, to run frantically for the door, although
he knew that it would probably be the death of him. Conversely, he
knew that he couldn't move a muscle should Hell itself open
beside his bed. He had been turned to stone. No, to ice. But ice
that made his brow sweat and his tongue burn in his throat with
the need to scream.

After what seemed an hour, he felt Phelippes move beside
him. He reached out with his left hand, hoping to alert him to
their danger, but without startling him. Phelippes felt the touch
of his hot fingers on his arm in his sleep and woke up from his
usual dream of coal scuttles and yelled at the top of his lungs.
Before the horrified Johns could stop him, he had jumped out of
the bed over him and lunged at the figure by the window, who
turned with a hissed curse, swinging his arm through the air.
Phelippes dropped like a stone and the intruder ran for the door,

jumping over the man's body as he did so. Johns closed his eyes and waited for death, which didn't come.

What came instead was a bubbling sound, a wet groaning that seemed to fill the room. Then it resolved into Phelippes' voice.

'Michael,' he whispered, 'Michael, he has cut me. Help me, help me, please.' Then there was a thump as the code-breaker's head hit the floor in a dead faint and Johns was himself again, a man who could fix life's little dramas, who, if he didn't know what to do could usually find a man who did. Getting up from the bed, he strode with what dignity he could muster, given the fact he was wearing only his shirt and went out into the narrow gallery outside their room.

'Solomon!' he called. 'Aldred, come quick! Light here, and help. A ruffian has broken into your house and murder is done. Solomon!'

Things were less exciting at the English College. Although the rooms would be considered austere by many, they were palatial by the standards of the scholars at any college in Cambridge. In some of the more poorly endowed, the scholars didn't have their own rooms, but had to lodge in houses around the town, often several to a bed. Even the dormitory in the English College would have seemed like heaven to them. The room was large and airy, with low partitions between the comfortable beds, with linen changed every term and the palliasses hung out of the window to air in the summer. The slightly more favoured scholars, those who helped in the library, those who had struck the faculty as being rather more devout – or whose fathers had deep pockets; in the end it all came to about the same – had rooms which they shared with just one other. A few, as well as temporary guests, had rooms to themselves.

Marlowe had got used to the faint scent of urine that the warmth of his body still released from his bed. He concentrated instead on the smell of rosemary and lavender and soon was drifting off and nearing sleep. As was his habit, he used the floating time, when he could no longer feel the bedding above or the mattress beneath but could still think clearly, to put all of his thoughts in order, then address and dismiss them one by one. He had always found that if sleep didn't come as the last thought flew away on the wings of night, he could always add a few lines to the constant poem that he kept in his head for the purpose.

In his time at the English College, he feared he may have been sidetracked for at least a while from his primary purpose of finding the missing conspirator. His instructions from Faunt had been couched in the man's usual roundabout way. Someone had slipped through Walsingham's net, a friend of the conspirator Babington. Intelligence ran that he had found his way to the English College. Marlowe was to go to Rheims, find the man and then proceed as he thought fit. He knew that however he did proceed, if it didn't suit the purposes of Sir Francis Walsingham and his own paymasters, then Marlowe would take the blame. Nobody, in the England of Gloriana, was indispensable and rotting heads jutted above London Bridge to prove it. If it did by some happy chance fit with their plans, then they would take the credit. That was how it worked and there was nothing he could do to change it. All he could hope was that when the mighty storm broke over his head in the event that he got it wrong, he would be adequately sheltered in the lee of a person more suited than he was to weather it. Sons of shoemakers were legion; university scholars ten a penny. Even titles were no absolute guarantee of safety, although titles helped.

Unfortunately, the only people he could hide behind at the moment were Solomon Aldred, a vintner with just a remaining trace of intelligencer left in him; Thomas Phelippes, a code-breaker and forger of high talent but little backbone; and lastly, Michael Johns, an innocent abroad who Marlowe would protect at whatever cost to himself. So, for that point to be adequately disposed of on his journey towards sleep, he had mentally to mark it as pending.

His secondary purpose was to avoid the razor intellect of William Allen; falling too far foul of him would mean discovery, capture and probably death. The man seemed to be everywhere and had a look in his gimlet eye that made Marlowe feel as though he stood before him naked. Not even Walsingham, not even, he would go so far as to say, his own mother, had ever made Marlowe feel so ill at ease. It was as though Allen could see into his soul, and the curtains had been down behind his eyes for so long, he had thought no one could penetrate into that secret room any longer. Nevertheless, he felt that his latest plan might solve this knotty problem. He had left Phelippes with a task to fulfil which would hopefully set his mind free to wander and possibly crack the uncrackable code as he worked his forging magic. So, that problem could be set free to flap on leathern wings into the night.

Which left him with just the murders to contend with, those annoying little circumstances that came between the tick and strike of the clock. Father Laurenticus was definitely murdered and he had access to a virtual eyewitness, should he need one, in the person of Sylvie. Mireille was easily found; in fact, he had received a merry wave from her already on two occasions, much to Solomon Aldred's amusement. But the details of the death of Charles, late of the flat Fens of Cambridgeshire, clearly strangled by person or persons unknown, remained a secret known only to his murderer and his God. With plenty else to occupy his mind, Marlowe decided to put the problem of strange deaths to one side for now. He could pursue it if he found that his other investigations were going nowhere and he needed to mull something over to keep his wits sharp. He opened his hands and blew softly on the black feathers of that thought and it hopped from his hand, about to take flight.

Before it could even get itself above the trees, the night was shattered by a scream so shrill it scarcely seemed to go in through the ears. It went straight to the bowels, turning them to water and seemed to go on so long he could hardly believe it came from a human throat. He opened his eyes wide, telling himself that if he saw anything apart from the dim outline of his window, he was dreaming already and could comfortably ignore the dreadful sound. The predawn light outlined his window and so he let instinct take over and he leapt from his bed and hurried to the door, pausing only to grab his dagger from beneath his pillow and hold it in his right hand, blade concealed along his inner forearm, below the sleeve on his shirt.

NINE

At the far end of the gallery, in the dawn's light seeping in grey fingers through the two long windows, a maid stood, her eyes wild, her hands over her mouth. The last strands of her scream filtered between her fingers but she was almost silent at last. Marlowe was at her side in an instant and touched her arm. She started, forced out of whatever Hell gripped her, and he led her away, back to his room, out of the light. He couldn't tell the woman's age as he sat her down on the wooden chest. She barely seemed to register him at all, just sat rocking gently, cradling her arms as if to hold herself together.

Marlowe slipped the dagger under the coverlet and knelt in front of the woman, gently uncoiling her fingers from around her arms and holding her hands down in her lap. He had seen this look before, the numbness of terror. It wasn't a mouse that had caused that scream. It was a body. Stiff and cold.

'Madame,' he said softly in his best French. 'What is it? What's happened?'

Slowly, as though waking from a dream, the maid's eyes began to focus. She saw the handsome young man in front of her, but not the concern on his face. She saw the bed, the crucifix on the far wall, the curtains and the sideboard. And suddenly, she knew where she was. This was Father Laurenticus' room. Her eyes widened again and her mouth opened to scream as she half rose. Marlowe recognized the signs and held her down with one hand while clamping the other over her mouth.

'No,' he said firmly, beyond the whisper he had used so far. Then he softened. 'It's all right,' he soothed, stroking her wild hair under the cap. 'You're safe here. Nothing can hurt you here.'

'Oh, Monsieur . . .' she tried to speak but her voice trailed away. The man had no idea. *Everything* could hurt her here.

'What is it?' he asked her. 'What did you see?'

She looked at him, blinking back tears, understanding what was happening for the first time before time had frozen and the only noise she could hear was the thump of her own heart and the blood rushing in her ears.

'The boy,' she said. 'The scholar. Edmund . . .' and she turned to the door, as if expecting the lad to be standing there, smiling at her in his grey fustian.

Marlowe lifted up the woman's chin, to force her eyes to focus on his. 'I will see to it,' he said. 'What is your name?'

'Antoinette,' she said.

'Antoinette,' Marlowe repeated. 'I will see to it. Where do I go? The end room?'

She nodded quickly. All her adult life she had worked in this house, long before the English came and she knew its stairs and landings like the lines of her own palm. Yet, one by one, these rooms were closing down to her, becoming places she didn't want to go. First, Father Laurenticus'; now this, the end room along the gallery.

'Antoinette,' Marlowe said, catching the woman's attention again, 'I am going along to that room.'

'Oh, Monsieur,' she said, startled.

'It's all right.' He smiled at her reassuringly and slipped the dagger out from its hiding place. 'You see, I am not alone. Antoinette, I want you to stay here. I am going to lock the door, so that you will be safe. Do you have keys of your own?'

She nodded, lifting up her jingling chatelaine, hung with keys of all sizes.

'I shan't be long,' he said and, stooping, kissed her softly on the forehead. He checked her as he closed the door behind him. Antoinette sat rocking again on the chest, and her arms circled her body and she hugged herself. If only to protect herself from the ghost of Father Laurenticus. She could almost feel his eyes on her from the darkest corner of the room and sensed the rustle of a monk's robe as he shifted position in the shadows.

Out in the gallery, all Hell was breaking loose. Scholars in nightshirts were crowding the confined space, each of them trying to see into the end room.

'Make way,' Marlowe shouted and one by one they fell back, especially as the man held a dagger in his hand.

The end room was typical of the attic accommodation in the

English College. There was a single window, its tiny panes closed against the rawness of the October dawn and two wooden beds wedged together under the sharp slope of the eaves. Marlowe took one look at the body on the furthest bed and turned, ushering the ghouls out of the room. 'Someone wake the Master,' he said before closing the door. He knew he didn't have much time before Allen arrived to close down Marlowe's particular line of enquiry.

Edmund Brooke lay on his back in his nightshirt. His lips were blue and tightly pursed and his eyes stared at the ceiling. Marlowe looked closely at those eyes, sunken and glazed as they were. There were tiny red spots in the whites and a similar rash over the cheeks and nose. He bent closer, as if to catch a last whisper of breath from the dead man and smelt the heavy aroma of wine. No doubt Solomon Aldred could have identified the vineyard. The bed itself was pulled about, the sheets pulled this way and that and the pillow was hanging half on the bed, with just one crumpled end looking as though it had been thrust under the lad's head after he was dead. The bed alongside was cold and virtually undisturbed. There was a Bible on the side table, open to a page of St Peter and another tome lying beneath it. Marlowe threw open the door of the makeshift cupboard and took in quickly what was there. A cassock, two or three shirts, two pairs of clogs, old and worn. Nothing that hadn't been hanging in his own humble wardrobe in Corpus Christi until recently. He was just closing the door when a shaft of weak light from the window fell on something on the cupboard floor. He opened the door again and rummaged under the clogs. It was a loose board, its end jutting proud of the surface as though it had been recently lifted. He prised it up again, easing the wood with his dagger point. It was a hole, perhaps a foot square and it was empty. Whatever had been there once was not there now.

The bedroom door crashed back and Gerald Skelton stood there, transfixed by the scene he saw. He crossed himself quickly and spun back to the scholars, still cluttering up the corridor and gabbling excitedly.

'You!' he snapped at the nearest lad. 'Time for Lauds. Ring the bell, for God's sake. And the rest of you, about your ablutions. Where is the praefectus for this floor?'

'Doctor.' A freckle-faced boy pushed himself forward.

'Whose room is this?' Skelton wanted to know.

The praefectus was a little dumbfounded by the question, bearing in mind Skelton had just seen Edmund Brooke's body. It was as though Skelton read his mind.

'The other one, you idiot. The one who isn't here.'

'Um . . . Martin, sir, Martin Camb,' the boy volunteered.

'Where is he?'

The name rang around the corridor and along under the eaves and scholar looked at scholar. There was no Martin Camb. No one had seen him since Vespers the previous night and heads were shaking in all directions.

'Ablutions!' Skelton roared at them all. 'Now!' Then he turned to Marlowe and let the door click closed behind him.

'Well, Dominus Greene.' The Bursar was calmer now, his public face gone and a horrified, confused bystander stood in his stead.

'Hardly well, Dr Skelton,' Marlowe said. 'The boy has been suffocated.'

'Suffocated?' Skelton crossed to the bed, peering down at the corpse. 'How do you know that?'

'The colour of the face,' Marlowe said. 'See, it's turning purple. The veins in his cheeks have burst as he fought for air.'

Skelton sniffed. 'Do I smell drink?' he asked.

'You do,' Marlowe said, nodding. 'Which is why, I suspect, the murderer could do what he did. I was at dinner with this lad the other night. He seemed strong and healthy then. Sober, he'd have been too much of a handful. In his cups . . . well, you've heard the phrase "dead drunk"?'

Skelton saw no mirth in Marlowe's gallows humour and was about to tell him so when the door opened again and Thomas Shaw stood there. 'Gerald, I heard there'd been another . . .' Then he saw Marlowe, saw the body of Edmund Brooke and crossed himself. The librarian was still in his nightshirt too, like everybody else, but Marlowe noticed he wore buckled buskins on his feet.

'Where are your rooms, Dr Shaw?' Marlowe asked him.

'Across the quad,' Shaw told him. 'Why do you ask?'

'Bad news travels fast in the English College,' Marlowe observed. 'I'm surprised the Master isn't here.'

'The Master is away,' Skelton told him. 'On College business. Thomas, Dominus Greene, this will be the talk of the College in minutes. It's important that we keep things on an even keel. Whatever happened in this room is for our ears only – is that clear? The scholars can speculate all they like. Officially – and until the Master returns, I *am* officialdom – the boy died of apoplexy.'

The librarian's mouth opened to say something but he thought better of it and closed it again.

'Who found the body?' Skelton asked.

'I did,' said Marlowe.

'Really?' Skelton was a little confused. 'I heard a scream.'

Marlowe ducked his head. 'That would have been me, I'm afraid,' he said. 'I have always been a little . . . theatrical, when alarmed. It is a habit I am trying hard to break myself of, but when there is a shock . . .'

Skelton narrowed his eyes. 'It was very shrill.'

'I was a choirboy,' Marlowe countered. 'If you make me jump somehow, I could do it again.' He closed his eyes and took a deep breath.

'No, no,' Shaw said. 'For heaven's sake, Gerald, leave the lad alone. Just because he has a habit of screaming once in a while there is no need to make a meal of it. We all came running, let that be the end of it. But why he was in here in the first place is an interesting conundrum. Dominus Greene?' He looked at Marlowe with a half smile on his lips.

'I just can't get my bearings in this place, especially first thing in the morning,' Marlowe said. 'I was looking for the jakes.'

'That way,' said Shaw, absent-mindedly picking up the book that lay beside the Bible and tucking it under his arm. 'I'll show you.'

'Many thanks.' Marlowe smiled and the two men heard Skelton lock the door as the bell for Lauds gladdened the hour.

It would not have surprised Marlowe to be told that Antoinette had the power to freeze time. She was sitting in exactly the same position in which he had left her. The room seemed to hold its breath so as not to disturb her perfect stillness. Even the grey light of dawn didn't seem any brighter in here, although it was almost fully light outside.

'Antoinette?' he said, crouching down in front of her and laying gentle hands on her knees. 'Antoinette? Can I send for one of your friends? Family?'

She shook her head, a tiny motion.

'Just someone to help you. Can I fetch the housekeeper? Doctor Skelton?'

This time the head-shake was much more vociferous. 'They can't know I was here,' she whispered. 'Please, M'sieur, keep my secret or I will lose my job. They have been angry with me since . . .' Her voice faltered and she looked anxiously around the room. 'Angry with me,' she said, this time with more of a note of finality.

Marlowe thought he might understand. 'Since you found Father Laurenticus' body?' he hazarded.

She nodded, tears squeezing out from under her tightly closed lids. 'It was horrible,' she breathed, half turning to the bed. 'There was so much blood.' She sketched an arc with one arm, which she then hurriedly clamped back across her body, for protection. 'On the window. The wall.' She glanced up. 'The ceiling, even.' She could see it still, grotesque splashes of crimson running in rivulets as the man's veins had emptied.

'Was he alone?' he asked.

'What are you?' she asked, leaning away from him. 'How do you know the questions to ask? The Evil One has sent you.'

'No,' Marlowe said. 'No. Look at me, Antoinette.' He trusted to his big brown eyes and his curls. No woman had ever thought him evil for long. 'Do I look as if I am from the Evil One?'

'He wears many guises, M'sieur,' she mumbled, crossing herself.

'I am just . . .' At this point, his French began to desert him. Words he needed like 'common-sense' were not in his vocabulary. He settled for second best. 'I am wise, Antoinette. You are uneasy in this room, so I guessed. But why were you in the boy's room so early in the morning? Surely, your duties do not begin so soon.'

'No, not so early. But I had forgotten to take clean linen to the room. The scholars change their own bed linen, but we must take it to them, leave it in their rooms. Doctor Skelton examines the beds once a week. He pulls back the covers and checks throughout. I did not want M'sieur Edmund to get into trouble for dirty linen. He was a sweet boy, that one. He would not have blamed me. So I thought I could quietly take it to the room, leave it just inside the door for the next day. If he was quick, he would have been in time, before the inspection.'

'That was good of you.'

'No, I had been wrong. I should have taken it the day before, but I am not very well these days. Finding –' again, her arm sketched the blood spray on the wall – 'finding this, my brain is not so clear. Doctor Skelton is not very understanding. If I make another mistake, he said, I must leave the English College and he will write me no character, nor give me my wages for the year.' She raised her eyes to his. 'I will starve. It is that simple. I have nothing but the clothes I stand up in.'

'Your secret is safe with me, Antoinette,' Marlowe said. 'And if the worst comes to the worst, I will see what I can do about a new place for you. It might not be in France, though. It may have to be in England.'

She shook her head and crossed herself. 'I am a good Catholic, M'sieur,' she said. 'England is no place for me.'

Marlowe looked down at her, a simple soul who would rather starve on the streets of a Catholic country than have a soft bed and a good life in a country that did not follow Rome. He couldn't help but admire her. 'Perhaps a place with Monsieur Aldred, then, the vintner,' he said.

She looked thoughtful. 'Perhaps in England they don't mind if their maids are Catholic,' she said, after a pause. Then, she smiled. 'Let's hope it doesn't come to that. But, I must go.' She jumped to her feet and smoothed out her skirt. 'The Lauds bell has stopped and I must be at my work.' She put a work-worn hand on Marlowe's sleeve. 'Thank you for keeping my secret, Dominus Greene,' she said. 'If I can ever help you, I will.'

He patted her hand and opened the door, looking both ways, then, the coast clear, ushered her out. When she had gone, wooden clogs pattering along the gallery, he turned and flung himself on his bed, with a sigh. Edmund Brooke wasn't going anywhere and Dr Skelton had sealed the scene of the crime. Marlowe had been in need of sleep when he had heard her scream. Now he was exhausted. He closed his eyes and drifted off, blissfully.

'Kit! Kit!'

He smiled to himself. This was a funny dream. Michael Johns was bouncing him on a big sheet, tied between four trees in a forest. The sheet was stretched taut and with every bounce, he flew higher, till he was in the sky. But still Johns bounced him, calling his name.

'Kit!'

He was in the clouds now, they were all wet. No. That was wrong. He was wet and people were still calling him. He sat up abruptly.

'Kit, thank goodness. Are you ill? I couldn't wake you.' Michael Johns looked like Hell. He was covered in blood and very green about the gills.

Marlowe was instantly awake. He took in the fact that although there was a lot of blood, it was mainly on the professor's sleeves and it was dry and browning. Although the man looked far from well, he clearly wasn't injured. 'Whose blood is this?' he asked. It wasn't the most perspicacious question he had ever posed, but it filled in the time.

'Phelippes',' Johns told him. 'He's been stabbed. Slashed, rather.' Johns wasn't familiar with the effects of weapons. He had to think about it. 'We had an intruder.'

'Is he dead?'

'No,' Johns said. 'He got away.'

'Not the intruder.' Marlowe still had the patience to be kind to his old tutor. 'Phelippes.'

'He'll live, the doctor said. He was slashed across the chest, but it was not a deep wound. Just very –' he glanced down at himself and ruefully shook out a sleeve – 'bloody. He'll be in bed for a while, until he gets back his strength. Solomon Aldred's . . .' Words failed him when he tried to give a title to Veronique. 'She looked as though she might be difficult, but I pointed out that it was the poor quality of her locks that had caused this and not any fault of ours. She seemed to think we had quarrelled and I had stabbed him. Stupid woman. Did you know that *she* is the vintner? Aldred is just the man who she sends out to sell.'

'I suppose she was right to suspect it,' Marlowe said. It didn't surprise him at all to find that Veronique was the brains behind

Aldred's business. If he was as bad at being a vintner as he sometimes seemed to be as a spy, he would have been bankrupt within weeks. But everyone was entitled to a bad day. Look at Spenser, for example; he seemed to have nothing but bad days whenever he picked up his pen.

'I disagree,' Johns said, suddenly on his dignity. 'Do I look like a sworder, Kit? Thomas and I get on very well, in the main. They will never have heard raised voices from us.'

'Are they searching for the intruder? Did you see him?' Marlowe thought he would get the investigation back on a more helpful tack.

'They say they are looking, but I don't think the Watch here are any better than in Cambridge. As soon as they realized we were English, they rather lost interest. I saw the man briefly in the light from the window. He was wearing a hood.'

'A monk's hood?' Marlowe could see a pattern beginning to develop, however tenuous.

'It could have been. It could equally have been a cloak drawn up over his head.'

'You call him "he", Michael. It was definitely a man, was it?'

Johns stopped to think. He was clearly letting his mind drift back to recent events. He scowled and narrowed his eyes, then nodded. 'Yes. It was definitely a man. I couldn't tell much about him, but I remember thinking that it wasn't you. It was too big around the shoulders.'

'Why should it be me? I wouldn't hurt you. Either of you.'

'No.' Johns tried a smile, but it was a little weak around the edges. 'No, not when Phelippes got hurt. Before. He stood very still, with his head turned. Just like you do sometimes when you are engrossed in something. Then he turned his head again and I could see he was just, well, as I said, bigger. Thicker set.'

'Well,' said Marlowe, 'that cuts us down to most of the men north of the Marne.' He looked at his friend, who had begun to shiver. 'You're in shock. Take that bloody shirt off and lie down here and rest. I'll go and see Solomon, see if he has any ideas.'

'Is that likely?' said Johns, his voice muffled as Marlowe helped him off with his shirt by pulling it over his head.

'I know you haven't seen Solomon in an altogether wonderful light thus far,' Marlowe told him as he pushed him back on the pillows and pulled up the covers. 'But he knows this town, and if anyone can help with a name or two, he can. Now, sleep.' But the instruction was too late. Johns, with one last sigh, was fast asleep and snoring. Marlowe drew the curtains to keep the man safe behind the velvet.

Thomas Phelippes was sleeping too when Marlowe reached him. Like Johns, he had had a shock. Unlike Johns, he had been gashed across the chest. And unlike Johns, Phelippes had been given a secret potion by the doctor that would have knocked out a horse.

'Strange business, this, Marlowe.' Solomon Aldred was at his elbow in this guests' room, oddly sober for this time of the morning.

'What do you make of it?' Marlowe asked.

The intelligencer-turned-vintner jerked his head towards the door and followed Marlowe out. They crossed the narrow landing and went into Aldred's inner sanctum, a tiny closet with ugly, home-made furniture and rushes on the floor.

'Cosy.' Marlowe nodded, ducking so that his head didn't collide with a beam.

'Handy,' said Aldred and nodded towards a wooden panel at his shoulder. He tilted it and the light shaft shot through like a crossbow bolt. 'Have a look.'

Marlowe did. The newly opened slit looked directly at Aldred's front door along the Rue de Valvert. Aldred flicked another one on the opposite wall and Marlowe could see the yard behind the house where the homely Veronique was hanging out her washing.

'Clever,' Marlowe said. 'But it didn't help last night?'

Crestfallen, Aldred let the shutters close. 'Not at all,' he said. 'One of Nicholas Faunt's little gadgets. Utterly useless after dark. And anyway, I'd have to be in this room at the time to have a commanding view of the back and front.'

'Veronique wouldn't like that?' Marlowe couldn't resist a smile.

'She *is* very demanding in that respect.' Aldred sighed and the thought of it made him reach for a goblet and decanter of wine. 'But that's not it. She knows nothing about my alter ego, so to speak. To her, as to the rest of Rheims, I am just Solomon Aldred, the English vintner.'

'And what are you to your visitor of last night, do you think?' Marlowe asked.

Aldred shrugged. He wasn't just turning into a vintner. He was turning into a Frenchman. 'I don't know,' he said. 'I've been racking what's left of my brain. I couldn't get anything rational out of Phelippes. If his attacker had horns and a cloven hoof, I shouldn't be at all surprised. Johns wasn't much better.'

'Was it wise to involve the Watch?'

'Johns' idea, backed up by Veronique. For some reason, which I admit escapes me, she seems to think that this is a respectable house. She has personally buried three husbands.' He paused to consider what he had said. 'I obviously don't mean she person- ally buried them, but she has been present when they needed burying.' He shook his head, still not sure he had made himself clear, but plunged on anyway. 'None of them was actually her own husband and the wives were a little testy, but she is a rich woman by anyone's reckoning, so paid them off. I am her latest . . . addition to the household and possibly a little more respectable than the preceding incumbents, in that my wife is—'

'Living with a fish-curer from Lowestoft,' Marlowe added, to show he had been listening.

'Quite.' Aldred took his first proper swig of the morning and shuddered as the burgundy hit his tonsils. 'But even without her support, Johns would have won the day. A determined bugger, isn't he? For a scholar, I mean? I refused at first, but he dashed off into the night and found a patrolling Watchman. I sent Veronique for a doctor.'

'This doctor,' Marlowe said. 'Can he be trusted?'

'Of course not,' Aldred snorted. 'He's a doctor. But Johns paid him over the odds so he'll keep his mouth shut for a while.'

'What about the Watch?'

'Apparently Johns had the very devil of a job to get him to come along at all. He took one look at Phelippes and then at Johns, said "Lovers' tiff?" and shrugged. I slipped him a couple of bottles and sent him on his way. Waste of space!'

'So that leaves you, Solomon,' Marlowe said, leaning closer. 'Have you received such a visitor before?'

'Never,' Aldred told him. 'Oh, I've had the odd run in with an aggrieved customer. Some nonsense about spoiled brandy and a watered-down Bordeaux – all rubbish, of course. But a thief in the night? No, never. There isn't a thief in Rheims who would risk meeting Veronique in the dark, I shouldn't think.'

'A thief?' Marlowe frowned. 'What was taken?'

'Nothing,' Aldred told him. 'At least I don't think so. Johns and Phelippes must have disturbed him. I checked the other rooms; nothing amiss there.'

Both men fell silent.

'A groat for your thoughts, Kit Marlowe,' the vintner said after a while.

Marlowe laughed. 'You can have my thoughts freely, Master Aldred,' he said. 'Though you might have to pay for my poetry and plays.' He looked at the man. He was far from ideal, but at this hour, between Lauds and Prime, he was all Marlowe had. And he'd have to do. 'I was sent to find a fugitive,' he said. 'One Matthew Baxter, one of Babington's plotters. You tell me he's here, under an assumed name, at the English College.'

'The scorpions' nest,' Aldred reminded him.

Marlowe nodded. 'Indeed,' he said. 'And the scorpions are killing each other in that nest. There was another one last night.'

'What?' Aldred sat up, slopping his drink.

'A scholar, name of Brooke. Nice lad. I had dinner in his company on one of my first nights here.'

'Another one for the crypt.' Aldred nodded, topping up his spilled drink.

'This one was suffocated,' Marlowe told him. 'Probably with the pillow he lay on.'

Aldred frowned. 'A scholar. Didn't he sleep in a dormitory?'

Marlowe shook his head. 'A shared room,' he said.

'And his ingle?'

'No sign.' Marlowe sighed. 'As missing as any pattern I can see – or rather can't see – in this whole wretched business. Three men are dead by my reckoning. Charles, hanged and thrown from an upstairs window. Father Laurenticus, stabbed to death in his bed. And now Brooke . . .'

'Two scholars and a tutor,' Aldred said, thinking out loud. 'Any connection between them? Other than the English College, I mean?'

'None that I can work out yet.' A sudden thought occurred to him. 'What time did the intruder attack Phelippes?' he asked Aldred.

'Two, three of the clock,' the vintner guessed. 'Why?'

Marlowe sighed. 'Nothing,' he said. 'It's all spinning in my head, Solomon, like St Catherine's wheel. Could the man who tried to kill Phelippes also succeed with Edmund Brooke? Could he have got into the English College from here in time?'

'The journey is possible,' the vintner said. 'But get into the College? That's impossible after cock-shut time. In fact, it's impossible at any hour. There are only two gates and they're both guarded night and day . . .' It was his turn to be visited by a sudden thought. 'Then, how . . .?'

'Did a mild-mannered Cambridge professor covered in blood get past the guard to bring me your little piece of news this morning?' Marlowe smiled, nodding. 'That is a very good question, Master Aldred. I wish I had an answer.'

TEN

They were whispering among themselves that afternoon as Marlowe turned the corner. Ahead of him, scattering as they heard his boots clattering on the cobbles, a knot of scholars went about their business. This was the second time that day that Marlowe had had to break through a cordon of ghouls and he hoped it wasn't for the same reason as in the morning.

The sun had reached its zenith now, surprisingly warm for October, and on a sudden breeze Marlowe realized what had drawn the scholars' attention. Puffs of smoke were wafting from the stable yard, but they were few, deliberate and not the harbingers of some conflagration. A grey gelding was standing on three legs in the courtyard while the fourth was held up by a blacksmith, nailing the newly forged metal to its hoof. The animal waited patiently for the procedure to be carried out, only the occasional flick of its tail marking his impatience.

Sitting on a bale of straw with his back to the wall sat the surly Londoner Solomon Aldred had told Marlowe about. He had arrived recently enough for him to possibly be the man the projectioner had been sent by Walsingham to find. But he was not surly this afternoon. There was a pipe in his hand and he was blowing smoke rings to the sky. A flagon of ale lay on the straw beside him and he seemed content with the world.

'A fine animal,' Marlowe said by way of greeting. 'We haven't met.' He extended his hand. 'Robert Greene.'

'John Abbot,' the Londoner said, catching it. The grip was firm, the eyes wary. He was giving nothing away.

'Yours?' Marlowe sat himself down and nodded to the horse.

'Bought him yesterday,' Abbot told him. 'I thought the London horse swindlers were a tough lot, but here in Rheims . . . Let's say they saw me coming.'

'You didn't bring your own horse over?' Marlowe asked. 'From home, I mean?'

'Not worth the cost,' Abbot said. 'And anyway, I wasn't sure what sort of welcome I'd get. You?'

'Ship to Rouen. Upriver from there. Is this your first time in the English College?'

'My first and my last,' Abbot grunted.

Marlowe looked surprised. 'Dr Allen's welcome not to your liking?' he asked.

'Oh, there's nothing wrong with Allen,' Abbot said. 'It's just that the place is just so damned . . . well, *foreign*, isn't it? I mean, the *English* College. I thought I'd find tobacco, ale, pigs' trotters, jellied eels.'

'Instead of which?'

'God knows.' Abbot shrugged. 'Things with eyes in. Horse. And snails. I mean, is that natural, Greene? Is it?'

Marlowe smiled at the man. 'You seem to be coping.' He pointed to the pipe and the ale.

'Ah, the last of my personal stash. I'd offer you some of both, but . . . well, replenishment might be a little tricky.'

'Where are you from?' Marlowe asked. He didn't expect a rush of confession from the man but the slow chip-chip at the outer shell might yield something.

'Just north of the city wall,' Abbot told him. 'The White Chapel. St Mary Matfelon. Know it?'

Marlowe shook his head. 'I'm from Cambridge, myself,' he said. 'Corpus Christi College.'

'Ah.' Abbot nodded, taking a selfish swig from the pitcher. 'I'm a Furnival's Inn man, of sorts.'

'Of sorts?'

'Never finished the course. Thought I was cut out to be a lawyer, then discovered I couldn't stand the buggers. Oh, don't misunderstand me. I'm as grasping and cut-throat as the next serjeant-at-law but they're so bloody arrogant, aren't they? Always quoting some damn law from the sixteenth of Edward I and expecting that to have some bearing on the state of things today.'

Marlowe sighed, leaning back against the wall in a postural echo of the Furnival's Inn man. 'Don't get me started on the state of things today.'

Abbot looked at him quizzically. Was it the ale or was there, sitting next to him, a fellow traveller in this vale of tears? 'You know England's finished, don't you?' he said in a half whisper.

Marlowe looked at the blacksmith still working with the horse and wondered how much English he knew. He decided to play dumb. 'How so?' he asked.

'Parma and Guise.' Abbot spread his arms, for all the world like the alien Frenchmen he now lived among. 'They'll carve England up between them. I can just see Philip of Spain now, sitting like a steaming turd on Elizabeth's chair.'

'Do I assume you don't altogether approve of the king of Spain, Master Abbot?'

'Well, there's the problem, Greene,' Abbot said, swigging again. 'You hit the nail on the head. Because of Henry VIII and his damned Great Matter; because the lad he fathered had a spine of jelly and died before he'd finished shitting yellow; because various lords listened to the ravings of the Reformers and set up a Godless church, you and I have a problem, don't we?'

More than you know, thought Marlowe, but he'd learned long ago that men in full flight let things slip. Let the man rant on. 'We either accept the Jezebel, in which case we have broken our faith with God and the Holy Father. Or we stay loyal to Rome and accept whatever damned foreigner shouts loudest for the throne of England. The Queen of Scots is the nearest Catholic we have to home grown.'

'Ah.' Marlowe nodded sagely, closing his eyes as he breathed in Abbot's smoke. 'And her cause is lost.'

'Lost?' Abbot repeated. 'In what way?'

Marlowe opened his eyes, sat bolt upright and looked at the man. 'Of course,' he said. 'You must have left London before it happened. Anthony Babington and his friends. All dead. Butchered to make an anti-Roman holiday.'

'By whose authority?' Abbot bellowed, startling his horse and making the blacksmith curse colourfully in a patois Marlowe was glad he didn't fully understand.

'The Queen's.' Marlowe shrugged. 'The Jezebel's, I mean. They say she stayed her hand on the second day of executions and let the hangman actually hang them first, to spare them the pain of the rest.'

Abbot snorted. 'That's damned good of her,' he said, leaning his back against the wall again.

The horse, spooked out of his previous somnolence, whickered and snorted in reply. The blacksmith, who had been stretching the job out to make it seem worth his inflated price, gave a final ringing tap on the last nail and put the leg down. Marlowe could see this little interlude was drawing to a close. Abbot stood and tapped out his pipe against the wall, the smouldering ashes hissing in the damp straw. The projectioner had to be quick. He sighed. 'All too late for my friend Chideock, I fear,' he said.

'Who?' Abbot asked him.

Marlowe looked askance. 'Chideock Tichborne,' he said. 'One of the so-called conspirators. Did you know him?'

Abbot shrugged. 'I meet a lot of people,' he said. Suddenly he stiffened. 'Is that why you're here, Greene?' he asked. 'On the run from Walsingham?'

Marlowe sighed again. 'You might say that,' he said.

Before Abbot could ask for any clarification, the blacksmith appeared at his elbow, the horse's reins in one hand, his hammer in the other.

'M'sieur,' he said. 'The shoe is mended.'

'What?' Abbot said, looking him up and down as though he had never seen him before. 'I can't really be doing with these country types, Greene. It isn't the French I was taught, at any rate. What does he say?'

'I think he is just saying that the shoe is fixed,' Marlowe said. He had to agree that the man spoke with the accent of another region, but it wasn't so thick that Abbot couldn't understand it. Any gentleman who had studied at Furnival's Inn could manage this much French.

'Tell him to send me the bill,' Abbot said, reaching for the reins.

Marlowe passed on the message, with some trepidation. The blacksmith looked a pleasant enough man but the gleaming muscles and the rather firm set of his mouth made Marlowe suspect that the tether he was on was not long.

The man looked at Marlowe, from his great height. 'Tell the M'sieur,' he said, enunciating clearly, 'that though I come from the country, I am not stupid. If he wants his horse, he will pay me for my work. We arranged the price before I even lit my fire.'

Marlowe dutifully translated, adding, for good measure, some advice about the possible consequences of taking on a man a head taller and twice as broad, with muscles where Abbot didn't even have fat.

The Londoner flicked his fingers in the blacksmith's direction. 'Tell him to send the bill, I said,' he snarled. 'And I will pay it when I am good and ready.'

This time, Marlowe didn't have to translate. The blacksmith picked up Abbot and tossed him across the yard, where he came to a skidding halt just on the edge of the hot fire the man had used to heat his iron. Then, he wrapped the reins once more round his hand and led the horse out of the yard and down the road.

'Greene!' Abbot screamed, rising up on one elbow. 'Greene! As an Englishman, stop him. He's got my horse.'

'No, I don't think so,' Marlowe said, watching the man go.

'Has he let it go, then?' he said, getting up and beating out a smouldering ember on his sleeve.

'No,' said one of the scholars, who had been watching with interest. 'He is leading it down the road, back to his forge, if I remember where it is correctly.'

'Then . . .?' Abbot was puzzled.

'What I meant,' Marlowe said, tired of the arrogant fool, 'What I meant was that he has *his* horse, until you pay your bill. We're not in London now, Abbot. We are ambassadors for our country, and I think paying up is what Englishmen do.'

'Not where I come from!' snapped Abbot, making for the road in hot pursuit of his mount.

'No, indeed,' Marlowe said to himself. 'Wherever that might be, Master Abbot.'

The Book of Days lay open at the dawning of the world on the lectern in Thomas Shaw's library. The whole room was clothed in books, their leather spines gleaming with a loving polish and the evening sun lent them a glow of their own, melting into gold.

'The only one of its kind in existence.' Shaw had slid in through a side entrance, his buskins gone now and soft sandals in their place.

Marlowe nodded, tracing the illuminated letters with his fingers. 'Magnificent,' he said. Then he snapped himself out of the scholar's worship of ink and the written word and smiled at the librarian. 'Rather belatedly,' he said, 'I have accepted your invitation to a tour of your library. Though now, I believe, we have other matters to discuss.'

'We do?' Shaw raised an eyebrow.

'The lad Brooke, Dr Shaw,' Marlowe said. 'Not ten hours dead. I seem to remember at my first dinner you didn't want him talking to me.'

'*Tristan and Isolde*,' Shaw said, patting the spine of a huge tome as he led Marlowe past it.

The projectioner knew a changed subject when he heard one and for now played along. 'A singularly secular book for the English College,' he observed.

Shaw chuckled. 'Don't let Gerald Skelton know it's here,' he said. 'He'd burn it.'

'Really? This book must have cost a fortune. I know it would pain the Bursar of my college in Cambridge to destroy something as valuable as this.'

'As a rule, I am sure Dr Skelton would be at one with your Bursar,' Shaw agreed. 'He is a bit of a spoon counter, is Gerald. But he is also a Puritan. Oh, not in the literal sense, of course.' He had noticed Marlowe's swiftly assumed expression of alarm. 'Ah –' his fingers found another volume – '*The Chronicles of Eden*.' He hauled it from the shelf and laid it down on a counter. 'The 1321 edition.'

Marlowe was impressed. Doctor Johns had once told him that no copies of this book existed. 'Tell me, Dr Shaw,' he said. 'Do you lend such manuscripts to the scholars? If I remember my Cambridge days, we were always pretty careless with our texts.'

'Some things we lend out, yes,' Shaw told him. 'But not, you can imagine, this. Look –' he pointed to a ripped hole in the leather of *The Chronicles*' corner – 'a reminder it was once chained. From the Monastery of Melk, on the Danube. Before that, it was owned, I understand, by a Doge of Venice. No, this one never leaves this room.'

'And the book you picked up in Edmund Brooke's room?' Marlowe asked.

Shaw turned to face him. 'You are persistent, Dominus Greene,' he said. 'I'll give you that. It was a copy, if you must know, of the *Iliad*, *not* strictly on Master Brooke's reading list. I don't know what he was doing with it.'

'It is a rattling good yarn,' Marlowe suggested. 'Must make a change from regular reading. Why did you make a point of taking it back?'

'The librarian in me, I suppose,' Shaw said. 'See a book where it shouldn't be, pick it up.'

'About Master Brooke . . .'

Shaw held up his hand. 'All in good time,' he said. 'First, I want to show you something.'

He motioned Marlowe to follow him through the side door he had entered by. Was there no end to the labyrinthine twists in this place? 'Watch your footing.' Shaw's voice echoed as he led the projectioner through a narrow dark passageway that twisted now to the left, then to the right. Little torches flickered in their iron brackets at intervals along the rough walls, giving just enough light to be a guide, but not enough so you could truly say you could see your hand in front of your face. A few in the sequence had gone out, and then the dark was almost complete. Clearly, this was not a part of the College where men walked often and there was a curious smell that Marlowe couldn't place.

They came to a door and here Shaw stopped and placed a warning hand on Marlowe's chest. He looked at him hard in what light there was. 'Do you believe in God, the Father and the Son?' he asked.

Marlowe nodded. 'Of course.'

'And in the primacy of the Holy Father and the Church of Rome?'

'Is there any other?' Marlowe asked, wide-eyed.

'Ah,' Shaw half growled. 'If only. What you will see behind this door, Dominus Greene, is a secret of a very special kind. It is a secret known only to a very few in this College. And it must remain a secret. Do you understand?'

'Perfectly,' said Marlowe.

Shaw nodded, still watching the man's face. Then he took a deep breath as a man might leaping into the abyss and pushed the door open. The light hit Marlowe like a wall and the noise followed it. Ahead was a huge frame with mechanical arms that slid and beat out a staccato refrain. Marlowe knew now what the strange smell was. It was paper and wet ink and the glue that stationers use to bind their books.

'A printing press,' he said, as much to convince himself of the reality of this bustling workshop as anything else. 'Dr Allen's tracts are printed here.'

'They are,' Shaw said. 'But that's not its main purpose.' He nodded at the monk scuttling past with sheaves of parchment. '*This* –' he reached across to a finished book – 'is its main purpose.' And he handed the book to Marlowe.

'The Rheims Bible.' Marlowe smiled.

'You've seen one?'

'Personally, no. But I know men who have.' He looked at Shaw. 'Some of them are dead.'

The librarian shook his head. 'Is that bitch of England still burning people for following the faith?' he asked.

'Oh, it's far more subtle than that.' Marlowe flicked through the newly inked pages and sniffed them. 'The late Queen Mary, may God bless her, used the flames. Elizabeth works through the law.'

'The law!' Shaw almost spat his contempt.

'And her minions. People like Sir Francis Walsingham.'

'Ah, the spymaster.' Shaw nodded grimly. 'You know he's top of the list, don't you?'

'The list?'

'Parma's list. When the invasion comes – and it will – the Duke of Parma has some very special treatment in mind for Francis Walsingham.'

Marlowe smiled. 'I should like to see that.'

'So should we all,' Shaw agreed. 'The man is often in my prayers. In the meantime, we do what little we can. Printing the Bibles here is relatively safe as long as the Catholic League holds Rheims.'

'And if they fail?'

'Oh, ye of little faith,' Shaw muttered, with unconscious accuracy. 'If they fail, the English College will have to move on again. It's not bricks and mortar that make this place, Greene, it's our unshakeable belief.'

'Amen,' Marlowe echoed. 'And now,' he said, placing the Bible back on its pile, 'Edmund Brooke.'

Shaw sighed and ushered Marlowe out of the printing room. The heavy door killed the rattle and thud of the machine instantly and they were in the half dark again. At first, Shaw took them back the way they had come. Then he turned suddenly to his left and began to climb a tight spiral of stone steps that looked more in keeping with a castle than a town house in the heart of Rheims. Another door at the top led out onto the leads and the whole city lay at their feet, twinkling as men lit their fires and smoke began to drift upwards to wreath into the fog that was breathed out by the chilly waters of the Vesle. It was a scene to make even the happiest man feel melancholy, up here on the cold roof, whilst down below, his fellow creatures were tucking themselves up warm before their own hearths. It wasn't just the chill that made Marlowe hug himself into his doublet against the clammy air, but a breath of his own mortality wafting softly on the back of his neck. He shook himself and turned to the librarian as the man spoke.

'What do you want to know about Edmund Brooke?' the librarian asked.

'Who killed him,' Marlowe said, simply.

Shaw leaned forward, resting both elbows on the parapet so that he looked not unlike the grinning gargoyles on the great cathedral which dominated the skyline from almost every rooftop in Rheims. 'God,' he said. 'We cannot fathom His ways.'

Marlowe adopted the same position and smiled at the librarian. 'In the macrocosmia, yes,' he said. 'But the devil is in the detail. God didn't press a pillow over that boy's face and hold it there until he died.'

Shaw said nothing, just stared out over the darkling city, the muscles in his jaws flexing.

'I was there, Dr Shaw,' Marlowe reminded him. 'As were you. Allen's "apoplexy" won't work here. We are discussing murder, you and I, whether we like it or not.'

'I don't like it.' Shaw pushed himself upright from the parapet and looked at Marlowe from his full height. 'Not one bit.'

Marlowe sighed, taking stock of the situation. Not for the first time in his life he wondered whether perhaps he had made a mistake to let someone have the advantage of him. But, he reasoned, he was still here to tell the tale, so either his mistakes had been few or his luck inordinate. He decided to plough ahead. 'I have heard it said,' he murmured, 'that if you want to know how a man died, you should look at how he lived. What do you know about the late Edmund Brooke, Dr Shaw? How did he live, would you say?'

'I know precious little, I'm afraid.' He caught Marlowe's look. 'I shut him up at dinner because like all scholars he had the habit of opening his mouth a little too wide. You were new then, Greene; I knew nothing about you.'

'And now?'

'Now, I have revealed to you my inner sanctum. And I don't do that to everybody. I pride myself on being a judge of men. The secrets of the English College are safe with you, I'm sure.'

'Not *all* its secrets, Doctor,' Marlowe said. 'There are some that are denied to all of us.'

Shaw fell silent, thinking. Then he turned again to the parapet and the city. Stars were peeping in the patches of clear sky, winking silently on and off as wisps of mist drifted over the streets and houses, as if there were no strife in the world. No Catholics. No Protestants. Just the eternal motion of the Heavens presiding over all. 'Brooke may have been a thief,' he said. He blew out a breath, and with it any indecision he had felt over sharing what he knew with the man at his side. 'It's nothing I can prove. It's just that a number of volumes have been disappearing recently. Nothing as obvious as *The Chronicles* of course, but lesser works, valuable in their own right. Always after Master Brooke had been working in the library.'

'So the volume in his room . . .?'

'Was not one he should have had,' Shaw admitted. 'I try to be charitable, Dominus Greene, but even I have to admit that some men are just naturally light-fingered.'

'How would Brooke have disposed of these books?' Marlowe asked. 'There was nothing in his room, except . . .'

Shaw looked at Marlowe in the gathering gloom. 'Except what?'

Marlowe smiled to himself. It was all falling into place. 'Except a little hidey-hole about so big.' He held up his hands to sketch a box shape in the air and then realized it was almost too dark to see. 'About the size where a book might fit. It was in the floor of his wardrobe.'

Shaw nodded. He wasn't surprised. 'There are a number of stationers in the town, booksellers by another name,' he said. 'Any of them would have made a killing out of the lad . . .' His voice tailed away as he realized what he had said.

A chapel bell began tolling from the quad away over the gabled roof behind the pair.

'Vespers,' said Shaw. 'Shall we?' He gestured with his arm towards the little door back onto the winding stair.

'You go,' said Marlowe. 'I have other business tonight, Dr Shaw. And thank you.'

'For what?' the librarian asked.

'Your honesty,' Marlowe told him. 'Your openness.'

'There's a quicker way down,' Shaw said. 'If you go that way and down the steps at the end you'll find yourself in the quad, just behind the main gate.'

Marlowe nodded and took his leave. At the bottom of the spiral steps he was out into the night air and nearly collided with a scholar leaning against a stone pillar. The lad looked pale and ill in his fustian and he mumbled something to Marlowe before he turned away to vomit in the shadows.

ELEVEN

Marlowe was studying the latest tract from Dr Allen that evening when he heard the rap at his bedroom door. He placed his dagger within easy reach and called, 'Yes?'

Gerald Skelton stood in the doorway, a grim look on his face. 'Dominus Greene.' He nodded to him. 'The Master would like a word. Now, please.'

Marlowe looked at the calibrated candle. 'It's late, Doctor,' he purred. 'Can't it wait?'

'No, Dominus Greene.' Skelton was firm. 'It can't.'

Marlowe closed the pamphlet and snuffed out the candle, gesturing to Skelton to lead the way. They padded up a staircase and along a gallery decorated with the martyrdom of Catholic saints, heads lying on pavements, executioners' swords crimson with holy blood. At the end, they turned sharp left and began a descent into darkness. Marlowe hadn't been this way before. The warm wood of the galleries had been replaced by the cold, damp stone of northern France and they were turning a tight spiral on the worn steps. Skelton carried the candle but knew his way instinctively and Marlowe was expected to follow suit. At the bottom, the Bursar swept around a pillar to his right and tapped on an oak door straight ahead. There was a muffled response and Skelton opened the door with a rattle of iron.

The dimmest of candles burned in a tiny chapel whose plain white walls glistened with moisture. The solitary flame flickered on the agonized face of St Peter, spreadeagled on his cross, upside down because he was not worthy to suffer the same fate as his Lord. The Master of the English College was at his devotions before the altar with its damask cloth and crosses. Marlowe heard the door crash closed behind him and the screech of a bolt. He was aware of two burly monks taking up positions on either side of the door, arms folded, hoods forward over their heads. Marlowe recognized muscular Christianity when he saw it; he'd known it all his life, from the early days at the King's School, Canterbury, and nothing surprised him any more. He wondered, very briefly, if either of these muscular Christians had been the one to take a slice out of Thomas Phelippes.

Allen crossed himself before the altar, turned and faced Marlowe. Then he walked over to a sedilia and sat down. Skelton stood next to him, his arms folded like the heavies at the door. 'Doctor Skelton has noticed, Dominus Greene,' Allen said, his ringed fingers twitching on the arm of his chair, 'that you do not attend divine service.'

Marlowe cast a glance at the Bursar. Clearly, the man was more observant than he looked. 'I am not a monk, Dr Allen,' Marlowe excused himself. 'You wouldn't expect me to follow the Orders.'

'The Orders, no,' Allen conceded. 'But Doctor Skelton tells me you don't attend *any* service, not even Matins. And in the time you have been here, you have taken Holy Communion only once.'

'I have been remiss,' Marlowe agreed, 'for which I apologize.'

'Oh, I think you have rather more to apologize for than that, Dominus Greene,' the Master said. 'You see, I received a letter recently from . . . let's just say a friend. In the University of Cambridge. Gerald.'

Skelton produced a sheaf of paper from his lawn sleeve and cleared his throat. 'Dominus Robert Greene is a scholar at St John's College, not Corpus Christi –' he was reading by the bad light, squinting at the tiny writing, but he was clearly familiar with the contents of the letter – 'and as I write, is very much alive and well. And residing currently here in Cambridge. I learn that he is reasonably travelled in Europe and has nonsensical ambitions to become a poet and a playwright.'

'Nonsensical indeed,' Marlowe said with a laugh.

'What is the date of that missive, Doctor Skelton?' Allen asked.

'Eight days ago, Master,' the Bursar told him.

'Yet you have been with us now for sixteen,' Allen was scowling at Marlowe. 'I think it's time you told us the truth, sir. I will not have lies in this College.'

'Will you not?' Marlowe grunted. 'Is that why three men are dead? And why you had me followed the other night?'

Allen's face changed not a jot in the candlelight. 'Who are you?' he said.

'Christopher Marlowe,' Marlowe said. 'Scholar of Corpus Christi College.'

'The same Christopher Marlowe you claimed to have killed?' Allen asked. 'The blasphemer and atheist?'

Skelton's jaw dropped. He knew none of this but Allen was in full flow. He'd long ago skated over secrets he'd heard in the Confessional, if only for the greater good. There was no going back now.

'Would I be here,' Marlowe asked the Master, 'if I were either?'

'Then why *are* you here?' Allen asked.

Marlowe straightened, then jerked his head in the direction of the monks at his back, 'Gog and Magog here,' he said. 'Can they be trusted?'

'Implicitly,' Allen said with a nod.

'Very well, then. You have a spy in your midst, Dr Allen – an intelligencer in the English College.'

'I knew it!' Skelton shouted, then fell abruptly silent at a wave of the Master's hand.

'Who is it?' Allen asked.

Marlowe chuckled. 'If I knew that, Master,' he said, 'I'd have left his head on your high altar by now.'

'Sacrilege!' Skelton was appalled.

'We live in a sacrilegious age, Bursar,' Marlowe rapped. 'Ask friends Luther, Melanchthon, Calvin. Every other jack's an Anabaptist. Have you all forgotten why you left England?'

'If you weren't telling the truth before,' Allen said, 'how do we know you're telling it now?'

Marlowe frowned, then slipped his hand into his purse and noted the monks behind him edging forward. 'Perhaps this will help. You have a lovely reading voice, Doctor Skelton. Read that to the Master.'

Skelton took the document Marlowe had passed to him. He saw the seal, the ribbon, the keys of Peter embedded deep in the wax. 'You know the imprimatur of the Curia?' Marlowe asked him. Skelton showed it to Allen who recognized it too and nodded. 'Read it,' he commanded.

Skelton unrolled the parchment and began. 'To Our Well Beloved Son in Christ, Dr William Allen.' He was reading in perfect Latin. 'Greeting. By these precepts know that our son

Christopher Marlowe has Our Dispensation to investigate the English College now at Rheims in Our belief that the antichrist is abroad in your cloisters. It is Our wish that you extend him every assistance to root out the Devil in your midst. May the Lord be with you in this time of Our trials, etcetera, etcetera . . .' His voice trailed away.

Allen glanced at the document. 'There's no signature,' he said.

'You know as well as I do –' Marlowe folded his arms – 'His Holiness only uses his quill on letters close. You and I, sadly, do not command such status.'

Allen wasn't looking at the paper any more, just at Marlowe. 'Top left,' he said to Skelton. 'The initials there . . .'

Skelton squinted at it, turning it towards the light. 'ACG,' he said. 'GC.'

There was a silence. Both men looked at Marlowe. 'Alessandro Castel Giovanni,' he said with a sigh, 'Gran Cardinale. When I was in His Eminence's palace last, I had the honour to dance with his daughter.'

Skelton tutted and rolled his eyes.

'Now, Gerald.' Allen smiled. 'Who are we to judge?'

'When the Curia finally sees sense and makes you a Cardinal, Master—'

Allen cut the man short. 'What do you need, Dominus Marlowe?'

'To find the Devil in your midst,' Master,' Marlowe answered. 'And I must be allowed to do that in my own way. I won't get very far if I'm prostrate in the chapel morning, noon and night.' He glanced at the monks behind him. 'Or, if I'm followed on an evening. My inquiries may well take me beyond the College walls.'

'You won't be hindered,' Allen told him. 'Gerald, I want you to give every assistance to Dominus Marlowe.'

'No, no,' Marlowe said hurriedly. Being marked out for special attention would not get him very far in his quest. 'Something tells me I'll get further as the runagate Robert Greene, failed poet and playwright than as a Papal Nuncio. People will be off their guard. Don't change your treatment of me in the slightest, please, either of you. I must maintain anonymity at all costs. Doctor Skelton, please feel free to carry on hating my guts as publicly as you wish.'

Allen considered it for a moment, then nodded. '*Genistho*,' he said in Greek. 'Let it be so.'

Skelton half bowed, an ironic smile on his lips. Nothing would please him better than to continue to hate Marlowe. The projectioner heard the bolts slide back behind him and the heavy door creak open. He crossed himself before the altar and waited for the Papal letters to be returned. They weren't. Instead, Allen slipped them into his sleeve. Marlowe bowed and made his way, groping for the stairs. Now, urgency quickened his steps. He had perhaps two weeks before Allen sent his messengers to Rome and before they got back, bearing the message that His Eminence the Gran Cardinale Alessandro Castel Giovanni didn't know Kit Marlowe from a hole in the ground.

Robert Greene had a plan. He had had plans before when trying to gain entry into Kit Marlowe's erstwhile rooms, but he had every confidence that this one would actually work. He had tried walking in boldly. He had tried creeping in and hiding, waiting for dark. This time, he would use a subterfuge as clever as a Trojan horse, and hopefully as successful. He knew the very place along the wall where the scholars crept in after hours. He knew the Proctors lay in wait for them but also knew that there were more scholars than Proctors. If he could insinuate himself in the crowd, climbing over the wall and into the tree at the right point, he could avoid the Proctors and be up the stairs in a trice. He might have to buy said scholars a few drinks first, to gain their confidence, but all should be well.

The first flaw in his plan was that he had severely underestimated the capacity for alcohol of the typical Corpus Christi scholar. His purse was deeper than theirs, but even so they had almost bled him dry by the time they all wandered, arms around each others' shoulders, singing snatches of catches down Bene't Street towards the crumbling wall of the College. Lomas and his cohort didn't even bother to conceal themselves. The smoke from their pipes drifted over the wall and they could be heard talking together from out in the street.

A scholar turned to Greene and tried to focus, first with one eye, then another. 'You're quite tall,' he said, 'when you stand upright.' He covered one eye to make it easier. 'Yes, there you are. Give me a leg up and I'll have a go at counting them.'

Greene locked his hands and bent down. The scholar stepped into the cup of his palms and Greene hoisted him to the top of the wall. The scholar could be heard counting under his breath and Greene let him down again. The boy leant on the wall and looked down at his own fingers, straightening and bending them experimentally.

'Six!' he said, triumphantly. 'Or twelve. Or three. They were moving about a bit. Hard to count.' He hiccupped violently. 'I think I'll go first. They put you to bed when they catch you and I could do with a lie down. Anyone else coming with me?'

The other scholars milled around, everyone trying to be at the back. Blurred and out of kilter as they were, they knew arrant nonsense when they heard it. The Proctors put you to bed all right, but the next day, on Dr Harvey's orders, they flayed the skin off your back. Greene found himself at the front and tried to bury himself in the pack.

'Nonononono,' the first boy said who seemed to be the leader, though he couldn't count. 'He bought us drinks. He can't go next. He'll get in trouble.' He listened to what he had said. 'Trouble? Is that the word?'

'Yes,' said Greene, out of the corner of his mouth, trying to drum up support for the idea.

'Trouble. Yes. Well, he's bought us all drinks. We can't get him into trouble. So, come on.' He reached into the crowd and hauled out a couple more scholars. 'You and you. Come with me.' And he swung himself up the wall and was gone, still unexpectedly limber even in his cups.

Greene began to feel old. He had been this carefree once, before bitterness and jealousy had bitten him. He gave himself a shake. He really shouldn't drink; it always made him pensive.

There was shouting beyond the wall and the sound of running feet. Another scholar went over and screamed that he was caught. And shouting from the Proctors confirmed it. So the ringleader's arithmetic was a bit awry, but surely no college had more than four Proctors on guard on any one night? Another one vaulted over and this time the sound from the other side of the wall was a triumphant whoop. Quickly, the others scrambled over, not forgetting to give Greene, their sponsor, a helping hand. Soon, he was at the entrance to Marlowe's room and was edging open the door.

Harvey was sweeping round Corpus Christi like a new broom, but he had not yet ordered the cleaning out of the rooms of absent scholars, so Marlowe's room was as he left it, with the addition of a few more spiders and another bloom of dust. Greene edged in, remembering his last visit and his hand twinged in memory of it. He sat down on the bed in the dark and closed his eyes, trying to put himself into Marlowe's shoes. If he wanted to hide a manuscript, quite a bulky one, where would he put it? The mattress? No; the mattress would be turned at random intervals and it might easily be discovered. The linen press? Again, not under Marlowe's control. It might be found by a maid or Proctor and although they probably wouldn't be able to read it, they would more than likely take it to the College authorities as something that had been hidden and therefore likely to be scurrilous, especially in the room of Kit Marlowe.

He needed to find a place in the room where no one would go except to hide something. It needed to be something permanent, yet movable, like a floorboard. His eyes flew open with the sheer simplicity of his idea and he was on his hands and knees in seconds. His first instinct was to get down and brush the rushes into corners and prise up the floorboards but the alcohol still in his system made him lazy and in his laziness he saw the hiding place, as though in a flash. As he sat indecisively on the floor, he saw a corner of the wainscoting which didn't seem to fit as flush to the wall as the rest. It was outlined, almost providentially, in a moonbeam and Greene leant forward and put the tip of his dagger under one corner and pushed. With a click, the piece of wood popped out and there, just inches from his hand, was a rolled manuscript, wrapped in oiled silk and tied with a length of red cord.

Remembering where he was, he prised the roll out with his dagger and rolled sideways, his hands and arms protecting his head, but nothing happened. Rising slowly and carefully, he took the roll and slid it into the front of his doublet and made his way out of Corpus Christi for the last time, just forbearing from cocking a snook at the darkened windows of the Master's Lodging.

In the shadow of the quad, a slender youth, Thomas Fineaux,

still very limber for all he had drunk Robert Greene's purse dry, smiled to himself. Tomorrow would be busy. First, he would pay his fine for being caught coming over the wall. Then he would take Lomas' whip across his back. Then, he had one or two letters to write.

The lad still looked green the next day when Marlowe found him. He was propped up against a stone pillar, his fustian robes wrapped around him, both to keep out the wind and to hold himself together.

'Someone told me you're Martin Camb,' Marlowe said.

Camb looked up and all he saw was a dark shape with a morning sun shining like a halo over wild hair and the collar of a roisterer's doublet. 'It's nice to be reminded now and again.'

Marlowe sat down next to the boy, spreading his cloak on the ground and crossing one elegant buskin over the other. 'I'm Robert Greene,' he said. 'Corpus Christi.'

The boy nodded. He wasn't in the mood for conversation and didn't care who knew it.

'Your ingle is dead,' Marlowe said, coming straight out with it. 'I'm sorry.'

Camb frowned, focusing now on the dark eyes, the soft mouth. 'No, you're not,' he muttered. 'And anyway, Edmund wasn't my ingle, as you put it.'

'No?' Marlowe raised an eyebrow.

'No!' Camb's response was louder than he meant it to be and he looked round, startled. Scholars were scuttling, late to lectures, across the quad. Brother Tobias scowled at him from the main gate. 'No,' he hissed. 'Such things are an abomination. Our Lord Himself frowned on sodomy.'

'Actually, he didn't –' Marlowe folded his arms – 'if I remember my scripture.

'What do you want?' Camb asked him. He wasn't up to rhetoric at this time of the morning, especially with an older man who knew more than he did. His head was banging, a slow and distant rhythm which nevertheless managed to drown out almost everything else and make coherent thought next to impossible. He wanted to lie down in a dark, cool room and wait until everything stayed still and the right way up, at the same time. Currently, it was either one thing or the other and the pain was so bad it reached to the ends of his hair.

'Information.' Marlowe produced a gold coin from his purse and watched it catch the light.

'About what?' Camb wanted to know.

'Edmund Brooke,' Marlowe told him and tossed the coin so that it spun in the air. Camb caught it and bit it. Marlowe smiled. 'You didn't learn that in the English College,' he said.

Camb's face creased into a smile for the first time and he looked the better for it. 'I'm sorry,' he said. 'The news about Edmund came as a . . . a bit of a shock. These things take a bit of getting used to. And I must say, I'm not feeling any too well at present.'

'You don't look it, if you don't mind my saying so,' Marlowe said. 'I was expecting quite an improvement on my glimpse of you last night, but if anything you look rather worse.'

'Oh, please,' Camb said, testily. 'Please don't be polite for my sake. I can take the truth.'

'I'll make allowances,' Marlowe said, with a small smile. 'How well did you know Edmund?'

'Oh, you know, shadows in the night.' He suddenly shuddered. 'I'm seeing a lot of those at the moment.' Marlowe took his hand. It was as cold as a stone. And the pupils of his eyes were tiny, lost in the irises of clear blue.

Camb instinctively pulled his hand away. 'Why do you want to know about him?'

'I have a curious nature.' Marlowe smiled. 'When a man is suffocated, I have a tendency to ask questions. I hope I may be forgiven.'

'Suffocated?' Camb was sitting upright, quivering in the cold of the morning. 'The Master said it was—'

'Apoplexy.' Marlowe finished the sentence for him. 'Yes, I know. It's his favourite word. When did you see the Master?'

'Er . . . I don't know. Last night, I think. He was asking me questions too. Dominus Greene, I don't understand. What's going on?'

Marlowe smiled at a hidden joke. 'The Master and I,' he said. 'We ask the questions. Where were you when Edmund died?'

'I don't rightly know. On the town . . . somewhere.'

'Are you often on the town, Master Camb?' Marlowe looked hard into the boy's eyes.

Camb looked back. Were there two Robert Greenes now? He couldn't be sure. He could keep them down to just the one if he closed one eye, but then the other one wanted to close as well and an ingrained sense of self-preservation made him want to keep both his eyes firmly on Greene. Greenes. He blinked several times and swallowed hard as the background swam out of focus. He wanted to speak up for himself, tell this interloper where to stick his inquisitive nature. 'Often,' he said. Not very compelling as answers went, but it was all his lips could manage.

'And when Edmund died?' Marlowe persisted. He felt almost sorry for the lad; his headache proclaimed itself in his furrowed brow and tight neck and shoulder muscles. He would have screamed with the pain, but for the pain it would have caused. Marlowe forced himself to be firm with him. 'Be specific, Martin. And be accurate. Your life may depend upon it.'

'Um . . . I left the College . . . let's see, it would have been after Vespers. It's easier to slip out when people are still moving. Once we're abed and it's lights out, there are creaking floor boards and marauding cats . . . Tread on a cat's tail and you can wake the College in seconds, from the gate to the attics.'

Marlowe nodded. It could have been him talking not so long ago as he crept out of the Court at Corpus Christi, making for the Brazen Head or the Eagle. He felt a sudden pang of homesickness for his room, his familiar walks. He shook himself out of it. 'Was anyone with you?'

'God, no. There used to be, of course, but now Drs Allen and Skelton have put the fear of God into the scholars. What does our Lord say about wine, Dominus Greene? You seem to know your scriptures.'

Marlowe shrugged. 'I know he turned water into the stuff,' he said. 'And His Father had some quite useful tasting advice, red, yellow, that kind of thing.'

'Exactly!' Camb prodded the air with his finger. 'So I don't see the Master's objection.'

'So, you went out after Vespers,' Marlowe said, bringing the lad back to the night in question. 'Where did you go?'

'Er . . . the Casque d'Argent. It's on the Rue Vervain. About half a mile away.'

'Did you meet anyone there?' Marlowe asked. 'Anyone who could vouch for you?'

'No one from the College, if that's what you mean. I take a few twists and turns before choosing where to drink. Less likely to get caught that way.'

Again, the wave of homesickness for the little back lanes of Cambridge swept over Marlowe, like a sheet of iced water from the crown of his head to the soles of his feet. He could almost smell the waft of stale ale that would envelop him as he pushed open the door of the Eagle. He could taste the smoke-filled air of the private room at the back of the Devil.

Camb was still speaking. 'A few locals were there, of course. I've drunk with them before, but they don't know my name. Least said, soonest mended. The English College exerts a powerful sway on this town.'

'But you know their names, surely,' Marlowe said. 'Just to say hello.'

'Jacques was there,' Camb said, then furrowed his brow. 'Or was that last week . . .? Pierre was definitely there, because he had borrowed money from Louis and . . . no, it wasn't Pierre, it was definitely Jacques . . .'

Marlowe wished that Camb would think inside his head, but he could see that the lad had the kind of memory that peopled the air around him with detail and he could see them, perhaps not clearly, but through a haze. Ask him to do his remembering quietly and there would be no remembering at all.

Finally, he came to a decision and turned to Marlowe triumphantly. 'Jacques,' he announced. 'Mireille—'

'Mireille?' Marlowe stopped him. 'The harlot who haunts this place?'

'Does she?' Camb asked. 'I don't know. I can't afford her. From there I went to . . . La Pucelle, was it? Yes, La Pucelle. Bit of a Hell-hole, really. They were playing lansquenet. I remember I was losing . . .'

'And?'

Camb shrugged. 'I was drinking.'

Marlowe's temper was suddenly at the end of its rope. He

grabbed Camb's hand and twisted it behind his back, pinning him under the weight of his body. 'I'm spending too much time on you, scholar,' he hissed into his ear. 'Stop all of this drunken reminiscence nonsense. Your room-mate, if we can properly call him that. Your ingle. The love of your life if you want to give it that gloss, whatever he was to you, Edmund Brooke is dead. So let's have it, the story of your wandering last night. What happened at La Pucelle, if that is where you were and not hiding somewhere in the College, with Edmund Brooke's last breath still damp on your hands?'

Camb went limp under Marlowe's weight, one hand trapped in the projectioner's vice-like grip, the other hopelessly tangled in his robe where he had tucked it to keep it warm. 'I don't know. I blacked out. I had the horrors of drink on me.'

Marlowe looked into the lad's eyes again and saw the pain. 'No, you didn't, Martin,' he said, releasing him. 'Somebody doctored your wine. Not very subtly, either.' He cast his mind back to Dr John Dee, who could send someone to sleep for as long as he wanted, although his claim of a thousand years had always struck Marlowe as overblown. How could he know? When they woke up, and Marlowe had witnessed it, they felt as though they had just dropped off for a second, no headache, no gripes, no nothing. Certainly, Dee's potions would never leave anyone in a state like this. The lad could have died. But he needed to check. 'Are you sure you have never felt like this before?'

'I have had bad heads,' he said, 'but never like this. I feel as though my skull has turned to glass.'

Marlowe nodded and patted the boy's shoulder. 'Do something for me, Master Camb.' He got up suddenly and straightened his cloak. 'Stay away from the Casque d'Argent.' He tossed him another coin. 'To cover your losses,' he said, in explanation, 'and to remind you to stay away from La Pucelle as well. Use the change to buy some candles for your friend. Will you do that for me?'

Camb nodded. 'Wait,' he said, trying to get up and failing. 'Dominus Greene, who did it? Who suffocated Edmund?'

'Suffocated?' Marlowe frowned. 'That was apoplexy, lad. You must have been drinking again.'

TWELVE

Walsingham hated Hatfield. The house itself was all right, and so too was the little church of St Ethelfreda's that sat squatly on the slope of its churchyard. It was actually getting there he hated. The roads of Hertfordshire were appalling and now that November was here with its creeping fogs and frosty nights, the iron-hard ruts of those roads jolted him around so that he resembled a dangled puppet and ached in every limb.

Burghley's finest claret only mollified him a little. Even his roast swan failed to hit the spot. Why, oh why, couldn't the Chief Secretary have stayed in London?

'So that's it, then?' Burghley asked him when the servants had retired for the night and the two Privy Councillors sat before the dying fire with only the Cecil hounds for company. 'That's the view of all of them?'

Walsingham shuffled the documents he had scattered on the side table. 'You've read it yourself, my lord,' he said. 'Twenty peers of the realm and forty knights of the shire want the Scottish bitch dead. We've done our bit.'

Burghley stared at the firelight dancing in his crystal glass and turned as a burnt-out log fell in the grate, like a burning kingdom put to the sword and the flame. 'Yes,' he said. 'The queen was allowed no counsel and given no jury. Small wonder we found her guilty.'

'Careful,' Walsingham warned with a smile on his lips. 'You're beginning to sound like Christopher Hatton.'

'God forbid,' Burghley growled. 'But tell me, Francis, Councillor to Councillor, did we do right?'

Walsingham shrugged. 'You have Her Majesty's letter?' he asked.

Burghley sighed. 'I have.'

'What did it say? Remind me.'

Burghley knew every word by heart. He knew he would never forget a syllable, as long as he lived. '"Let the wicked murderess know her vile deserts compel these orders",' he quoted. '"Upon the examination and trial of the cause . . . "' His voice tailed away as he shook his head.

Walsingham finished the sentence for him, '"You shall by verdict find the said Queen guilty of the crime she stands charged with." Rest easy, my lord, our mistress herself is judge, jury and executioner.'

'Executioner?' Burghley laughed. 'That I doubt. When will that petition be presented to her?'

'Next Tuesday,' Walsingham told him, 'at Richmond.'

Burghley nodded. 'She'll hedge,' he said. 'She'll whine about being on a stage and in the limelight. "*Who shall cast the first stone*" et cetera, et cetera. She'll probably play the sex card too – frail womanhood and so on: *even now, if Mary confesses, I will counsel my God to spare her life*.'

It was one of the best impressions of the Queen Walsingham had ever heard and the fact that it bordered on treason didn't faze him one bit. It was the sort of conversation that he'd had with himself on many an occasion. Looking at Burghley now was like looking into a glass. 'Will she do it, do you think?' he asked the Chief Secretary. 'Will she sign Mary's death warrant?'

Burghley looked into the eyes of the spymaster and saw only himself reflected there. 'Yes,' he said, after a while. 'Yes, she will. But when she does, it'll be our fault and personally I shall be well away from the Presence when that quill hits the parchment.'

Both men sat in silence as their thoughts overtook them.

Burghley broke the silence first. 'In the meantime, what news of the English College?'

'None.' Walsingham helped himself to more claret. 'We could have done with Phelippes at the trial. How he's faring in the scorpions' nest, God only knows.'

'But this man Marlowe,' Burghley said. 'He's in safe hands, surely? Phelippes, I mean.'

'Oh, Phelippes is in safe hands, my lord. As for Marlowe, that I can't answer.'

La Pucelle lay on the wrong side of the cathedral and a stone's throw from Solomon Aldred's house near the tanneries. The

familiar smell of curing hides followed Marlowe all along the
narrow, winding streets of another autumn night. There was no
moon tonight, peeping past the chimney pots, no stars to twinkle
in Heaven to remind the great and good of God's light. But the
way was lit by the welcoming glow from the open frontage of
La Pucelle. A solemn wooden girl, painted white and wearing
plate armour, looked down at Marlowe from her wooden perch.
He knew all about Jeanne the Maid. She was a mad woman from
Domrémy whom the French called a saint and who had taken
Orleans back from the English when Marlowe's great-grandfather,
Richard, was a tanner in Canterbury and nobody fought anybody
over religion. In the end the French church had become concerned
that the Maid was more central in men's affections than they
were and they handed her over to the English who burned her
in the market square. She was younger than Marlowe was today
and all her life already played out.

But it was another girl who caught his attention tonight and
she was very much flesh and blood. Mireille was flirting with
La Pucelle's clientele in a far corner, half hidden by the joists
that held up the low roof and she suddenly found herself whisked
away by a dark Englishman in a scarlet doublet.

'You,' she said with a smile when she realized who it was.
'Had a change of heart, have we?' She squeezed herself against
him.

'Not exactly,' he said. 'Tell me about Martin Camb.'

'Who?' Marlowe's French wasn't bad, but she had never heard
the name.

'The lad from the English College,' he explained. 'Likes a
drink. Out of his depth.'

'Don't know him,' she said with a shrug. 'We get lots of the
English boys in here. And some of the men. And I'm not here
all the time, you know. I have a living to earn. You are lucky to
have caught me.'

Marlowe could recognize hedging when he heard it. 'This one
hangs out at the Casque d'Argent. You were there with him two
nights ago.'

'With him?' Mireille was becoming bored with this conversation. 'I don't think so. He couldn't afford me.'

'"With" can mean a lot of things in this language, it seems,'

Marlowe said. His eyes were everywhere but on the girl. This was a rough crowd; he could recognize the types in any inn on either side of the Channel. They watched him too, noting the expensive clothes, the purse that bulged at his hip. A sheep for shearing. 'And it's my guess you followed him here.'

'What if I did?' she asked.

Now he looked her full in the face for the first time. 'Unless you do what you do for love,' he said, 'I can't imagine what Master Camb had that would interest you. You have already told me he couldn't afford you. Had you asked him?'

She shrugged an expressive shoulder. 'He's a scholar. He's got no money.'

'But you did follow him,' Marlowe insisted.

She broke away from him and stood with her hands on her hips, breasts jutting in the half light. 'So what if I like breaking in the young ones for nothing now and again? Life should not all be work. Perhaps you might like to think on that, sometime.'

'*J'ai affaires à vous en dehors*,' a gruff voice snarled in his ear. He half turned to face an ox of a man who also had his hands on his hips. It was defiance of a different kind.

'I can't imagine what business we might have together, sirrah,' Marlowe said.

Mireille shrieked with laughter. 'It's a phrase we have around here, Englishman,' she said. 'Business outside means David here intends to skewer you like a chicken.'

Marlowe smiled. 'Does he now? Well, Mireille, thank you for the explanation, but I'd rather play cards.'

'Cards?' David scoffed. 'I hadn't got you down for a coward, Englishman. A popinjay, yes. *And* you're bothering Mireille here.'

'Yes,' Marlowe mused. 'I probably am.' He looked up at David, half a head taller and twice as broad. 'A friend of mine,' he said to him, 'an English scholar called Martin Camb.'

'What of him?' David asked.

'He was here two nights ago, playing cards. Lansquenet. Did he play with you?'

David chuckled and glanced back to his companions around a table. 'He might have done.'

'You fleeced him,' Marlowe said, 'to the tune of fifty blancs.'

'Fifty be buggered,' David grunted. 'Twenty at best . . .'

Marlowe smiled, the smile of a basilisk on a rock. 'Twenty it is, then,' he said and brushed past the Frenchman to sit at his table. 'I'd like a chance to win it back.'

David turned. 'You're sitting in my seat, Englishman,' he growled.

'Am I?' Marlowe expressed amazement. 'Well, I won't be here long. Just long enough to relieve you of your twenty blancs.'

David looked at his companions. Each of them was grinning at him, willing him to flatten the popinjay. David couldn't disappoint them. He raised a massive arm.

'Outside!' the landlord's voice roared over the din. 'I won't have my tables buckled. Take it outside.'

Marlowe stood up. He wasn't smiling now. 'Very well,' he said. 'Since you . . . David . . . have called me out *and* effectively chosen the time and place, I believe I have the right to choose the weapons.'

'Choose away,' the Frenchman grinned and the next second he was face down on the table, Marlowe's dagger tip sticking in his ear. The card players had leapt back, the landlord's chairs crashing in all directions and they formed a half circle, facing the pair. There was no noise now and the whole of La Pucelle seemed frozen, all eyes turned to Marlowe, everyone wondering what he would do next.

'I know,' said Marlowe, holding the big Frenchman down with an iron grip on his neck. 'I can see why you are amused,' he said to the card players, some of whom, the ones who wanted to see David get his comeuppance, were grinning broadly. 'It *does* look silly, doesn't it, to see a man with a knife stuck in his ear? But we all know, don't we – especially you, David – one tiny bit more pressure from me and this dagger tip goes straight into what passes in that skull of yours for a brain.'

The silence was deep enough to hurt the ears, even the ones with no dagger in them. David hardly dared breathe. Marlowe lowered his head and whispered past the blade, 'Now, I am only going to ask this once. What did you lace Martin Camb's drink with while you were taking his last blancs?'

'I don't know what you're talking about,' the Frenchman hissed as clearly as he could with a mouth full of tabletop.

'Stop!' a female voice shattered the silence and Marlowe's flexing elbow held firm. Mireille crossed the floor to the pair and looked into Marlowe's face. What she saw there terrified her but she went on anyway. 'I'll tell you what you need to know. David's telling the truth. He's not involved.'

Marlowe blinked for the first time in minutes. He kept the dagger point in place and half straightened, fumbling in David's purse. He grabbed a handful of coins and counted out twenty blancs by the guttering candles. The rest he threw on the floor. Then he jerked the knife back and kicked the Frenchman's legs away so that he thudded heavily to the ground.

'Now,' he said to Mireille, grabbing her arm and keeping the dagger at arm's length in front of him, backing to the door, 'I have business with *you* outside.'

The silence was shattered again, this time by laughing, clapping and whistling. The last Marlowe saw of David was his companions hauling him upright and slapping his shoulders. The popinjay and the harlot were gone into the night.

This wasn't a part of the city that Marlowe knew at all. They skirted the river once, then climbed the hill. The Watch, leaning on their halberds as the bells of the cathedral called the hour, saw them go and said nothing. They all knew Mireille and half of them had had her. One or two of her customers hailed her, but took one look at Marlowe and decided against engaging her services tonight.

'What is he to you?' Marlowe asked her after minutes of trudging in silence. 'David?'

'Nothing,' she said. 'Except he's a Frenchman.' She cast him a glance under her eyelashes. 'Saving your presence. I thought you might have killed him.'

'There's no "might" about it,' Marlowe said. 'Where are we going?'

'I hope you don't mind if I don't give you the address,' she said. 'I wouldn't want you finding it again.'

'I hope I won't have to,' he muttered.

Mireille suddenly ducked under an awning to her right and she led Marlowe under a low archway. They were in a dingy courtyard where no torches guttered and Marlowe kept his hand on his dagger hilt. She pushed open a small door and closed it once Marlowe was inside. She lit a candle and he took in the room. There was a bed, a chair and a table and a pale mark on the wall where a crucifix had once looked down on the scene.

There was a rhythmic grunting coming from the next room, behind the mark of the cross.

'She won't be long,' Mireille said. 'Wine?'

Marlowe shook his head and leaned back against the far wall. From here he could take in the door, the little window and whoever might come hurtling out through the curtain that screened the other room. The grunting came to abrupt end and there was a long sigh that ended in a curse. Mireille busied herself hanging her cloak on a hook and a burly rough pushed through the curtain, tying up his points. He threw a glance at Mireille and made to brush past her, but the girl stood in front of him, blocking the door, with her hand out.

'Get lost!' the lout snarled. 'She's damaged goods, that one. Like shagging a door.' And he pushed Mireille aside.

'You!' Marlowe shouted, kicking himself away from the wall and standing with his hand still behind his back. 'Pay the lady what you owe.'

The oaf hadn't taken in the dark figure in the shadows but he did now and the sight made him reconsider. 'How much?' he growled.

'The usual,' Mireille said. 'Five blancs.'

The man fumbled in his purse.

'Make it ten,' said Marlowe. 'Or next time you won't be shagging a door; you'll be lying on one.'

The client hesitated, then threw a stash of coins onto the table and was gone. Mireille picked up each one, weighed it, bit it and then stashed them away in her bodice, laughing. 'You should do this for a living,' she said.

He half smiled and let the dagger hilt go. 'You couldn't afford me,' he said.

A pale face peered around the curtain, a frail elfin child in a thin chemise. She looked ill and much older than her years.

'Did he hurt you?' Mireille asked, teasing the girl's hair away from her face and tucking it behind her ears.

She shook her head.

'Monsieur Greene.' Mireille put her arm around the girl and pulled her further out into the room. 'This is Sylvie. This gentleman is from the English College, Sylvie. He wants to ask you some questions.'

Sylvie's eyes widened and then her lids drooped again. She lifted her chemise and moved back towards the bedroom. 'No,' Marlowe said and took her gently by the hand. 'My name is Robert Greene. And I really do want to ask you some questions.' He sat her down by the table. 'Where's that wine you spoke of, Mireille?'

Sylvie was a strange girl and Marlowe couldn't really fathom her. He'd known harlots of all shapes and sizes in his time, from All Hallows in Canterbury to Petty Cury in Cambridge. On his fleeting visits to take ship from London he'd seen the Bishop of Winchester's 'geese' flaunting their wares as far east as Deptford Strand. But he'd never met a whore like Sylvie. She seemed ethereal, like a faerie, not quite of this world. When she'd told him all she knew and wandered out into the night again in search of another five blancs, Mireille had sensed Marlowe's curiosity and told him all she intended to. 'What's the matter, Monsieur. Never seen a French girl with a broken heart before?'

It may have been doubly broken now, or at least bruised with guilt, because in her own way, the girl Sylvie had contributed to the death of Edmund Brooke. On the night the boy died she had been approached by someone she didn't know. Or perhaps she did. There had been something about his voice that she couldn't quite place, but his face was in darkness. He'd met her at the Porte des Cappuchins and had kept well back in the shadows. He had given her gold and told her he wanted her to help him play a trick on a friend. The friend was a scholar from the English College and he would be somewhere in the Strangers' Quarter soon after Vespers. He described the boy. He wouldn't be wearing his college robes but he had clear blue eyes and a thatch of auburn hair. His name was Martin and he was partial to a hand or two of cards, not to mention wine.

And the man in the shadows had handed her a glass phial and told her to pour its contents into young Martin's beaker.

'It won't kill him, will it, Monsieur?' the girl had asked.

'God save you, no,' the man had said, laughing. 'Just put him to sleep for a while. And it may put him off the demon drink for a while too. Now, be off with you.'

Marlowe had asked her how old the man sounded, but Sylvie didn't know. Her usual experience of men was when they were lying down and they all sounded the same then. She had found the lad the man had described at the Casque d'Argent after what seemed like forever and got friendly with him. She sat on his lap while he groped her and lost ever more money in La Pucelle. Primero, Gleek, Laugh and Lie Down, Lansquenet – it didn't matter what the game was, Martin lost them all. It came as no surprise to Sylvie – David and his cronies fleeced somebody every night. Martin just happened to be their current target.

When he was well into his cups, the girl wound her arm around his neck and drove her tongue into his mouth, as French girls do. With her spare hand, she sprinkled the contents of the glass phial into his drink and snatched up another to drink the boy's health.

'Your deal, Englishman,' David had said, as if he was doing the lad a favour by taking his money. How much more Martin could have remembered, Sylvie didn't know. Whatever the stuff in the phial was, it had acted quickly, because the carousing scholar suddenly slumped sideways and toppled off his stool onto the floor. That was the last Sylvie had seen of him.

'Is he all right, Monsieur?' she had asked Marlowe. 'I meant him no harm. He was a sweet boy.'

'He still is, Mam'selle,' Marlowe assured her. 'He still is.'

Marlowe had wanted to ask Sylvie more questions. About Laurenticus, the tutor of Greek in whose bed she had lain so happily; whose throat had been cut alongside her. But now, he sensed, was not the time. And the next time, he'd learn more when Mireille was not there, listening to every word.

Marlowe had meant to go and see Johns and Phelippes that night, but it was late and he was tired. Veronique was also a strict landlady and would not be pleased to be woken at this hour. Aldred preferred her sleeping too, as she tended to turn her back resolutely when she dropped off and he could pursue his own thoughts and nightly habits without being called on to do his duty. Marlowe could hardly suppress a smile when he thought of how Faunt would react to a description of Aldred's life in Rheims. He would have him recalled quick as winking and would reassign him somewhere out of harm's way. Veronique would be desolate, at least for a while.

Michael Johns had slept off his shock in Marlowe's bed and then with his usual gentlemanly air slipped away quietly, having somehow found the right person to take away and replace the bloodstained bedding. Marlowe had gone back to his room expecting to find his old tutor and friend still in his bed, but had found just crisp sheets and a note scrawled in his terrible scholar's handwriting on a scrap of paper on the table, held down by the ink bottle.

'*The antidote for fifty enemies is one friend.*' M.

Marlowe had smiled when he read it. How like Johns to leave a quote from Aristotle. And how like him also to write it in English; he had stopped testing Marlowe's Greek at last.

As he made his way back to the English College from Mireille's room, he promised he would visit Johns and Phelippes first thing the next morning.

'*Oui? Puis-je vous aider?*'

'Madame Veronique?' Marlowe applied his mouth to the door-jamb so he didn't have to shout and wake the whole street. 'It is Monsieur Greene.'

'*Oui?*'

Marlowe sighed. So, it was going to be like that, was it? 'Yes, Madame. I would like to speak to Dr Johns and Monsieur Phelippes, if that is possible.'

'Pardon?'

Desperate times, desperate measures. 'If you could just fetch your . . . I would not say husband, Madame, your . . . I am not sure I have the French word for it . . . your . . .'

The door flew open and a beefy arm shot out, gathering Marlowe to the accompanying bosom. The door slammed shut again, shaking itself from its hinges as was its habit. 'How dare you shout such calumnies in the street?' Marlowe could hardly breathe where he was situated, let alone shout. 'I am a respect-able widow,' the woman hissed in the general direction of his ear. 'I would thank you to remember that.'

Solomon Aldred came out of the back room in his nightshirt,

absent-mindedly scratching the small of his back. 'What are you doing with Master Greene, Veronique?' he asked, mildly. 'Do put him down.'

She turned to him in a fury, releasing Marlowe, who drew a grateful breath. 'He was airing our scandal in the street,' she yelled.

'The door is open, sweetness,' Aldred said, reasonably. 'You've been slamming it again, haven't you?' He walked past the woman and his visitor and reseated it on its hinges with a practised hand. 'You're here to see our friends, I assume?' he said over his shoulder to Marlowe. 'Go on up. Master Phelippes is in Veronique's late mother's bed. Doctor Johns is in the best bedroom. You can't miss them. They are both at the top of the stairs. I will be up shortly.' He swept an explanatory hand over his *déshabillé*.

Keeping a careful eye on the volatile Veronique, Marlowe squeezed between the racks of Aldred's stock in trade and climbed the narrow stairs. The first thing he saw when his head rose above the level of the last riser was John's head peering short-sightedly round a door.

'Kit. It *is* you. I thought I heard your voice outside.'

'Yes,' the poet said, speaking for the first time since his near suffocation. 'Mistress Veronique let me in.' A master at verse, he was also the master of the understatement.

'She is a very assiduous hostess,' Johns said, without a shred of irony in his voice. 'Come with me, we will see if Thomas is awake.'

'You have a room each,' Marlowe observed.

'Thomas couldn't sleep for his wound and I couldn't sleep for worrying whether I might roll over and hurt him in the night. I must say, it is nice to be sleeping on my own again. Until recently, I hadn't shared a bed since I was twelve. And then there were seven of us, so it wasn't quite the same.'

Marlowe thought he would let that one go.

Johns pushed open the next door and peeped in. Then, he spoke to the occupant of the room. 'Are we awake?' His voice was pitched a little higher than normal and was full of sunshine and pretty flowers. At least, that was the aim of the exercise. It just came out sounding as though he was a little bit gone in the head.

From the room, a rather testy voice replied. 'Well, I am. I

don't know about the rest of us. Men? Are we all awake.' There
was a pause during which Marlowe moved awkwardly from one
foot to the other. 'Yes, it seems we are all awake. Do come in,
Michael.'

Johns looked back over his shoulder at Marlowe. 'Still a bit
cross grained, I fear,' he said. 'It must be the shock.'

'Have you ever looked after anyone who has been stabbed before,
Michael?' Marlowe asked as he pushed past him into the room.

'There has never seemed to be the need,' Johns said. 'Until
recently, there haven't been too many stabbings in my life.'

Phelippes' room was dark and fusty. It smelled vaguely of
very old women, perfume which had faded away to leave just
the civet behind and just a touch of dried urine. Overlying that
was the smell of a rather angry and sweaty male, cooped up
beyond the measure of his temper. Marlowe pulled back the bed
hangings, wrenched back the curtains at the tiny window and
threw it open to the cold morning. Fresh air flooded the room.

Johns immediately flew to close it. 'He'll get a chill,' he cried.

Marlowe held him back. 'He's been knifed, Michael,' he said.
'And that only slightly, if what I hear is right. He should be up
and about, not sprawling around in bed. Can you get up?' he
asked Phelippes.

'I can if he'll let me,' the code-breaker said, turning round on
the mattress to dangle his legs over the side. 'It's been like prison
in here. All we need is the Queen's Rackmaster in here and it
would be complete.'

Johns looked mortified. Marlowe took pity on him. Any wound
looked deadly at the time. A spot of water and a clean bandage
generally brought it down to earth a little. Johns was just an
overzealous nurse. 'He will be all right, if he's careful,' he reassured him. 'Sitting in the chair will be a change and he can
always go back to bed if he wants to. Thomas?'

'Yes, please. Anything rather than this dreadful room.'

'It was Veronique's mother's, apparently,' Marlowe ventured.

'She's welcome to it,' Phelippes said and, mustering as much
gravitas as he could, he swept through the open door, clutching
one arm to his side.

'Where are you going?' Johns asked, waspishly.

'Downstairs. Anywhere.'

'In your nightshirt?' Marlowe asked, mildly.

Phelippes looked down. 'Perhaps not,' he capitulated. 'Into the other room, then. There is a table in there we can use as a desk.' He turned to Marlowe. 'I assume you are here about the code, rather than to ask about my health.'

'A little of both, to be honest,' Marlowe said. 'But more the code than the health, perhaps. Have you got anywhere with it?'

Phelippes looked at him and raised his eyes. 'Did I explain?' he said. 'Did I not tell everyone that without the original text, a substitution code no matter how simple is bound to fail?'

'Yes, you did,' Marlowe agreed.

'Well then, why are you asking have I got anywhere with it? Where can I have got with it?' He was beginning to look a little hectic round the eyes and Marlowe ushered him to a chair.

'I understand, Thomas,' he said. 'I think I had just hoped that you might be familiar with the pattern of the letters. I thought that . . . I was just hoping, that was all.' He looked very crestfallen and Phelippes relented.

'There are very many codes that are being used and they are changing all the time,' he said. 'Some are literally codes made up for the purpose and everyone who has to read the message has a copy of the cipher. If they use it a lot, they can become very adept at it and can write it as fast as their mother tongue.' He pulled a piece of parchment towards him, unstoppered the ink bottle, dipped his pen and began to write. After a moment, he passed the parchment to Marlowe. It contained a short line of very tiny writing.

'U.I.J.T J.T B W.F.S.Z F.B.T.Z D.P.E.F.' he read. He looked at it for a moment. 'This is a very easy code,' he said, smiling broadly at Phelippes and Johns.

'Indeed it is,' Phelippes agreed. 'It is one of the simplest of all, just a letter ahead in the alphabet from the one you intend to use. As you saw, I can write that as fast as I can write English.'

'Why are the letters so small?' Marlowe asked. 'I could hardly read them in this light and my eyes are strong.'

Phelippes shrugged. 'Force of habit. Codes are often left in odd places. Sometimes they are written on the edges of the pages of a book and there is little room. They can be any size. Here—' He held out his hand for the parchment. 'I'll do you another.'

The room was silent except for the scratch of his pen and the tinny clink as he tapped the excess ink off against the rim of the bottle. 'Try that one.'

The writing was just as small, but this time, Marlowe could make nothing of it. 'These are just shapes,' he said, passing it back.

Johns looked over Phelippes' shoulder. 'It says the same as the last one,' he said.

'How do you know?' Marlowe said.

'The letters, or shapes perhaps I should say, are spaced the same and the shapes repeat, look, here and here –' Johns pointed – 'like the letters do in "this" and "is".'

'Well done, Michael,' Phelippes said.

Marlowe was a little disgruntled. Who was the spy around here, after all? 'That was a lucky guess,' he said.

'Most code-breaking is, in the main,' Phelippes said. 'Then, you see a pattern and it suddenly unravels.' He looked up at the two men, who were looking dubious. 'Well, it does to me, at any rate. That might be why I am Sir Francis Walsingham's chief code-breaker.'

'True.' Marlowe laughed. 'So, you have no clue at all as to what the piece of code I found might say?'

'None. I have looked at it and cross-referenced it with all the codes I know by heart and nothing seems to make sense. Sometimes it looks as though a word is emerging, but then it is gone again. Either I haven't cracked it yet, or the code changes with every line. I have known codes which change with every word.'

'When you say change . . .?' Marlowe was a man of words, but not gibberish. Codes gave him a headache.

'If it is a substitution code, it is made by using a book. Well, not always a book, but usually.' He looked up at Johns. 'Just pass me that Aristotle, would you?'

Johns reached onto the shelf where the remains of his once proud personal library stood, trying hard to keep each other upright. He took one very thumbed and travel-worn volume down and passed it across but Phelippes did not take it.

'Better yet, choose a line at random. Er . . . I suppose you would prefer it if I didn't write in the book.'

Johns snatched it back and held it between both palms, eyes wide.

'I thought not. Well, read me a line then, any line at random but from the top or the bottom of a page.'

Johns flicked carefully through and then paused. 'This is in English, you know.'

Phelippes sighed. 'Don't let's be purists, Michael. I am just making a point here.'

Johns resumed his flicking, and then said, 'All human actions have one or more of these seven causes: chance, nature, compulsion, habit, reason, passion and desire.'

'Excellent,' Phelippes said, scribbling.

'That's odd,' said Marlowe. 'I had remembered that in a completely different order.'

'So had I,' Phelippes said, not looking up. 'That's why it is important to use a book. Now, look at this. If Michael was not so careful with his books, I would have written this in his copy, but I think it is clear enough.'

Marlowe took the page from him and saw that he had now written out the Aristotelian quotation and above it, but only on some letters, he had written the alphabet. Then, below, he had written a short sentence.

'Why have you only put letters above some words?' Marlowe asked.

'Because each letter of the alphabet needs a different one as a substitution,' Phelippes explained. 'So, you will see at once that A equals A and B equals L. Then the next L is missed out and C equals H. D and E equal U and M respectively, but then we miss the A out because we have already used it and so F equals N. Do you see?'

'Yes,' Marlowe said, a smile spreading over his face. 'Yes, I do see. So, you can use this as often as you like, making superimpositions on every page or even every sentence if you want to.'

'Yes,' Phelippes said, getting excited with the joy of teaching. Then, he sagged. 'So you also see, I hope, that even something as simple as a superimposition code is impossible without the original text.'

Marlowe handed him the parchment back. 'Yes, I do,' he said. 'I have a few ideas. I have made some kind of friend of the librarian at the English College.'

'Just has the one book, does he, in his library?' Phelippes asked, snappily.

Marlowe shook his head, though the question was rhetorical only.

'In that case, unless you like the man, don't worry about making him a friend.' Phelippes threw down his pen. 'We have to face facts, gentlemen,' he said. 'It will be as well that this code is not important to the safety of our realm, because I won't be able to crack it. Not with what I've got.'

'A stab wound to the chest,' Johns broke in. 'You're exhausting yourself. You should be in bed.'

'Lord, give me strength,' Phelippes said, pushing himself away from the table. 'Kit, go and find me the book the code comes from and you will have your murderer in hours.'

'Murderer?' Marlowe looked confused. 'I thought we assumed this code was to do with the Babington conspiracy.'

'Yes?' Phelippes looked at him as a teacher might look at a favourite pupil newly proved to be an idiot; more in sorrow than in anger.

'Well . . . I know murder is part of the case against –' habit made him look behind him – 'the Queen of Scots, but, still . . .'

Phelippes looked at Johns, who shrugged. 'We had assumed that the person murdering the English College one by one was also our plotter. Is this not the case?'

Marlowe had been so wary of putting two and two together and making five that he suddenly realized he may actually have been coming up with three instead. 'I may have been missing the nose on my face,' he said. 'I'll be back, gentlemen, with a text if possible.' He reached over and patted Phelippes' shoulder, but gently. 'We will crack this code, if I die in the attempt.'

The two men watched him go. They both knew he never said anything he didn't mean, but one had his head full of the text and the other of the dying as the sound of his boots died away on the stairs.

THIRTEEN

Marlowe sensed that someone was there even before he opened the door. The hairs on the back of his neck prickled and instinctively his hand was behind him, resting on the dagger hilt. He twisted the knurled knob quickly and kicked the door open; if someone was behind it he'd have a ringing head by now and probably double vision too.

In the event there was no one behind the door, just Peregrine Salter sitting in Marlowe's chair at Marlowe's desk.

'Good morning,' the Yorkshireman chirped. 'I hope you don't mind. The door was unlocked.'

'Yes,' Marlowe said with a nod. 'Unusual around here, isn't it?' He checked his books. Allen's treatise was open to the page at which he'd last read it. The level in his wine decanter seemed the same. His colleyweston cloak still hung behind the door. He crossed to his cupboard and checked the corner. His sword was still there, oiled and ready in its scabbard.

'Master Greene, I'll come to the point. I'm worried.'

'You are?' Marlowe closed the door. 'There are priests a-plenty here to hear your confession, Master Salter.'

'Hah!' Salter scoffed. 'You'd expect that, I suppose, at a seminary. No, it's not a priest I need; it's some answers.'

Marlowe opened the decanter and poured them both a drink. 'If memory serves,' he said, 'you've been here longer than I have. What can I know that you don't?'

'A-hah!' Salter took the glass and raised it in salutation. 'But you're not quite what you seem, are you, Master Greene?'

Marlowe suppressed a smile. No man could walk a tightrope like his for long and perhaps his moment had come. 'Really?' he frowned. 'I don't follow.'

'I've been watching you,' Salter said. 'You're looking for somebody.'

'Aren't we all?' Marlowe sighed. 'Someone to walk this vale of tears with us.'

'Well, you won't find her here.' Salter laughed. 'You've probably noticed the English College is singularly short of women.'

'What makes you think I was talking about a woman?' Marlowe sat on the edge of the bed.

'Oh . . .' Salter was momentarily nonplussed. 'Oh, I see.'

Marlowe smiled. 'No, I don't think you do. Tell me, Master Salter, since you have been at the College, how many people have died?'

'Precisely!' Salter jabbed the air with a triumphant finger. 'My point exactly. Oh, we all know the Lord takes away as he pleases and who are we to deny it . . . but this? Well, it's odd.'

'In what way?'

'Well . . .' Salter was about to launch into what he knew, but he checked himself. 'No,' he said. 'First – you. Am I right? Are you what you seem?'

'That very much depends on what I seem.' Marlowe could fence with this man all day.

Salter looked him up and down. 'If I didn't know better,' he said, softly, 'I'd say you were a sworder. A professional killer.'

'Tsk, tsk.' Marlowe shook his head. 'My dear, white-haired old mother would be horrified to think that her little boy . . .'

There was a silence between them, each of them deciding which way to jump next.

'But you're right –' Marlowe blinked first and felt Salter tense, as if he might be next to feel his knife between his ribs – 'and you're wrong. My name is not Greene, it's Marlowe, Christopher Marlowe. The Curia sent me.'

'Rome?' Salter was impressed.

'I carry His Holiness' writ.'

'I see.'

'I'm still not sure you do,' Marlowe said. 'You're right that things here are not as they seem. Murder is being done.'

'Murder?' Salter paused in mid swig and crossed himself.

'Three men have died – two scholars and a tutor. Two of them at least were taken since you've been here, Master Salter.'

The Yorkshireman's eyes narrowed. 'It's nothing to do with me,' he said flatly.

'That,' Marlowe said, 'is what they all say. Did you know Father Laurenticus?'

'I met him once,' Salter admitted. 'I can't say I formed any real opinion of him.'

'What about Edmund Brooke?'

'Who?'

'The scholar who was found dead in his bed the night before last.'

'Was that his name? I'm afraid I don't have much to do with the scholars.'

'Too juvenile? That's a little condescending, don't you think, Master Salter? A few years ago you and I were scholars ourselves, though in my case at least, not much like these lads.'

'No, no, it's not that. As you say, Master Marlowe, we were seventeen ourselves once and not too long since. No, I'm not a university wit. I was educated privately. At home.'

'By a Jesuit,' Marlowe remarked, without inflection.

Salter laughed. 'Holy Mother of God, is it that obvious?'

'It's difficult to be educated at home in the true faith these days without a Jesuit. I hope you had a suitable hole for him to skip back to when anyone knocked at the door.'

'As I was going up the stair,' Salter said, 'I met a man who wasn't there. He wasn't there again today. I wish, I wish he'd go away.' And he tapped the side of his nose.

'Let's not wish that,' Marlowe said. 'If the Jesuits leave England, what hope is there for any of us? I put the same question to Anthony Babington before I left.'

'Anthony Babington?' Salter asked. 'Why does that name sound familiar?'

'He stood trial with other friends of mine for carrying letters to the Queen of Scots. Walsingham had him hanged, drawn and quartered.'

Salter spat copiously onto Marlowe's floor. 'May he rot in Hell, that one,' he said.

'Oh, I'm sure he will. But in the meantime, I have more pressing matters. Someone is targeting members of the English College, killing them, one by one. There is no pattern to it, except that they were all within its walls. The three victims scarcely knew each other, as far as it is possible to be strangers in such a closed community as this. The methods are not the same – in my small experience, a strangler is always a strangler, a knife man swears by his blade. I have to find who is behind these crimes, Master Salter. Will you help?'

'Root out a Puritan?' Salter asked. 'My hand on it,' he continued, and he shook Marlowe's hand warmly. In a second, the projectioner was on his feet, his finger to his lips. He crossed the room in a single stride and wrenched open the door. Antoinette the maid stood there, broom and cloths in hand, gasping at the sudden movement.

'Pardon, Monsieur,' she said with a bob. 'I can come back.'

'No, no,' Marlowe said, smiling. 'Master Salter was just going. Weren't you, Master Salter?'

'Oh, absolutely, yes indeed.' The Yorkshireman finished his wine and patted Marlowe's shoulder. 'Here's to rooting out Puritans,' he whispered and he clattered off down the passageway.

Marlowe watched him go and closed the door behind Antoinette. The woman trembled as she ferreted around with her feather duster.

'Antoinette.' He was standing with his back to the door and she knew there was no way out. 'We need to talk.'

She ignored him at first, not making eye contact, finding something fascinating in every nook and cranny of the room and rubbing it feverishly with her cloth.

'Antoinette . . .' he repeated.

'I can't,' she suddenly blurted out, turning to him with a red face and trembling lip. 'I promised Dr Skelton.'

Marlowe took the little minion by her shoulders and sat her down on the bed. He took the feather duster from her, then the cloths and looked deep into her eyes. 'What?' he asked her. 'What did you promise Dr Skelton?'

'That I wouldn't tell a soul what I know, Monsieur. Not a soul. For the sake of my own soul. Not a word. I have already said much too much.'

'Your own soul?' Marlowe frowned. 'What do you mean, Antoinette?'

She looked frantically around the room. Laurenticus' room. And there was no escape. 'Dr Skelton,' she whispered. 'He said the Lord's wrath would be visited on me if I told.'

Marlowe put a comforting arm around the terrified woman, as a son might squeeze his mother. 'He was thinking of the College's reputation, Antoinette,' he said. 'It's his job. He didn't want you talking to the wrong people. He didn't mean me.'

'But you . . . you're an Englishman, Monsieur.'

Marlowe laughed. 'Almost to be expected in the English College, surely? Who do you take me for, Antoinette? Beelzebub? Asmodeus? Lucifer himself?'

She crossed herself and, since Marlowe had used the names of three demons, did it twice more. He took those shaking hands and held them together in an attitude of prayer, clasped between his own. 'I am ready to hear your confession, daughter,' he said. 'Place your burden on the Lord.'

'Confession?' she repeated, staring into his dark eyes. 'You mean, you're . . .?'

'A priest? Of course,' Marlowe lied smoothly. 'Why else do you think I'm here?'

Antoinette hesitated, her eyes swivelling wildly from side to side. She saw again the blood on the coverlet, the one they sat on now, washed clean of crimson. She saw the sprays of blood on the wall, the ones she herself had washed and scrubbed away. She saw the dead man sprawled on his pillow, his throat another mouth gaping open. But this man didn't look like a priest. He was young and handsome, though that was no bar to the priesthood, as many a village maiden had discovered over many a long century. But he didn't have the air about him . . . she couldn't put her finger on it. She made her decision.

'I . . . I will speak to my God myself,' she said at last. It didn't sound rehearsed, but it took Marlowe aback.

'My child,' he said, 'that is the way of the Lutherans. *Solo fide.* By faith alone. It is not the way of our mother church.'

She looked at him as if transfixed, her lip trembling again, her whole body cold though beads of sweat stood out on her forehead. She wrenched her hands free and fumbled in her placket. Out came a crumpled piece of parchment and there was blood dried brown on one corner.

'What's this?' he asked her.

'I found it, Father,' she said, on a sob, 'bless me, for I have sinned,' and she fell into his lap, crying helplessly. He lifted up her head and made the sign of the cross over her, muttering the old Latin incantation he had known as a child. Then he took a corner of her gown and gently wiped her eyes.

'Where did you find it?' he asked her.

'There, Father –' she flung her left arm behind her in the direction of the bed – 'on the morning I found poor Father Laurenticus. It was in his hand. I don't know why I picked it up. Why I touched it. I shouldn't have. God forgive me. I shouldn't have.' She held his hand tightly. 'Is it a curse, Father? Is it a curse, written down to hurt Father Laurenticus?'

'No, no,' Marlowe said, patting her white knuckles with his free hand. 'Of course it isn't. It wasn't magic that killed Father Laurenticus. Only men wield knives. And God has forgiven you, if you needed forgiveness.' He slipped the parchment into his doublet. 'Now, wipe your eyes or you will be late with your work.'

She jumped to her feet, grabbing a cloth to show her willingness to sweep the dust behind the door. 'There was something else . . .' She sniffed, feeling much better now that she had confessed and found absolution. 'There was a ring.'

'Oh?' Marlowe raised an eyebrow. Perhaps he had blessed her prematurely.

'I didn't take it, Father,' she said quickly. 'I didn't even touch it.'

'And where was the ring, Antoinette?'

'There, Father.' She pointed to the bed again.

'On the right side?' he checked. 'Away from the body?'

She nodded.

'It was nothing,' he said. 'A meaningless trinket.'

'Oh, but it was valuable, Father,' she told him. 'That's why I didn't touch it. A man's ring, it was, gold with a funny design.'

'A *man's* ring?' Marlowe frowned. 'Tell me, Antoinette, this design. What did it look like?'

'I don't know, Father. It had . . . it was an eagle on one side. And a key, I think it was, on the other.'

Marlowe crossed to his table. He dipped the quill into the ink and sketched quickly on the parchment that lay there. He showed what he had done to the maid. 'Like this, Antoinette?' he asked. 'Did the ring look like this?'

*   *   *

William Allen was dining in his private quarters that night and Gerald Skelton was with him. Marlowe batted the little monk at his door aside and crashed into the solar.

'What the devil . . .?' Skelton was on his feet, the knife he was using on his bread suddenly a dagger in his hand.

'It's all right, Gerald,' Allen said. 'You see how I am fussed over, Dominus Marlowe?' And he patted Skelton's sleeve to make him sit down again. 'Wine? Cheese?'

'Thank you, Master, no.' Marlowe stood across the laden table. 'Forgive this intrusion, but I must have words with you.'

'And I take it they can't wait?' Allen cut himself another chunk of bread.

'I'm afraid not. And this *is* private, Master.' Marlowe nodded in Skelton's direction.

'If I haven't made this clear already,' Allen said, 'I am doing so now. Gerald is my right arm in this College. Talk to the whole man.'

'Very well,' Marlowe said and threw his rough sketch across the table.

'What's this?' Allen asked, turning it this way and that.

'I was hoping you would tell me,' Marlowe said. No one had asked him to sit and he felt like a naughty scholar again on the Persian carpet in old Dr Norgate's study.

'Where did you get this?' Skelton asked, narrowing his eyes.

'I drew it,' Marlowe told him, 'from a description given to me.'

'By whom?' Allen wanted to know.

'That damned maid!' Skelton shouted.

'Maid?' Marlowe was at his most convincing when he played the idiot. 'I know nothing of any maid. I got this from a strumpet.' Marlowe folded his arms to emphasize what he was about to say. 'A strumpet who was lying with Father Laurenticus on the night he died.'

The silence in the room was almost deafening.

'This strumpet.' Skelton was the first to break it. 'Does she have a name?'

'I expect so,' Marlowe said. 'I didn't ask her. The point is, Doctors, you have not been honest with me.'

'You'll forgive us.' Allen put his goblet down and teased a

morsel of cheese around his teeth. 'But in your case, Marlowe, it's rather a case of pots and kettles, isn't it?'

'You know I have the writ of His Holiness,' Marlowe said, 'and yet you didn't tell me of Laurenticus' . . . shall we say, extra-curricular activities.'

Allen and Skelton exchanged glances. 'All right,' the Master said, as if his mind were suddenly made up. 'You're right. When we found Laurenticus the morning after he died, it was clear to us that there had been someone in bed with him. He was a man, after all, as we all are. We all struggle . . .'

'What about the ring?' Marlowe asked.

'It was on the bed,' Skelton said. 'Presumably the strumpet's. We don't know what became of her. Or how she could get in and out of the College with no one seeing her.'

'You have at least confirmed one thing for us, Dominus Marlowe,' Allen said, sitting back in his chair and resting his hands together calmly. 'I for one, and I think Gerald also, had wondered who Laurenticus' bedfellow might be. Gerald thought of an outsider at once; I was more inclined to wonder whether it was a member of the kitchen or household staff. Or, perhaps . . .' He left a silence, hanging in the air.

Skelton looked at him askance. 'I told you Laurenticus did not have that kind of appetite, did I not?' he asked, triumphantly. 'Now we know for certain. But it still does beg the question, how did she get in and out?'

'Any one of a dozen ways,' Marlowe said. 'Your security is pretty lax, Bursar, considering how many secrets this place keeps. And besides, the ring is not hers.'

'Not?' Allen raised his head.

'It was a man's ring, she said,' Marlowe told him. 'Heavy and gold. That –' he pointed at the sketch – 'was worked on it.'

Skelton shrugged. 'So, what are you saying, Marlowe? That Father Laurenticus, as well as his weakness for women, wore expensive jewellery? So what? Hair shirts belong to the saints. We are ordinary men.'

'Indeed.' Marlowe nodded grimly. 'But that is no ordinary ring.'

'Isn't it?' Allen asked him.

'The double eagle,' Marlowe said, 'and the keys of St Peter.

I'm surprised they haven't dropped that by now. Symbol of Rome and all.'

'What are you talking about?' Skelton asked.

'The eagle and key, Dr Skelton,' Marlowe said, 'is the coat of arms of Geneva, as I'm sure you know.'

Allen and Skelton looked at each other.

'Geneva, gentlemen –' he felt as though he should spell it out – 'is the Protestant Rome. That Machiavel Calvin stole it, you will recall, some years ago. He banned our church, tore up our tracts, tortured our brethren. So, I have to ask, how did Father Laurenticus come by this little trinket – "a present from Geneva" was it? I don't think so.'

'It *must* have belonged to the strumpet,' Allen persisted and looked at Skelton for backing. But the Bursar looked troubled. 'Cat got your tongue, Gerald?' he snapped.

'Master . . .' Skelton was trying to formulate the words, 'Dominus Marlowe *is* from the Curia.'

Allen scowled at them both. His messenger had not returned from Rome yet and there was no definitive proof who he was. Even so, things were getting out of hand at the English College and something had to be done. 'Very well,' he said, 'Gerald and I had our suspicions about Laurenticus. Had them for some time, in fact.'

'Suspicions?' Marlowe helped himself, unbidden, to a chair.

Allen continued to look at Marlowe, watching for a sign, anything that might give him a clue as to how far he could trust this man. 'Tell him, Gerald.'

'For some time,' the Bursar said, 'snippets of information have been leaked from the College. Some of it is careless talk – you always get that. But some of it . . .'

'Some of it is code,' Allen said, finishing the sentence for him, 'as from a projectioner to his people on the outside. Gerald here thought it was me, didn't you, Gerald?'

The Bursar looked outraged. 'Certainly not, Master, I . . .'

But Allen was chuckling, raising his hand. 'Just joking, my old friend. Laurenticus' ring is not proof, of course, but as soon as I saw it, I knew.'

'And is that why he died?' Marlowe asked. 'The natural justice meted out to a projectioner – and a traitor to God's word?'

'The thought had occurred,' Allen said, nodding. 'The Protestants would say we're all fanatics here. What do they call us in Richmond and Placentia? The nest of scorpions? And don't scorpions kill their own?'

'I'd be the first to share your view, Marlowe,' Skelton said, 'on security, I mean. Father Tobias is a little long in the tooth to be ever-vigilant and there *are* ways in and out other than the main gate.'

'And out there . . .' Marlowe was finishing the man's train of thought. 'In Rheims there are any number of Catholic zealots who would do God's bidding at the drop of a piccadill.'

'Indeed,' Allen mused. 'But what of the others?'

'Master!' Skelton warned.

'It's too late now, Gerald. The man *knows*. This lad Brooke; didn't you say he was a thief?'

Skelton shrugged. 'Dr Shaw thinks he has been helping himself to books, yes; selling them to the town's stationers.'

'What if it's more than that?' Allen asked.

'I don't follow,' Skelton said.

Marlowe helped him out. 'What if it wasn't the books themselves?'

'Go on,' Allen said.

'What if there was something *in* the books? A code, perhaps, that Brooke smuggled out.'

'My God,' Skelton muttered.

'And there was Charles of Westley Waterless,' Marlowe added.

'Ah, Charles Russell.' Allen checked him with a raised hand. 'Now that was just a tragic, tragic case, Marlowe. I blame myself for not having seen the depths of his despair. The boy was disturbed and took his own life. We shouldn't really have allowed him to be added to the crypt.'

'The crypt?' Marlowe played the innocent.

Skelton fidgeted. 'Our dead,' he said. 'Those who pass over in the College. The Douai martyrs. They are all down there. Beneath the east wing.'

'There can't be many, surely?' Marlowe said. 'You haven't been here very long. How many deaths have there been?'

'No, no,' Skelton said. 'We brought our dead with us when we left Douai. We couldn't leave them behind and all alone.'

'I see.' Marlowe tried to keep the surprise out of his voice. Even though he had already seen the serried ranks of the dead, it still struck him as a very odd thing to do. 'I would like to see them,' he said.

'Why?' Allen asked him.

'Dead men sometimes tell tales,' the projectioner explained. 'If you listen carefully enough.'

'Master,' Skelton said. 'I really don't think . . .'

'What harm can there be?' Allen said suddenly, his mind made up. 'Gerald, take Dominus Marlowe down, will you? Any light he can shed . . .'

They heard the Watch calling beyond the College walls as they crossed the quad, its stones gleaming silver in the moon. The place was asleep now except for the few revellers Marlowe guessed were still out, breaking the Master's curfew and risking the Master's wrath. One thing was certain: Martin Camb would not be among them. He would be lying in his bed with a ghost for company. And it was that ghost that Marlowe was looking for now. Not for the first time he pondered the questions – were there such things as ghosts? Did they haunt their last abode, forever trapped in the four walls where they died? Or did they hover, roaring their silent vow of vengeance, above their earthly corpses as they rotted?

He followed Skelton down the narrow, dark passages he had found before when Solomon Aldred had told him of the crypt. Skelton eased open the iron-ringed door and both men felt the cold, clammy blast of dead air hit them. Only a solitary blue candle lit their way as they passed the rows of bodies. Skelton crossed himself and kissed the end of the stole around his neck. The rows of bodies were held upright in their niches by bolts of iron that here, in the damp below ground, were already beginning to rust. They looked at the intruders through sunken, sightless eyes, as though wondering who it was who had come to disturb their rest. The skulls lolled to left and right where the sinews of the neck had long ago given up the uneven struggle to keep them upright. It gave them all a rather pensive air, as though they had relaxed as they pondered on deep and secret things which they only knew now they were dead.

'Edmund Brooke,' Skelton murmured, even his soft voice a violation in that great silence. The boy was covered in a shroud from neck to foot and his skin was already grey under the lifeless thatch of hair. Marlowe gazed at the face again, the face that had already told him all he could learn. The face of a projectioner? An intelligencer? A thief? Or just a luckless scholar, playing jack-the-lad in a world too big for him?

'Father Laurenticus.' Skelton had already moved on. Marlowe looked up at the corpse. For all it was hunched now, the Tutor in Greek had been a tall man, well built. Whoever had cut his throat had been powerful and, Marlowe suspected, quick. With the element of surprise, with the man muzzy with love and sleep, it had been a relatively simple matter to kill him with a single swipe. His killer would have been lucky to get a second chance.

'Charles Russell.' Skelton introduced Marlowe to a boy he had met before. The sinews of the spine had snapped now and the skull lay on the chest as though he had been decapitated. 'He was a strange boy, introspective, secretive. No one really seemed to know him, he was always skulking about on his own. As a suicide, he will not be at God's right hand, poor boy,' he said, piously.

Marlowe was glad all over again to be done with God and the cruelty done in his name. Something – and he never knew for certain what – made him pass to the body in the next niche. He lifted a corner of the shroud that covered him. The skin was still there, like the old parchment covers on the books in Shaw's library and there was a black stain over the chest as though the man's heart had burst. It was a stain Marlowe had seen before.

'Who was this?' he asked.

'That?' Skelton replaced the shroud's corner as a matter of respect. 'That was Leonard Skirrel. He was a poor priest of Herefordshire until the Protestants drove him out. His soul is with the saints, I trust.'

'Amen,' said Marlowe.

FOURTEEN

'Found your horse, then?' Marlowe was in the College Buttery that morning as John Abbott arrived with his mug of ale and dish of oatmeal.

'Horse, my arse!' The Furnival's Inn man was not in the best of moods. 'What is it about these bloody Frenchmen?' he wanted to know. 'Are they all crooks?'

'Probably,' Marlowe said with a chuckle. He watched the man toying with his porridge, pushing the lumps about disconsolately. 'Starting to miss it, are you? The White Chapel? St Mary Matfelon?'

Abbott growled, 'Yes, I suppose I am. I didn't think I would. I can't go back, of course.'

'Which of us can?' Marlowe nodded. 'Until the great day.'

Abbott frowned at him, then suddenly remembered. 'Oh, yes,' he said. 'Walsingham's after you, isn't he?'

'In a manner of speaking,' Marlowe said. 'Who's after you?' He wasn't looking the man in the face and carried on tucking into his oatmeal, lovingly prepared, lumplessly, by Antoinette on her breakfast duties. He even had a golden curl of honey bedded gently into its creamy top. He threw out the question casually, as though he had asked Abbott to pass the salt.

'What makes you think anybody's after me?' the Londoner asked, somewhat put out.

Marlowe paused in mid-spoonful. 'Look around you,' he said. Abbott did. Scholars cramming their food as if their lives depended on it. Tutors muttering in corners. Priests counting their rosaries. 'Somebody's after all these men,' Marlowe said. 'This place is the last bastion of English sanity, but it's also full of edgy, dangerous souls.'

Abbott shrugged. 'I don't see it.'

'Edmund Brooke,' Marlowe murmured. 'Father Laurenticus. Charles Russell.'

'Who are they?' The Furnival's Inn man was momentarily thrown. And now, Marlowe could throw in a new name.

'Leonard Skirrel,' he said.

'I'm none the wiser.' Abbott got back to his trencher.

'Edmund and Charles were scholars here,' Marlowe told him. 'At the College. Father Laurenticus was on the staff; taught Greek. Leonard Skirrel was a priest from Hereford. That's all I know about him.'

'Wait a minute . . .' Abbott's head snapped up. 'Brooke was the lad who died, wasn't he? Apoplexy?'

'Apoplexy, my arse,' Marlowe smiled. 'Charles Russell was hanged. Edmund Brooke was suffocated. Laurenticus had his throat cut. And the priest of Hereford? Stabbed would be my guess.'

Marlowe had Abbott's full attention now. 'What's going on?' he asked. His question had been too loud and faces turned towards him. He dropped his head and started eating for England, lumps and all.

Marlowe closed to him. 'Murder is going on, Master Abbott,' he said. He leaned back, crossing his ankles as he relaxed. 'Now, tell me,' he said. 'Why can't you go back, exactly?'

But there was no answer because Abbott had snatched up his trencher and was gone.

If there was one thing Francis Walsingham hated more than trotting along England's rutted roads in winter, it was sitting freezing in a barge down the Thames. The Queen was travelling downriver to her palace of Placentia at Greenwich. News had come that the Earl of Leicester was in the sea roads off Essex and making for the estuary. Elizabeth wanted to be there to meet him.

'Will she kiss him or box his ears, do you think?' Nicholas Faunt was at Walsingham's elbow, as ever, as the oars groaned in their rowlocks and the scarlet-clad oarsmen bent their backs. He was looking ahead to the first barge in the little convoy, the arms of England fluttering above the crimson canopy.

'None of your damned business, Faunt!' Walsingham snapped. The cold of November was chilling his bones to the marrow. 'Remember where you are,' he growled. '*And* whose badge you wear.'

'Sir Francis.' Faunt bowed extravagantly. If you couldn't tease

England's spymaster now and again, what was the point of it all?

Walsingham had thought about it and he tucked his hands under his armpits for comfort. 'She'll kiss him in public – after the usual toadying and ring-licking, of course. In private? Boxed ears will be the least of it.'

'Bollocks, do you think?' Nicholas Faunt enjoyed ruminating on the discomforts of others.

'For taking on the mantle of Stadtholder of the United Provinces without Her Majesty's express permission? Count on it.'

Faunt was delighted. He'd never liked the Earl of Leicester. The man's neck was too long and his arrogance knew no bounds. And then there were those rumours about his wife and those stairs. In all his time as intelligencer and projectioner, Nicholas Faunt had never heard of anyone breaking their neck falling down just three steps. If Faunt had his way he'd put a noose around that long neck himself.

'The English College,' Walsingham murmured in case any of the Queen's boatmen had ears. 'Anything?'

'Not since last week, Sir Francis,' Faunt said. 'Aldred says Marlowe is doing what he can but he's run into what he calls a little local difficulty.'

'And you didn't think to mention this to me?' Walsingham's cold gaze could freeze a man.

'You know Aldred.' Faunt shrugged, wincing a little as a gust of wind caught him as the little convoy took to mid-river at Rotherhithe. 'Always moaning. You could write a book about his whinges.'

'Is he sound, do you think, Nicholas? Can he be turned?'

'Aldred?' Faunt frowned. 'Straight as a die, Sir Francis. One of the best. Not terribly bright, of course . . .'

'I didn't mean him.' Walsingham blew on his numb fingers now. 'I was thinking of Marlowe.'

'Ah.' Faunt raised an eyebrow. What did the spymaster know that he didn't? Probably quite a lot.

'He's sound,' Walsingham told himself aloud. 'I know it. It's just . . . that damned place, Nicholas. The English College.'

Faunt took up the horn beaker on the little table beside him and passed Walsingham the other one. He raised it high. 'May it fall through the Rue de Venise and into the bowels of Hell!' he toasted.

For once, Marlowe allowed himself the pleasure of visiting the wine shop in daylight, so he didn't have to run the gauntlet of the redoubtable Veronique. Her sturdy shadow was lurking at the back of the shop, doing something arcane with muslin, sieves, bottles and Solomon Aldred. Marlowe gave her a small wave as he passed through on his way to the winding stair, calling over his shoulder, 'If I could pray your indulgence, Master Aldred, when you have a moment?'

He rapped on the door of the chamber that did not smell of old lady and was pleased to see Thomas Phelippes, without his bandaging, sitting at the small table, an ill-smelling candle at hand, surrounded by piles of paper, mostly covered with inky daubs and scribbles. Phelippes was only marginally less inky, but he looked happily occupied and so Marlowe, having tipped him a nod, went to the window, where Michael Johns sat, a book in his hand.

Marlowe smiled to see him sitting there, absorbed in his work, just like the old days. He scarcely recognized him without some writing or another in front of his nose.

'Doctor Johns,' he said, his voice just a breath above a whisper. 'How is it going?'

Johns closed the book, but kept his finger in the page. 'Hello, Kit,' he said. He nodded down to the book. 'Excuse me for keeping this to hand. It is a translation into French from Greek of an early biography of Augustine of Hippo. I am finding it fascinating as a study; translating it in my head is refreshing.'

Marlowe looked at his tutor with affection. It wasn't every man who would be so exercised by translating a text in French, written by a Greek on an Algerian bishop. 'Have you been shopping?' he asked. He was sorry that his tutor was not venturing out more into Rheims. It seemed a shame, having come so far.

'I got it from the librarian at the English College,' Johns said, absent-mindedly, his eyes wandering back to the book. 'When I was resting in your room, after . . . well, you know.' He tipped his head at where Phelippes sat, engrossed, at his table.

'I didn't know you'd met,' Marlowe said, surprised.

'Not met as such. He came into your room as I was tidying up. I was a bit surprised the way he just came in. I thought that might just be the English College way. Anyway, he had this with him, and he lent it to me. It is very fascinating. I am translating in reverse, trying to see what happens when different voices take on the task.' He sighed. 'It is hard to concentrate with so much happening.'

So Marlowe had been wrong to worry about Johns' closeted life. He didn't want to go outside where people were talking real language. He preferred his words to be dead. Phelippes preferred his buried. Marlowe hoped his tiny bit of news wouldn't deflect Johns too much from his somewhat peculiar purpose. 'I think I may have something to help with the code,' he said, quietly.

Phelippes spun round, in a welter of ink, parchment, quills and cries of pain. 'What do you have?' he yelled, rather louder than he intended.

'Excuse him,' Johns said. 'I've noticed this about Thomas. When he hasn't used his voice in a while, he can get a bit loud.'

'Sorry,' Phelippes said. 'Was I shouting? I do that, or so I'm told. Shall I begin again?' He mopped a little ineffectually at a pool of ink which was dripping onto his leg. 'What do you have, Master Marlowe?' He made a face like a smile and sat, expectantly. A casual observer may have thought him relaxed, but his non-inky leg was trembling with excitement under the table.

Marlowe was suddenly aware of how little he had brought with him. The little scrap of inky parchment didn't look like much, but it had come from Laurenticus' room and was stained with the man's last blood as it pumped from his body. It had to be important; a man may have died because of it. He reached into his doublet and drew it out. Phelippes and Johns jostled him to see what he had in his hand, then drew back, disappointed.

There was a pause, filled with the sound of Phelippes' last hope leaving the room on ghostly feet. Finally, Johns spoke for them all. 'Is that it?'

Marlowe suddenly felt more than a little testy. It was true that Phelippes had had a nasty stab wound and that Johns was lucky to be unscathed. It was true that they were not really used to being anywhere but their studies, looked after, fed, clothed, watered, by people who knew that they had more brains in their little fingers than they, their servants, had in their whole family. It was true that they were in a strange country, assaulted, given snails to eat and vinegary wine to drink, sharing a bed with each other and foreign pests which bit and irritated. Added to which they were both discovering that the beautiful French of Molinet and Marot was not the French of the streets of Rheims. Marlowe accepted all of that, and more, but was still rather irked that they didn't even bother to find out the risks he had run to get this possibly vital clue. He was about to unburden himself in no uncertain terms when the door opened and Solomon Aldred poked his head into the room.

'Oh,' he said, 'you are here. It was so quiet, I wondered. What's happening?' He glanced at the ink, dripping now onto the floor. 'I wouldn't let Veronique see that, if I were you.' He looked from one man to the other, his eyes as bright as a blackbird squaring up to a worm. He finally read some of the mood. 'Is everything all right?'

Marlowe drew a breath to tell him exactly what wasn't all right, but Johns forestalled him.

'Kit here has brought something he thinks might help with the code unravelling,' he said.

'Excellent!' Aldred said, stepping forward and rubbing his hands together.

'But it is rather . . .' His voice died away. Like all men of normal height, he tried to avoid the next word around the diminutive vintner, but had no choice. 'Small.'

Aldred's enthusiasm was undimmed. 'Let's have a look at it, all the same,' he said. 'The best things come in small packages, or so they say.' He smiled brightly. 'Come on, Master Marlowe. Let's see it. Where is it?' He looked around, excitedly.

Marlowe reached out his hand and uncurled the fingers, to show the small folded square of parchment lying in his palm. It had been folded so tightly and for so long it looked even smaller than it was. Aldred looked at it, goggling disbelievingly, then, with the same amazed expression on his face, he looked up at Marlowe.

'It's rather small,' he said. He reached for it. 'May I?'

Marlowe inclined his head in the briefest of nods.

Aldred took the parchment between finger and thumb and carefully unfolded it. 'Blood?' he asked, with a flick of a nail at the stain.

'Sadly, yes,' Marlowe agreed.

'Whose? Laurenticus'?'

'Again, yes,' Marlowe said. 'We are lucky, though, that it hasn't obscured the writing.'

'What's this other piece of parchment that it's wrapped in?' Aldred asked, preparing to throw it down.

'Oh, no, Solomon, don't throw that away,' Marlowe said, holding out a hand. 'I had forgotten that was there. It's just a sketch of the cartouche on a ring that was also found in Laurenticus' bed.'

Aldred smoothed it out, turned it round and grunted. He held it out to Phelippes for him to see. 'Geneva?' he muttered to him.

'Where else?' Phelippes agreed.

'That's an interesting wrinkle,' Aldred told Marlowe, 'but not much of a surprise, with his general behaviour, as I've heard it.'

'Geneva?' Johns asked, puzzled.

Marlowe reached behind him and patted his tutor on the shoulder, absent-mindedly. 'Not important,' he said. 'No bearing on the code, except that possibly Master Phelippes might need to bear a few more languages in mind, to be on the safe side.'

'I always test a number of languages,' Phelippes said, a touch pompously, as experts often tend to do.

'This writing is minute,' Aldred said, carrying it to the window. 'It is very clear, even so.'

Phelippes drew himself up. 'Every man who claims to be a code-writer must learn to write neatly and smaller than an imp might do. When we are plucked from the obscurity of our colleges and trained to use our logical brains, we spend no less than six weeks learning to whittle a goose feather down to less than the thickness of a baby's first hair. We learn how to mill and distil the smoothest of inks, so that no grain can impede the progress of our cipher. Neatness and attention to the smallest detail are our watchwords . . .'

As though housed in one head, all the eyes but his in the room swivelled to the chaos that was his desk. Drifts and avalanches of parchment and feather were spread over the surface, with the odd trencher and slice of bread amongst them. Johns had remembered a cat liking to visit them when they had first arrived and he feared that it might be in there too, possibly with a litter of kittens by this time.

Phelippes caught the direction of their gaze and dismissed it with a shrug. 'Of course, I am not *writing* a code at present, merely punishing my poor brain trying to break one. That's different. Where was I?'

'Neatness,' Johns offered.

'Ah, yes. Um . . . did that have anything to do with anything?' Phelippes had lost his thread.

'Not really,' said Aldred, sighing. 'I was simply saying this writing is extremely tiny. And neat, as you say. The letters are all stacked up in groups of –' he paused as he counted, using the tip of his finger to trace the lines – 'five by five.'

'Five by five is usual,' Phelippes said, dismissively. 'That gives the letters of the alphabet.'

Aldred was the only one who counted silently for a moment on his fingers. 'Not really,' he said. 'It's one short.'

'Indeed,' Johns said, 'but not really. Many people interchange I and J.'

'I personally usually interchange U and W when trying out codes,' Phelippes said. 'But, yes, Master Aldred, that is how it works. It still makes sense, when you have the rest of the word.'

'I see,' said Aldred, doubtfully.

'Let's see your piece of paper, then, Master Marlowe,' Phelippes said, sounding like a mother soothing a fractious child. Aldred handed it over and the code-breaker took it over to his candle. He took up a lens mounted on three little brass legs and passed it over the pages. The others waited patiently, one less patiently the others.

Eventually, Aldred spoke. 'Well? What does it say?'

Phelippes smiled acidly. 'Precisely?' he asked.

'Yes.' Aldred's reply was full of breathless anticipation, but the others were ready for what came next. Even so, Marlowe, over his irritation, was hard pressed to keep a straight face.

'Wofnut,' Phelippes remarked. 'Tufurufuh, arfptun, talwul, marmsa. Seffa, vewuls, g . . . sorry, there's a tiny bloodstain

there, so I'm not sure . . . I think it's gustufwuh, begpucl, ampnut.'
He paused. 'Unless I miss my guess.'

Aldred narrowed his eyes at the code-breaker and suddenly
the temperature in the room seemed to drop. Marlowe almost
expected to see icicles form on the edge of the table, made from
the dripping ink. He knew that someone would do this one day.
That someone would underestimate Aldred. He just hoped he
could move fast enough to save Phelippes from another nasty
stabbing. This time, the smiler with the knife would know exactly
what he was aiming at.

'Sometimes,' Aldred said, 'I think that people underestimate
me. You, for example, Master Phelippes, think that I am an idiot
vintner, at the beck and call of a large woman. You think that I
have forgotten that I am a projectioner, in the pay of Francis
Walsingham. You think I have become a Frenchman in all but
blood, and that I don't notice when I am being made fun of. That
would be a very big mistake on your part, Master Phelippes.'

Phelippes tried a smile and reached a hand out towards the
little projectioner, but whether in friendship or to prevent him
coming nearer, it wasn't clear. Johns took a step behind Kit
Marlowe, in his view the very best place to be when there might
be violence.

Aldred was still speaking. 'So, I am wondering, Master
Phelippes, why Sir Francis Walsingham sent me here, to sit and
watch the scorpions' nest. There are not many animals which
are immune to a scorpion's poison, Master Phelippes. The best
way to live long in the company of the creatures is to be quick
on your feet and watch out for the sting. Are you quick on your
feet, Master Phelippes? Can you avoid a sting?'

As Marlowe had been expecting, Aldred suddenly had a blade
in his hand, a nasty-looking thing, thin as a needle and almost
singing with sharpness. He doubted he would use it, but he could
see from the set of the man's shoulder that his temper was well
and truly lost and in moods like this the most phlegmatic man
can strike first and think later.

'Do you know how many countries I have lived in, Master
Phelippes, how many different people I have been? I speak more
languages than you have cracked codes and am fluent in every
one. I can swear in Flemish to make a sailor blush. I can order

whores in Spain to do things that even they had never dreamed of. I can't speak your dead Greek or Latin, but where would that get me? Could it save my life? I doubt it.'

'*Nollit ergo soliciti est, non intendit laedere*,' Marlowe said, easily, with no inflection.

'Oh, but I do,' Aldred said, looking over his shoulder at the playwright. He held his pose for a minute and then burst out laughing, sheathing his deadly needle so neatly that no one saw where it went. 'God's teeth, Marlowe, you shouldn't make me laugh when I am putting my little misericorde away,' he said. 'I could skewer a kidney.'

Marlowe slapped his shoulder. 'Apologize to Master Phelippes,' he said. 'You shouldn't tease guests, it is very uncouth.'

'He was making fun of me,' the vintner complained. 'He thought I didn't know what a substitution grid looked like.'

'You play the idiot a touch too well, Solomon,' Marlowe said. 'Sometimes I think you have forgotten yourself and believe what you tell the rest of us.'

Phelippes still looked mutinous. 'Do you mean to tell me,' he said, through gritted teeth, 'that you could have solved this code yourself?'

'God, no,' Aldred said. 'Of course not. But that isn't to say I don't know one when I see it. I wouldn't know where to begin when it comes to finding the most popular letter and what word goes where, all of that nonsense.' He rubbed his nose and looked for a moment like a naughty schoolboy. He wasn't sure how much further he could push Phelippes. And he wasn't sure which of them Walsingham would value more, if push really did come to shove. 'I know what comes in fives, though.' He stole a look at Marlowe under his sparse lashes.

Phelippes snorted. 'Toes? Fingers?'

'No,' Johns said, having regained the power of speech at last. 'Kit's syllables. He writes his plays and poetry in iambic pentameter, with five beats to a line.'

'I'm not alone there,' Marlowe was quick to admit. 'But you have a point. I can't imagine that Father Laurenticus would have memorized anything of mine, though.'

'He wouldn't have had to memorize it, Kit,' Johns said. 'He might have a copy of your translation of Ovid.'

'Hardly likely, surely,' Marlowe said. 'My stationer tells me it has sold less than twenty copies and that at knock down prices. I don't imagine it has reached Switzerland.'

'Twenty copies?' Aldred spluttered. 'Kit, you surprise me. You seem to know your way about the world, but you don't know when you are being gulled well and truly. There is hardly a man alive who doesn't like a bit of . . .' He had had a word in mind, but with the man himself in front of him, he was shy to use it.

'Smut!' spat Phelippes, still in a nasty temper brought on by fright.

Marlowe looked at Johns, who smiled and shrugged. 'He's right, Kit. Every College Master in Cambridge has banned it, which is why it is under every pillow. When you get back to Cambridge, you should see your stationer, I think.'

Marlowe was touched that Johns just assumed he would be going back to Cambridge, that he would be alive to go back there. There was a murderer on the loose and he was chasing him. But sometimes he worried that it might be the other way around. Nothing was quite what it seemed in this peculiar town and he wondered sometimes as he paced its streets whose footsteps he was hearing; his own, his murderer's or just the steps of Nemesis.

'I don't remember it, you know,' he said. 'I can't tell you if what you have is from my book. It's more likely to be from something in Latin, surely, or from some German thing.'

'Let me see,' Johns said. He took the scrap of parchment and held it to the light. Marlowe took it gently from his hand and turned it round ninety degrees. Johns peered again, then shook his head. He smiled at the other three. 'My arms are too short for my eyes,' he said, handing it to Aldred. 'Can you read it to me, Solomon. Properly.'

Aldred took the scrap and cleared his throat to begin. 'Oh, hang on,' he said. 'There's a letter and number outside the square. It's . . . something one. Does that help?'

The others shook their heads.

'The first line is W, O, F, N, T. Then comes T, F, R F, H. After that . . .'

'Comes R, F, P . . .' Johns paused and moved his lips silently.

'T, then N.' He drew a deep breath and adopted the nasal tone which men with no dramatic ability adopt when speaking verse and putting heavy stress on some syllables, he intoned, 'We *which* were *Ov*id's *five* books *now* are *three*, for *these* be*fore* the *rest* pre*ferr*eth *he*. If *rea*ding *five* thou *plainst* of *ted*ious*ness*, two *ta'en* a*way* thy *la*bour *will* be *less*.'

'First elegy,' Marlowe said, with a blush on his cheek. 'Well done, Michael. Fancy you knowing that by heart.'

'Yes,' Aldred said. 'Most of us have learned the naughty bits. That Elegy Three, eh? Oh, yes, I've got my end away to the tune of those lines well enough. Oh, yes.'

'Thank you, Master Aldred,' Phelippes said, quickly stopping him in full flow. 'I think we have the general idea. But I still don't see why some Catholic priest would have some dirty poems in his possession.'

'Don't forget, he wasn't all he seemed,' Marlowe said. 'Although quite what he was may never really come to light. But according to his mistress, he had one thing on his mind from dusk till dawn. Perhaps he liked to have something to remind him of her from dawn till dusk.'

Phelippes looked suitably appalled, then shrugged and turned to his desk. 'Come, Michael,' he said. 'From the letters we have I already know that this is not the key. But somewhere in Master Marlowe's dirty verses, we will find it. Do we have a copy to hand? Master Aldred?'

'I lent it to a friend,' Aldred said. 'And then he . . . you know how these things go.'

'Perhaps there are only twenty copies,' Marlowe said, slapping him on the back.

'I know it, more or less,' Johns said. 'It is very easy verse to learn. Well, it's the tumpty tumpty rhythm, Kit. Sorry.'

'Tumpty tumpty?' Marlowe was appalled. 'We'll leave you to your ciphering, gentlemen. Shall we, Solomon?' He opened to door and went out. 'I believe we may have some projectioning to do. Unless you are all vintner today?'

'I'm never all vintner, Master Marlowe,' the little man said, passing him in the doorway. 'I am never *all* anything.'

Phelippes and Johns didn't even hear them go. Johns was reciting at snail's pace, beating time on the edge of the desk, while Phelippes compiled his charts. Sooner or later, they would get their man.

As Marlowe made the turn in the stairs, he heard Phelippes ask, 'By the way, Michael, how many of these Elegies are there?'

He didn't hear Johns' reply but as he reached the shop doorway he did hear Phelippes' plaintive, 'How many!'

FIFTEEN

'He's not there.' Thomas Shaw was leaning on the door-frame of Peregrine Salter's room having heard Marlowe's knock on Abbott's door. 'And I've tried twice now.'

'A sudden impulse to hear the old Middlesex vowels again, Dr Shaw?' the projectioner asked.

'Yes.' The librarian smiled. 'An unlovely sound, isn't it, London? No. Ever since Edmund Brooke I confess I've become a little suspicious about who has my books. Master Abbott borrowed a couple when he first joined us and he hasn't returned them since. My shelves are beginning to look a little devoid of good literature. It's odd about Abbott. He moans about the breakfast but he never misses it. And he's usually at Matins, too. Well, if you see him, you might tell him I'm on to him.' He swept away down the corridor.

It was nearly Terce and the maids would not be about their business for another hour. Besides, this was Antoinette's floor and Marlowe knew he could do no wrong in her eyes. He tried the heavy oak door. Locked. He checked the landing, to left and right, then clicked the point of his dagger into the lock and twisted to the left. There was a jarring of metal and the door swung inwards.

Marlowe was inside in a second. The bed had not been slept in and there was a new, unlit candle in its stick alongside it. Two books lay on the table – the possessions of Dr Shaw, no doubt. Marlowe had not sheathed his dagger. Men died in the English College and their bodies stood in the crypt, like somebody's macabre collection, awaiting Judgement Day. He whisked the arras aside, ready for anything, but all that was beyond it was a washbasin and towels.

He rummaged in the drawers of the press. There were two shirts and a belt, along with a pair of hose and an ornate pair of spurs. The cupboard above yielded a plumed hat and a velvet doublet, slashed and lined with silk. Marlowe slid the dagger home behind him. This made no sense. If Abbott had left of his own accord, why hadn't he taken *all* his clothes with him? And why had no one seen him go? Or perhaps they had – he had yet to talk to Father Tobias, the eternal gatekeeper. But Shaw had said Abbott had missed breakfast and Matins. But the last Matins was in the small hours of the morning. Did that mean that the Furnival's Inn man had got up and gone in the middle of the night, or had he been gone for longer than that, since yesterday, in fact? Marlowe slammed his way out of the room. He had places to be, people to see.

'Not there?' Solomon Aldred was checking the strapping on his wine cart, tugging the strips of thick leather to make sure they would hold.

'Not anywhere,' Marlowe told him. 'I checked every nook and cranny I know – including nooks and crannies I'm guessing Abbott didn't know. Father Tobias didn't see him leave, but in the kingdom of the selectively blind, I fear Father Tobias is king. His horse is the key.'

'His horse?' Aldred wasn't sure which head he had on this afternoon – the projectioner's or the vintner's. He wanted to be sure the train of thought was his too.

'John Abbott seems inordinately fond of his horse,' Marlowe explained, 'on account of the inordinate amount of money he spent on it. It's there, in the College stalls, unridden, I'd say, for days.'

'In the habit of riding out, is he, Abbott?'

Marlowe smiled. 'I'm glad you brought that up, Master Aldred,' he said, 'because I'd like you to look for him.'

'I barely know the man.' The vintner shrugged before checking the hames of his own horse.

'Come on, Solomon,' Marlowe said. 'Don't give me that. The man's built like a brick privy and after "how much is that?" his French is pretty non-existent. How far is he likely to get in Rheims?'

'Well,' Aldred said, screwing up his face, 'I could put the word out, I suppose. I know a few people. It'll cost.'

'See Phelippes about that,' Marlowe said. 'I've been here too long. I'm fast running out.'

Aldred sighed. 'Yes, Walsingham's slush fund doesn't go far, does it? But, tell me, Master Marlowe. This Abbott. Why the fuss? Is he our man?'

Marlowe looked at him. 'He is *a* man, certainly,' he said.

'No, I mean, is he the bloke we're after, conspirator and killer?'

'What makes you think they're one and the same?' Marlowe asked him.

And Solomon Aldred shook his head. Today, he was definitely a vintner.

'Dominus Greene.' Father Tobias stood in the playwright's doorway, looking for all the world like the gatekeeper to some faerie world. Marlowe had not seen him other than hooded and girdled, his robe sometimes caught up in the rope around his middle, to keep it out of the mud if the day had been wet. Now, he stood there, his hood thrown back, his white hair a nimbus around his head, with the light behind him. 'There is a boy here –' and he reached to one side and dragged an urchin into view by the ear – 'who says he has something for you from the vintner. But since he doesn't seem to have a bottle about him, I assume it must be a reckoning.' He clapped a hand over both of the boy's abused ears and mouthed over his head, 'Don't let him rook you, Dominus Greene. The man is not to be trusted.'

Marlowe unwound himself from his bed, where he had been resting with a book, a brief interlude from his usual frantic scurry through life. 'I have bought no wine from Master Aldred,' he reassured the old man who was simultaneously releasing the boy's head from his iron grip while the lad still had some feeling in his ears. The child staggered slightly, then righted himself, tipping his head experimentally from side to side, as though emptying water from a jug.

'Then this boy is up to no good,' Father Tobias rumbled, reaching for a lobe to tug.

'Let me find out what the lad is after, Father Tobias,' Marlowe said, 'and if his purpose is indeed nefarious, I will bring him straight to you for a good, sound whipping. Does that seem like a bargain to you?'

The old monk looked dubious, but wandered off down the passageway regardless, looking back every few steps to see that

the lad was not stuffing the College silver down his ragged
britches.

'Thank you, Monsieur,' the boy piped in an uncertain treble.
'He is mad, that one. My friends and I make sure we use the
back gate if we wish to enter the College.'

Marlowe couldn't resist a smile. He had known that there was
at least one other way into the English College from the street,
and now it seemed there were even more. But still, a projectioner
is a projectioner, and there was a puzzle here. 'Why do you want
to come into the College?' he asked.

'Some of us have sisters who work here, or aunts. If they work
in the kitchens, there are good pickings to be had. If we can save
our mothers having to feed us a plate or two, it is worth running
the gauntlet of the Old One.'

'And the ones who don't have sisters and aunts?' Marlowe
probed.

The boy ducked his head. 'There is money to be made,
Monsieur, if you don't mind how you make it.' There was a
heavy silence. 'For myself, I have two sisters in the College.
Both in the kitchens. And my father, he has a stable. We are not
poor. I do not need the money.'

Marlowe realized he had touched a raw nerve, but it was
nothing he hadn't expected. A College full of men sworn to
celibacy was bound to hold a few who found it too much for
their willpower. And some had strange tastes; not everyone was
as straightforward in their requirements as Father Laurenticus.
'I can see you don't,' he said, looking down into the boy's anxious
eyes. 'What have you got for me, then? Something from Master
Aldred, is it?'

'He said to bring it straight to you and you would give me
five blancs.' The boy looked hopeful, but not sanguine; he had
learned through bitter experience that any promises of money
made by Solomon Aldred were unlikely to come true.

'I'm sure we can do better business than that,' Marlowe said,
ferreting out a gold coin from the purse at his hip. 'Now, what
do you have for me from Master Aldred?'

The boy reached into his jerkin and brought out a piece of
paper, folded and folded then folded again. It was held closed
by a dab of red wax, with the imprint of Phelippes' ring on it;

a knot being cut in two by a sword. Marlowe could hardly contain his excitement and also his amazement. For the code-breaker to have an answer this soon was almost unbelievable. He took it from the boy with studied casualness, twirling it in his fingers as if he didn't care if he ever got round to opening it or not. He spun the coin in the boy's direction. The lad had it in his hand and was halfway down the corridor almost before it had left the projectioner's fingers. Marlowe turned into his room, shut the door and sat down at his table, turning the parchment wax up, ready to break it open. Then he stopped, went back to the door and turned the key. He pulled the curtains across the window and lit the candle. He almost felt as though he should mark this moment somehow. The end to the puzzle of where Babington's man had gone, or the answer to who had killed Laurenticus and the others; either or both could be inside this small parcel.

Scarcely breathing, his slipped his thumb into a fold and pulled the parchment flat. He looked up at a corner of the ceiling and counted to ten. He wanted to be ready for the revelation that was now in his hand. He dropped his eyes.

The candle was still settling in to its steady burn and he turned the parchment towards it, narrowing his eyes against the flicker. But no matter how carefully he looked and how much he concentrated, the words wouldn't change. He couldn't help but read aloud, if only to convince himself of what he saw written there, in Phelippes' tiny, exquisite hand.

'Let me confess that we two must be twain, although our undivided loves are one: so shall those blots that do with me remain . . .' His voice died away and he read the rest silently to himself. Then he dropped the paper onto the tabletop and, drooping his head, massaged his temples. This must be wrong. Phelippes had broken the code, to another code, surely. How long could this chain continue, everyone spiralling round each other, more people dying, more paths leading nowhere. Suddenly, all Marlowe wanted was to be back in his room in Cambridge, with nothing more to worry about but an untranslated passage for Dr Lyler. But his eyes were drawn to the rest of the verse, and he read each line carefully, looking for a hidden meaning. Then, he reached the bottom and knew there was no meaning other than what he could see in plain sight. 'For Sylvie,' he read, 'who will never be mine, but who will always be, in my heart, my wife.'

Marlowe had made assumptions about Father Laurenticus, based on others' views of him. A philanderer, a heart-breaker, a spy; now, to this list, he had to add a man in love. Which was the right one? This one, surely, the one who had sat, hour after solitary hour, pouring out his heart to his love, in codes culled from Marlowe's own words. He read the lines again and knew that his lines had become greater in their retelling, no translation of old bawdiness here, just love laid bare on the paper. He refolded the parchment and slipped it into the breast of his doublet. There was someone he had to go and see, before he changed his mind.

There was a tap at the door, and he went to open it. The lad from Aldred was there, with another parchment in his hand.

'I'm sorry, Monsieur,' he gasped. 'I forgot this other one.' He held out the gold coin forlornly. 'I will understand if . . .' Although the coin was in the flat of his palm, even so he seemed to be holding it fast.

Marlowe ruffled his hair and was immediately sorry. It was stiff with some kind of grease. He tried to resist wiping his hand until the boy had turned his back.

'It's goose grease, Monsieur,' the boy said. 'My grandmamma says it is good for the chest.'

'But it seems to be in your hair,' Marlowe couldn't help but remark.

The boy shrugged the French shrug involving his whole body. 'To be safe,' he said. 'One cannot have too much goose grease.'

'Indeed not,' Marlowe said. 'Keep the coin, you didn't mean to keep the note and I have it now. *Au revoir.*'

'*Merci, Monsieur,*' the lad said, already running down the corridor.

Marlowe wiped his hand on the curtain and then opened his second note. This was from Johns. 'Kit,' it began, 'I hope you don't mind that I have translated the verse from the German. Such an ugly language for poetry, don't you think? If you want the original, we have it here. After I had done the work, I realized that perhaps the original had a code inside the code. Kit, I know this sounds mad, but being with Phelippes so much has made me a little mad, I think. I see shadows in every corner, an assassin in every shade. I think I will go back to Cambridge soon, Harvey or no Harvey, but I will see you before I go. With my fondest wishes. Take care and God will go with you, whether you want Him to or not. M.'

There was something in the tone of the note that made a goose step over Marlowe's grave, with or without its grease. Something about this afternoon, begun at such leisure, reading a book in peace, had turned the world and started something in motion that no one would be able to stop. It was no good trying to think it through. It was time to let the feeling in his blood lead him, and hope that his blood would stay inside his skin.

The sun had long since set by the time the Queen's First Secretary took off his spectacles and closed his tired eyes. All day he had been reading correspondence, the private sort that not even his secretaries saw, not even his wife, nor young Robert, the son waiting in the wings to assume his father's mantle of state. His hounds lay dreaming before the fire and the glass of mead was shot through with the reflected embers in the grate.

It was then that one final letter met his gaze as he sat upright again, shaking sleep from him. He knew that crest – the golden eagles on the green field. That was the Fineaux coat of arms and he and old Walter Fineaux went back a long way. He ripped the seal and adjusted his candle to give him a better light.

'My lord,' it read. 'Regarding Corpus Christi and the successor to Dr Norgate. May it please you that one Dr Gabriel Harvey has assumed the powers of . . .' His voice tailed away.

'Vernon!' he roared and a distant voice answered, 'My lord?' A ferret of a man scuttled into his presence, bowing curtly.

'Get me our best horseman,' Burghley barked. 'And send me Collard. I need to get a letter to John Copcott, Vice-Chancellor of Cambridge. I must, it seems, use a prerogative or two.'

Marlowe had a skill, innate rather than learned, of feeling at home in any city and knowing his way around like a native in no time. He put this down to his choirboy years in Canterbury, when he would spend more time ducking and diving round the alleyways, twittens and snickets which would lead him out of trouble with his schoolmasters and into trouble of a far more enjoyable kind, involving games of bat and ball, not five-part harmonies by Tallis, God rest his soul. So, although his journey with Mireille had been in the dark, he let his feet do the thinking and was soon outside the little, dark door in the dingy courtyard. He tapped politely and waited. No one came, so he risked pushing the door a little, to see if it was open. It creaked, but it gave on its sagging hinges, and Marlowe slipped into the room.

There was no light at all inside, just a faint glimmer through the grimy window, but it was enough in that tiny space for Marlowe to know that he was alone. He edged along the wall to the curtained doorway that led to the other room, where Sylvie seemed to do most of her business. Mireille was more at home in the lights and bustle of the taverns in the town, happily giving her customers what they wanted against any convenient wall. Sylvie was more the choice of those who wanted privacy, no talking, no reaction or emotion, just somewhere to get some quick release as cheaply as possible. Feeling like a voyeur, he craned his neck to listen at the gap.

The frantic, angry grunting of his previous visit was absent, but it was obvious that Sylvie was earning a crust beyond the curtain and he drew back to wait. This time there was no crashing boor of a man flying through the room, just a thin and unkempt boy, if anything younger than Sylvie herself, who crept round the tattered hanging and, seeing Marlowe lounging against the wall absently polishing the blade of his dagger on his well-clothed thigh, ran for the door, wrenched it open and flew across the courtyard as though the hounds of Hell were at his heels.

Marlowe gave the girl a moment to collect herself, then called her name, softly. 'Sylvie?'

'*Moment, Monsieur*,' she called back, not happily, but with more spirit than he had heard in her voice before. As she came into the room, her face fell. 'Oh, it's you. Are you looking for Mireille?'

'Not today, Sylvie. I came looking for you.' He pointed vaguely at the door. 'A friend of yours?'

She laughed, flatly. 'No, bless him. He has come here every night for the last three weeks. This was the first time I got him to even unlace his britches. One of these days he will get so far as to lose his precious virginity. He will find it is not all it is cracked up to be.'

'Virginity, or the losing of it?' Marlowe was curious to find out how this strange girl ticked along. When Mireille was around, everyone else just seemed to become background noise.

'Either.' She shrugged. 'Both. But how can I help you, Monsieur?'

'For once, I think I am here to help you. Can we have some light in here?'

'Not in here,' she said with a smile. 'A light in this room only means one thing: open for business. Perhaps you would like to go elsewhere? There are taverns . . .'

'No, this is something private,' he said. He had no intention of reading a love poem to her in the noise of even the quietest inn. He had made a rough translation of it in his head and wondered how much of the man Laurenticus could remain; even lines written from the heart lose a lot when translated into and out of code and then through two more languages to the ear of the intended recipient. But it was something that had to be done.

'Come into the back room, then,' she said. 'It is quite tidy, nothing to offend you. My last client, as you saw, wasn't one to wrinkle the sheets. Come.' She crooked a finger and pulled the curtain to one side.

Whatever Marlowe had been expecting, it wasn't this austere little cell. There was just a bed, neatly made, a table with a jug and a bowl on it, half full of water. A towel was neatly folded alongside. 'Do you live here?' he asked, looking round.

'No. Mireille and I share a room across the courtyard. We rent this for . . . business. It works better this way, especially when the weather is bad. We can use both places. Even Mireille comes inside when it snows.' She smiled. 'Don't get me wrong when I criticize Mireille, Monsieur. I love her like a sister, but we don't have much in common, other than this.'

Laurenticus seemed to hover between them like a ghost. Marlowe could almost see him, a little vague as to face, but otherwise he had the measure of the man, he thought. Big, quick to temper and also, as it turned out, to love. Full of appetites which the English College had failed to stifle. Even his spying had taken second place to his passion for this little, sad girl.

As if she could read his mind, she spoke. 'So, what do you have to tell me, Monsieur? Time is money, you know, in my line of work.'

Marlowe took out a gold coin and put it on the table. 'Take the rest of the night off,' he said. 'Consider it a gift from Father Laurenticus.'

She flinched, but said nothing.

'Do you have a candle? I think I can remember what I need to tell you, but it will help if I have a light.'

She looked at him oddly, then dipped through the curtain and came back with a stump of candle, with many dribbles and very trimmed as to wick. This was a candle that was lit often and for short periods. She lit it with a practised hand, striking the flint just the once. She handed it to him.

'Make yourself comfortable, Sylvie,' he said. 'I am going to read something to you. It's only short, don't worry.'

Obediently, like a child, she lay on the bed, on her side, with her head in the crook of her arm. In the candlelight, her eyes glowed as she looked at him.

He took the paper from his doublet and unfolded it. Resting it in his lap to jog his memory, he began. 'Let me confess that we two must be twain,' he said, haltingly in French, 'although our undivided loves are one: so shall those blots that do with me remain, without thy help by me be borne alone.' He glanced at her and saw that her eyes had closed. A silver trail led down across her cheek to the corner of her mouth, but she made no move to wipe the tear away. 'In our two loves there is but one respect,' he continued, 'though in our lives a separable spite, which though it alter not love's sole effect, yet doth it steal sweet hours from love's delight.'

She suddenly sat up, dashing away the tears with the back of her hand. 'Did he write this for me?' she asked, her voice thick and dry.

'Yes, Sylvie,' he said, gently. 'Yes, he did. He sat day by day and wrote you poetry, in code, because he couldn't say what he felt in his heart.'

'You weren't there,' she said, smiling through her tears. 'You don't know what he said to me, in the dark. No one does, and no one will. If there is more, Monsieur, don't read it to me.

Take the poem, read it to others if you will. And if you want to, tell them it was written by a man who loved a woman and who had to leave her, by someone else's fault, not his.' She looked around her with big eyes. 'He has gone at last. He has been here, you know, since that night. I have been so angry with him for leaving me, so guilty that I ran away as he was dying and left him alone, but I have let him go now.' She looked at Marlowe, sitting there in the candlelight, the paper on his knee. 'Thank you, Monsieur.'

'Are you sure . . .?' He held up the paper.

'No. I have heard enough. You have taken a weight from me. I can see the whole thing clearly now, for the first time since it happened. As the knife went home, he –' she swallowed hard, and grabbed a handful of bedding as though to steady herself – 'he grabbed at me. He was dying. I didn't know. I was fright-ened, so I jumped up and ran, past a man on the gallery outside. He frightened me. His face . . .'

Marlowe was on his knees at her side in an instant. 'You saw his face?'

'I . . . think so.'

'How can you think so?' he almost shouted. 'You either saw it, or you didn't.'

'It was in deep shadow. But if I saw it again, I would know it, I'm sure.'

He leaned forward and held her face between his hands. 'Sylvie,' he said, 'you are a miracle. I may need you to help me later. Will you do that?'

'If I can,' she said.

He leaned forward and kissed her sweetly, tasting the salt of her tears. 'Take care, Sylvie,' he said. 'I think Father Laurenticus would have wanted me to tell you that.'

And he was gone.

SIXTEEN

Philip Henslowe was feeling very pleased with himself. He already ran three bear-pits where the great and good of Southwark paid ridiculous money to watch dogs torn apart by the black-furred beasts from the forests of Russia; or to watch the ravenous curs sink their teeth into the animals' noble hides – it could all turn on the random slash of a claw. And he also made a modest return collecting rents from the Winchester geese who sold their charms all along the South Bank.

Now, fortune had favoured Henslowe further. He and his partner, John Cholmley, grocer, had just built a theatre, The Rose, and the smell of newly planed timbers and damp wattle was still in his nostrils that Tuesday morning as the post boy thudded up the stairs to Henslowe's solar.

'Master Henslowe?' the lad asked, breath in fist.

'Yes.' Henslowe was poring over his latest play returns.

'Master Philip Henslowe, the dyer?'

'Yes.' The man was irritated already. Little things like a reminder of his origins took the gilt off his profits.

'Are you the bloke what owns the Rose?'

'For God's sake, man,' Henslowe thundered. 'Yes, I am. Why all these questions?'

'Sorry, sir.' The lad rummaged in his purse. 'But I've rid all the way from Cambridge and was told to give this to no one but *that* Philip Henslowe. You can't be too careful in my profession.'

'Indeed not.' Henslowe took the letter from the lad's hand. 'What's this?'

'It's a letter,' the lad said, privately wondering what sort of people were running London's theatres these days.

Henslowe scowled at him. The post boy wasn't to know that dyers-turned-theatre-impresarios didn't suffer fools gladly, if at all.

'From Master Thomas Fineaux,' the boy said. 'See, there's his crest on the seal. It's on the letterhead too . . .' His voice tailed

away. 'It's three eagles on a field of verte, if my heraldry serves
me right. Only, I've got a bit of a gift for heraldry, if I say it
myself.'

'Have you?' Henslowe smiled. 'A pity you haven't got much of
a gift for delivering letters. Get out.'

The lad was shocked. 'Er . . . it is customary for the recipient
of a letter to give some sort of remuneration, sir,' he said.

Henslowe looked at him. 'Of course,' he said. 'How remiss of
me. Have you heard of Edward Alleyn, the actor?'

'No,' said the post boy.

'Oh dear.' Henslowe looked glum on the actor's behalf. 'He'll
be prostrate to hear that. Anyway, to cut a very long prologue
short, he's the man who handles my petty cash and he'll see you
right. Good morning.'

'Er . . . thank you, sir, but where will I find Master Alleyn?'

'Let's see.' Henslowe crossed the narrow room and peered
through the wobbly panes to catch a glimpse of the pale sun. 'It
must be about eleven of the clock. You'll probably find him in
the Marshalsea about now.'

'The Marshalsea?' the lad repeated. 'Isn't that a prison?'

'Is it?' Henslowe asked. 'I never enquire too closely about the
private lives of my actors. It doesn't pay. Any more than I do.
So –' he bundled the boy towards the door – 'if it's remuneration
you're after, Alleyn's your man. If finding him is too much
trouble, well, there it is. Life's a bitch and then you die –' he
crossed himself – 'saving the Almighty's presence, of course.
Can you see yourself out?' The lad found himself outside on
the landing, the door firmly slammed in his face.

Henslowe read the letter. The lad was right. The arms of the
Fineaux family were stamped firmly across the top of the page
and in a spidery scrawl beneath were the words, 'A play called
Tamburlaine the Great may be on its way to you, Master
Henslowe, and its author purports to be one Robert Greene of
St John's College. Be assured this is a lie. The play is brilliant
but its real author is . . .'

'Christopher Marlowe,' a voice murmured in Henslowe's ear.

The theatre manager jumped visibly and turned savagely to
the man behind him. 'God damn you, Ned Alleyn, do you always
read other people's letters over their shoulders?'

'Always, if I can,' the actor told him, removing the parchment from his boss' grasp. 'It saves having to search through drawers; so demeaning, that, don't you think? And I always read them if they concern me.'

'And that concerns you?' Henslowe snatched it back.

'Marlowe does,' the actor said.

'That's right,' Henslowe remembered, throwing himself back into his chair again. 'Didn't you pinch another play of his? Um . . . *Dido*, wasn't it?'

'It may have been,' Alleyn said, pouting.

'Well, well . . .' Henslowe chuckled. Ned Alleyn's ego was the size of St Paul's – it was good to see it demolished every now and again.

'If this play *is* by Marlowe –' Alleyn sat down next to him – 'it'll be worth your while getting hold of it.'

'Will it?' Henslowe asked. 'Why?'

Alleyn looked at the man with a smouldering hatred. 'Because Marlowe is a genius,' he said, as though the Queen's Rackmaster had ripped the words from him with red-hot pincers. 'And because it will make us a fortune.'

'Us?' Henslowe raised an eyebrow.

'Philip, Philip.' Alleyn chuckled, leaning back with his hands locked behind his head. 'We are but the buttocks of the same arse, you and I. You have a theatre. Brand spanking new. State of the art. I have a talent that will not be matched in a thousand years. Together . . . well, we're irresistible. The third corner of our great triangle of the Muse belongs to that man –' he flicked a finger at the letter – 'Kit Marlowe.'

Henslowe was nodding, groat signs reflected at the back of his eyeballs onto his brain. 'Who is this Tamburlaine?' he asked.

'No idea,' Alleyn said, shrugging. 'But whoever he is, I'll make him immortal.'

'Well, then.' Henslowe crossed the room again and produced a bottle of claret and two beakers. 'Here's to the great Tamburlaine,' he said. 'And the great Kit Marlowe.'

'What about this Greene?' Alleyn asked. 'The man who's stolen the play?'

'Do you know him?' Henslowe checked.

Alleyn shook his head.

'I'll just wipe him off my shoe,' the theatre-manager said.

Marlowe sat through breakfast more quietly than usual. Once the jealousy over his lumpless oatmeal had worn off, he was a popular companion at the day's first meal, as he was witty without cruelty and was a ready mimic of authority, when authority was conveniently looking the other way. This morning, though, he was not on his usual form and one by one, the scholars who had flocked to his table got up to get second helpings and didn't come back. He scarcely noticed.

'Good morning, Dominus,' a voice with a twang in it broke his conversation and he looked up into the face of Peregrine Salter. 'Do you mind if I join you?'

'Not at all,' Marlowe said, looking around at the empty table. 'There is plenty of room, after all.'

'Where are your audience today?' Salter asked, without malice.

'They seem to have heard all of my best lines,' Marlowe said with a smile. 'I don't seek the bubble reputation and I don't mind a quiet breakfast now and again. To be truthful with you, Master Salter, I have a bit of a head on me. I was out late last night in some rather dubious company and the lads are good company when I feel well, but with both my eyes feeling as though they are on one side of my nose, I couldn't bear their chunter.'

'Their . . .?'

'Their talk,' Marlowe said, covering one eye and attempting to focus on Salter's face. 'They will go on.'

'Well, boys will be boys,' Salter agreed. 'Where were you last night? Anywhere you would recommend?'

'Oh, no. A tavern of a very low sort. I met with a –' he lowered his voice – 'a couple of ladies of very low type.' He smiled, but without using too many muscles, as a man will whose head is splitting. 'I lost track of time somewhat as well as goblets.'

Salter sat back on the bench and placed his hands flat on the table on either side of his platter. 'Do you know,' he said, carefully not using the projectioner's name, because of listening ears, 'you don't really strike me as someone who would get much pleasure from that kind of night out.'

'Not as a rule, Master Salter, not as a rule,' Marlowe growled, addressing his oatmeal with little relish. 'But now and again one's animus drives the body, not the other way around.'

Salter cocked his head on one side, considering. 'I'm not sure that is a doctrine we follow in the English College, is it?' he asked.

'Oh, Master Salter,' Marlowe said in a low voice, letting go of his forehead for a moment and leaning forward. 'I think in the English College it might be said that doctrines are there for reading and talking about, not necessarily following. But I did hear an interesting thing, when I was out and about and before I forgot myself in the arms of the lovely ladies – we were chatting.'

'I hope you weren't paying by the hour,' Salter said, spooning in his oatmeal but keeping his eyes on Marlowe.

'Pardon?'

'Paying your two drabs by the hour. Just for talking. It seems an awful waste of money.'

'Oh, I see.' Marlowe's hand went back to supporting his head. 'They weren't as low as that. They have an evening rate. Where was I?'

'Chatting.' Salter was concentrating on Marlowe now, his dish of oatmeal slowly congealing in front of him.

'Yes, that's right. Chatting.' He closed his eyes as if retracing his words. 'We were chatting, and one of them said she had seen something suspicious when one of the murders happened. Father Laurenticus. Murdered in his bed.'

'So she . . .?'

'Was with him. Or so she says. Whatever the truth of it – and how can you trust a woman of the street, no matter how pretty? – she claims she saw who did the deed.'

'Why didn't she tell the Watch?' Salter asked.

Marlowe sounded testy. 'The Watch weren't involved. And besides, she would hardly do that, would she? She isn't exactly on the right side of the law, in her . . . business.'

'True,' Salter said, nodding slowly. 'So . . . did she tell you who this man is?'

'No,' Marlowe said, finishing off his oatmeal and pushing the dish away. Antoinette had excelled herself this morning and it had pained him to eat it with so little relish. If he lived to see another breakfast, he would do it better justice next time. 'She doesn't know who he is. She just told me she would know him next time she saw him.'

Salter shrugged. 'The woman was lying, to get your attention.'

Marlowe looked down at the table and traced a random doodle in the spilled ale by his plate. It looked a little like a double-headed eagle. 'She had my attention, if you take my meaning,' he said, quietly, with a silly smile on his face.

Salter looked at him for a long minute, as the silence between them filled with skittering spoons and the hum of conversation. 'I see,' he said at last. 'You do surprise me, Master M . . . Dominus. But we never really know a person, do we?' He swung his leg over the bench and stood up. 'Well, I must be away. I am sure I will see you later in the day. Perhaps when your head is better?'

'Yes,' Marlowe agreed, with a wan smile. He watched under his lashes until Salter was through the door, then sat up straight and flexed his shoulders. 'Chunter, chunter, chunter, Master Salter,' he murmured. 'It's just all so much chunter.'

'Dr Shaw?' Marlowe stuck his head round the door of the library and spoke in the hoarse whisper of library users everywhere. 'Can I have a moment?'

Shaw didn't look up, but raised a finger in the air. When it had had its effect in silencing the young man in his doorway, he turned it round and beckoned with it. Marlowe approached the table where the librarian was working and pulled out a chair, which squeaked along the stone floor like the fingernails of some demon in nethermost Hell. Shaw looked up, a sardonic eyebrow raised.

'Sorry,' Marlowe mouthed, looking around the room and meeting the outraged eyes of the scholars reading there.

'And, we're done,' whispered Shaw, releasing the book he had been holding in a vice-like grip in his other hand. 'Just doing some running repairs,' he said quietly. 'The glue needs a little encouragement in the early minutes. Let's go into my room. It's quieter.'

'That is quite a strong grip you have there,' said Marlowe when they could speak normally.

Shaw turned his hand this way and that. 'It's nothing,' he said. 'Librarian's fingers, that's what I have. Good for mending broken books and apprehending anyone trying to sneak out of my library with something they shouldn't.' He mimed pinching Marlowe's ear.

'And yet you didn't apprehend Edmund Brooke,' he remarked, taking a seat.

'No,' Shaw said sadly. 'No, someone else did that for me. A shame. He was a nice boy.'

'And Charles Russell?'

'No,' Shaw looked Marlowe straight in the eye. 'I have no idea who that is.'

'Died by hanging.'

'Was that his name? How sad that we only remember him because of the hanging. There were . . . rumours, of course. Boys from the town, that kind of thing.' His voice dropped to a whisper. 'The sin of Sodom.'

'Leonard Skirrel?'

'No, you really can't just drop these names like this, you know, Master Marlowe. I really don't know that one at all.'

'He was a priest. He was with the College in Douai.'

'Ah, well, there we are, then. I wasn't librarian in Douai. Well, I was *in* the library, but not in charge. Much more humble than I am now, if possible. I didn't know everyone.'

'Father Laurenticus.'

'Well, obviously I knew Laurenticus. He was in here all the time, poring over books and writing, writing, always writing. We have his papers somewhere . . .' He looked around vaguely. 'I'm sure we will come round to cataloguing them some day.'

'Do you know his mistress, Sylvie?' Marlowe asked.

Shaw froze, looking away from Marlowe on a fruitless visual search for Laurenticus' papers. When he turned his head, his face was a mask, immobile and waxen. 'I never met the lady,' he said, 'although, of course, there were . . .'

'Rumours. Yes. The sin of Gomorrah. Well, she has now remembered who she saw outside the room on the night he died.'

'Really?' Shaw plumped down in his chair and leaned on his elbows on the table. He blew out his cheeks and smacked his lips, a parody of amazement. 'Really? Well, out with it, man. Who was it?'

'I don't know,' Marlowe admitted. 'She didn't know who it was, just that she would know him again.'

'That must be quite frightening for her,' Shaw remarked.

'She's very brave. She has met him once since, when he paid her to poison Martin Camb.'

'Well, in that case . . .'

'Yes?'

'I was about to say she is no better than she should be, but that rather goes without saying, doesn't it.' The librarian bared his teeth, in what might pass for a smile.

'I think that he feels he does have that crime to use against her, should the day of his accusation dawn. Well –' Marlowe got up – 'I must be off. Things to do, you know, Dr Shaw. Busy. Busy.' And he was gone.

Shaw looked at the door for a moment. 'I wonder what he came for?' he asked the inkwell, for lack of anyone else to ask.

Marlowe tapped on the door of Dr Allen's room. This was his last piece of bread that he must cast upon the waters before he started his wait to see what fish the bait brought to the surface. He had left this particular eel until the last. Whenever he was with the Master of the English College, he was never sure who was watching whom.

'Enter.' A clever choice, Marlowe thought. It didn't really matter who was standing outside, English or French, they would at least get the drift.

He pushed open the door and stepped in, closing it carefully behind him. 'Master,' he said, 'I can't stay long. I have promised to help Mr Salter with a trans . . . Oh, Dr Skelton. I'm terribly sorry. I didn't see you there.'

'Gerald does tend to skulk,' Allen said, jovially. 'It comes with being a Bursar, I have always thought. Watching to see if he can catch any of those groats going down a drain. That is where they all go, you were saying, isn't it, Gerald?'

Skelton gave a wintry smile. 'We must look after every tiny expenditure, Master,' he said. 'Money doesn't grow on trees.'

'Sadly not,' Allen said. 'However, I am almost certain that

Dominus Marlowe didn't come here to talk about economics, did you, Dominus Marlowe?'

'Not really, Master, no,' the projectioner admitted. 'Although it is a fascinating subject, in its way.'

Skelton smiled a slow smile, the smile of the accountant who knows his books are in perfect balance.

'No, I have come with some good news. Not wonderful news, but a good way to putting a lid on a little problem of yours, once and for all.'

'This sounds marvellous, Dominus Marlowe. May I call you Christopher, I wonder?'

'Kit, Master, if you wish. I usually only get called Christopher by my mother, when I have done something wrong.'

'Yes, indeed,' the Master said. 'Mine was the same.' It was hard to think of the Master having had a mother, but biology dictated that it must once have been so. 'Well, Kit, what is your news?'

Marlowe flicked his eyes at Skelton, who moved towards the door, prepared to leave.

'Kit, Kit,' the Master said. 'Have we not already agreed that anything you have to say to me, you can say in front of Dr Skelton?'

'Of course, Master. I am sorry, Dr Skelton. I didn't mean to throw you out so rudely. No offence taken, I hope.'

'None in the world, Dominus Marlowe,' the Bursar said, sitting in a hard chair by the window.

'I am agog, Kit,' the Master said. 'What *is* your news?'

Marlowe squirmed slightly. 'I hope I haven't given it too much emphasis, Master,' he said. 'It may be nothing.'

Allen waved a hand, his expression getting steely. This was like pulling teeth with no pliers.

'I met with the girl Sylvie, Father Laurenticus' . . . erm . . .'

'Harlot,' Skelton said, calmly.

'Come, come, Gerald,' Allen said, gently. 'Live and let live. There but for the Grace of God . . . well, not literally, of course, but . . .' Thoroughly tangled in his sentence, the Master waved Marlowe to continue.

'Shall we call her his mistress? He would have made her his wife, had he not been caught between his God and a hard place. Call her what you will, I met with her last night . . .'

'How did you get out of the College?' asked Skelton, aghast. 'Where is the gate roster, Master? Heads will roll.'

'I just walked out, Bursar,' Marlowe said, with an apologetic shrug. 'I walked out and then back in, just as the scholars do and for all I know half the town. Father Tobias is not much of a watchdog, I fear.'

'Make a note, Gerald,' the Master said, mildly. 'Speak to Father Tobias.' He turned to Marlowe. 'Let's assume for the moment that we are already at the home of the girl Sylvie,' he said. 'Then we may have this news before nightfall.'

Marlowe took a deep breath and delivered his tale at last. 'For reasons I need not dwell on, Sylvie has remembered the man who was outside Father Laurenticus' room on the night he died.'

The Master and Bursar were on their feet in an instant. 'What?' they chorused. The Master looked Skelton in the eye and he subsided once more into his chair. 'Who?' the Master asked.

'She doesn't know,' Marlowe said, spreading his hands helplessly. 'She only knows that she will know him again.'

'We must get the girl here,' Allen said.

'How will that help?' Skelton asked.

'She must be made to look into the eyes of every man here, to see if she can recognize him,' the Master said. 'See to it, Gerald.'

'With respect, Master,' Marlowe said, 'I interrupted her night's work last night. I paid her, as seemed only fair, but she has regular customers.' He shrugged. 'You know how it is.'

'Not really,' Allen said, drily. 'But if I read you aright, Dominus Marlowe, you are suggesting that we bring her here tomorrow in her . . . off-duty hours, if I may put it like that?'

'Exactly,' Marlowe said. 'Tomorrow.'

'We will do that, then.' Allen turned to the Bursar. 'Gerald, make a note.' After a moment, he looked up and saw Marlowe standing there. 'Don't let us keep you, Dominus Marlowe. I believe you have some translations to be getting on with.'

'Hmm?' Marlowe was a little foxed for a moment.

'Master Salter? I understood you to say . . .'

'Indeed, yes.' Marlowe made for the door. 'I have to help Master Salter with some translations.'

'Close the door on your way out,' Skelton barked.

And with a whisper of wood on wood, Marlowe was gone.

Marlowe smiled gently to himself as he walked purposefully back to his room. He was not a countryman by either upbringing or inclination, preferring the buzz of humanity to that of the bees, but he felt now as he thought a gamekeeper might. He had baited his trap. All he needed to do now was to wait for nightfall and see what fell into it. A quick visit to Solomon Aldred, a quick rummage through his clothes for something that would neither rustle nor gleam in the darkness, and then he was all ready to catch a murderer. The only slight weak link in his plan was that he needed Aldred to watch one gate while he watched the other. That the vintner was still mostly projectioner was not really in doubt, but he was a well-known figure on the streets of Rheims and he would find it harder than many to pass without being hailed by some wandering drunkard. But sometimes there were no choices but second best, so Solomon Aldred it would have to be.

SEVENTEEN

They met in the blackest shadow the cathedral had to offer. Aldred was excited; he hadn't trailed anyone in years and was looking forward to resurrecting old skills. He knew he was a little shorter in wind these days, as he had always been of limb, but age and cunning were on his side against the youth and inexperience of Peregrine Salter.

'It is Salter I am after, Kit, isn't it?' he asked for the hundredth time.

For the hundredth time, Marlowe patiently told him that this was not necessarily the case. 'Solomon, please listen. I have told four people that Sylvie knows who the murderer is. For all I know, those four could well have told four more, who could have told four more . . . ad infinitum. Do you see what I am getting at? We are looking for anyone creeping out of the College tonight.'

'Come on, Kit,' Aldred said. 'The place leaks like an old sieve. We could end up running all over town.'

'I think that the gates will be secure tonight, Solomon,' Marlowe told him. 'Father Tobias won't be much of a gatekeeper for many nights, but I think that he will have been reminded of his duties this afternoon and so anyone coming out of the College will be our man.'

'Salter.'

'Solomon . . .'

'Just joking, Kit,' Aldred said, hurriedly, having seen the projectioner's right arm slip behind his back. Their nerves were on edge; not only did they have to catch a killer, but also keep Sylvie safe. 'I will take the back gate, you take the front. Anyone who comes out, we follow. Even if they don't seem to be going in the right direction. We are dealing with someone here who is cunning, cruel and desperate.'

'Right,' Marlowe said, withdrawing his hand and using it to clap Aldred on the back. 'And, Solomon . . .'

'Yes?'

'No heroics. Just keep Sylvie safe. Don't tackle our man unless she is in danger. Just keep him in sight and, if possible, stop him from getting back in to the College.'

'Yes, Kit. And the same goes for you, does it?'

'Very likely,' Marlowe agreed, slipping from the shadow. 'See you tomorrow.'

'*Deo volens*,' Aldred murmured.

'Very likely,' Marlowe repeated and disappeared round a buttress. After a moment, Aldred followed on soundless feet. The playwright had already disappeared into the rabbit warren of streets.

Solomon Aldred had trailed men before. He'd sometimes lost them, sometimes been given a bloody nose for his pains when someone he was following had doubled back round a blind corner and given him a smack. It was all in a night's work when you were in the pay, however intermittently, of Francis Walsingham. But this night was particularly foggy, Fall blurring into winter as December drew near and the mists came creeping up from the Vesle and past the quays into the labyrinth of alleyways that men called Rheims.

All there was to do now was wait. It was no night for a man to be waiting outside in the dark. The cold was the seeping kind, that crept into your clothes and drove out every ounce of heat the body in them had stored against the day. The first thing to go was the soles of the feet, with only thin, soft leather to ensure a silent tread between the skin and the slick stone. Aldred could feel his feet becoming numb and eased them one by one, wanting to stamp, but unable to make even the slightest noise. He knew that the front door of the College had a little wicket in it, for use at night. He also knew it had a squeak, so he relied on that to alert him, as he wrapped his cloak around his face to avoid the flash of an eyeball or a tooth giving him away in the dim light. It seemed like hours before he heard it, then he had just a few seconds to unwrap himself from the wool and slide away after his quarry.

The brazen bastard. He was just walking out, bold as brass, yet there was still something furtive in his movements. Aldred couldn't make him out, especially as he'd had to dodge backwards into the shadows to avoid being seen. He was a large man, certainly, with a satchel under his arm and a hooded cloak billowing out behind him. His buskins clattered on the cobbles as he ducked under the archway into the Rue de Lyon and on across the square. He skirted the outer precincts of the great cathedral, dwarfed, as all men were, by its Gothic magnificence. Vespers would be tolling soon, and the black shadows would flicker with movement as the faithful made their way for their evening meeting with the Almighty. But this man wasn't going there. And neither was the one who followed him.

Aldred nearly broke his ankle spinning fast to hide behind an archway. His target had stopped, looking from right to left and listening. Aldred had tried to time his steps to the rhythm of the man but that wasn't easy when he was so much shorter in the leg than his quarry. In the murky light there was always one cobble that gave you away, one stone that slipped. The man tapped on a low door twice and waited. Aldred knew the street he was in but the particular house meant nothing to him. He saw the light fill the street as the door opened. There were muttered words, then the door closed and the street was in darkness again.

Kit Marlowe was pressed to the stonework of a warehouse opposite the back wall of the English College. He was sure of one exit; he had used it himself when he had been up on the leads with Shaw, but he was almost certain there was at least one more. There was no way of watching the fourth side of the building – Aldred needed to be in his position to see the front door and couldn't alter that – but from where he stood, he could see the other side and the back. Surely, from here he would be able to get his man. He tucked his hands under his armpits for warmth and sank his chin on his chest, breathing long, slow breaths, deep down in his abdomen, just like his old choirmaster had taught him to do.

Time slowed down, but his attention was high. It needed to be; right at the very end of the building, almost on that blind fourth corner, a window went up and a figure, dark against the dark, slipped out of it like black quicksilver and slid away, straight up the hill, straight towards Sylvie. He knew there was no time to waste, so, throwing caution to the winds, he ran in the shadow of the warehouse until he reached the end of the College wall. The light from a window picked out a glint of metal in the road and Marlowe slowed a pace to peer at it. Tiny caltraps littered the road and if he had run through them it would be the last running he would do for a while. Whoever this man was, he was indeed cunning, cruel and desperate. He looked up the hill to see the man he sought disappear around a corner. He gathered himself like a greyhound in the slips and gave chase.

The projectioner-cum-vintner checked his weapons. There were at least two men in that house, that house that was nowhere near the hovel where the harlot Sylvie lived. Perhaps she was inside, however. Perhaps this was a house of assignation and the killer he was hunting knew that. Perhaps, even now, the girl was in mortal danger, her throat naked to the knife. Aldred had a soft spot where women were concerned, Veronique notwithstanding, and his gallantry ruled his head now. Any sensible projectioner would have marked the place out, gone back in broad daylight, used a subterfuge of some kind to gain admittance. But Aldred had long ago stopped being a sensible projectioner; there were those who said he had stopped being a projectioner at all.

He found a window to one side of the house. It looked to be large enough for a grand entrance. The man he had been following had his back to him and he couldn't, in the candlelight, make out who it was. Another man stood sideways to them both. He appeared to be handing something to his visitor. Aldred could wait no longer. He grabbed the lintel with both hands and, lifting himself off the ground, launched himself, lashing out with both feet so that he crashed through glass and splintered wood and collapsed onto the floor.

In a second, he was back on his feet, trying to preserve anything that may have been left of his dignity. His rapier was in one hand, his dagger in the other. And he blinked at the others, who just stood there, blinking back at him.

'Dr Shaw,' Aldred said.

'You're the vintner, aren't you?' Shaw said, pulling his hood back for the first time that night. 'What the devil are you doing here?'

'I might ask the same of you,' Aldred said, adjusting his grip on his weapons, to be better prepared. This man was an unknown quantity; he could do anything at any moment.

'If you must know,' Shaw said with a sigh, 'I am buying this book from Monsieur de la Grange here. The Bursar's purse strings are kept as tight as a goat's arse and he'd never let me run to this.' He held up de la Grange's volume lovingly, running his hands over the worn leather. '*Chronica Turcica*,' he said triumphantly. 'I'll wager not even the Parker Library in Cambridge has one of these.'

'And you're buying this . . .?' Aldred was trying to make sense of it all.

'Clandestinely, I admit,' Shaw said. 'On my reckoning for Dr Skelton, it will appear as glue, hides and thread. And in a way, it is, although the ingredients were separate many years ago. As for Monsieur de la Grange, secrecy suits him too. If his many creditors, currently happy enough to be so, knew that he was selling off his books to make ends meet, they would be on him like wolves. Now, would you put those blades away and explain why a vintner should give a tinker's damn about all this.'

'So . . . you weren't on your way to see Sylvie?' Aldred felt he had to check.

'Who?' Shaw frowned. 'No, I wasn't.' And he glanced at the de la Grange. 'Unless, François, there's something about you I may have missed.'

'Nothing that you need worry about, Thomas,' de la Grange said, chuckling. 'And of course, Monsieur Aldred didn't miss a single pane of my window. No doubt he intends to pay for the damage before he leaves.'

Aldred stepped over the sill, turning back and peering in from outside. 'I'll take it off your bill,' he said. 'Terms strictly one day from receipt, Monsieur de la Grange, if you please.' And, crunching over broken glass, he stalked off into the mist.

Marlowe stopped, confused. He had been sure that the man he followed would make straight for Sylvie's room, but he didn't remember the lanes he was running through from his walk with Mireille. It could be that she had been trying to confuse him, or possibly that was the purpose of this circuitous route they were taking now. He decided to stay on his man's tail and see where that led. As long as he wasn't a decoy, sent to confuse him, all would be well. And surely, a decoy would take him further from Sylvie's room. They must be within a street or so of it by now, even though they were approaching from another direction. He set off again, anxious not to lose his man.

As he sped off, staying in the shadows, running on his toes so that his heels, though soft, would make no ring on the cobbles and give him away, a man peeled himself out of the shadow of a doorway. With his hat pulled over his eyes and his cloak wrapped around him, the only pale part of him was around his eyes and they gave nothing away. He watched Marlowe turn the next corner and then was off, the hound chasing the hare; or was it two hounds in pursuit of the same quarry?

Unaware of his pursuer, Marlowe put his head down and ran. His breath was coming like acid into his lungs and down his side he felt the pain of a stabbing stitch. He began to think that Aldred must be right; only Salter, or the missing Abbott, could beat his pace. The other men were older, unfit, used to spending their days behind desks or seated at ease at high table, eating the fat of the land. But then again, the man he followed had kept an equal pace, whereas he had been forced to stop and start, running twice as fast just to keep up. An open mind; that was the important thing.

Around the next corner, he skidded to a halt and nearly fell, his fingers brushing the greasy cobbles in the entrance to the yard. The man from the English College was silhouetted in the doorway of Sylvie's room, lit by the candle burning there. Marlowe heard him call out.

'*Est-ce que tu fais ce soir l'enterprise?*'

Now there was a man who had never visited a prostitute before. The formal request was not what any girl making a living on the street would recognize. Usually it was a grunt and a quick jump, money on the table and out of the door before your britches were laced. Some men didn't even bother with unlacing, just hauling out what was necessary to do the business and expecting the girl to do the same. He quickened his pace and was flattened against the wall outside the door in a wink.

'Madame?' he heard the low voice call. 'Madame?' There was

a susurration of heavy fabric as the curtain was drawn aside. 'Madame?' The wheedling voice was much fainter now and Marlowe sensed rather than heard the swish of metal on metal as the man drew his dagger, to plunge it over and over and over into the shape on the bed.

'Bitch!' Ah, now, that was loud enough for anyone to hear. Even Sylvie and Mireille, in their little room under the eaves across the courtyard probably heard it. Certainly, Marlowe's pursuer heard it, hidden in the darkness of the entry to the yard. He stepped forward a pace, keeping the same distance between him and the projectioner until he stepped into the room. Then the second hound in the chase moved up to take his place, flattened against the wall outside the low door.

The curtain quivered and a dark shape stepped through, the dagger still in its hand. The head was hanging low under its monk's hood and the shoulders were sagging. But only for a moment. At the sound of Marlowe's clearing of the throat, they squared for battle and the blade came up to point ahead, exactly at his throat.

Marlowe blinked, then collected himself. 'Well,' he said, as though the tip of a blade was not a pace away from killing him where he stood. 'I had not expected you, Dr Skelton.'

Skelton laughed, a sudden, harsh sound in the tiny room. 'May I ask why not?' he said.

'That is not quite true,' Marlowe corrected himself. 'I had you on my list, but you were not at the top. I hadn't had you down for a passionate man.'

'What has passion to do with it?' Skelton said, edging his foot a fraction nearer and with it the tip of his blade. His eyes flickered to Marlowe's right hand. 'Please hold your hand – both hands, perhaps, for safety's sake – out to your sides. Now, without bringing your hands in more than you must, put your hands on your head.'

Marlowe did so. 'This must look very foolish, Dr Skelton,' he said.

'There is no one to see, sadly for you,' Skelton said. 'And if it prevents you from stabbing me, you may wear a daisy in your arse for all I care.'

'Arse, Dr Skelton? I had no idea you could be so very Rabelaisian.'

'If I can't sound like a Catholic monk around here, Dominus Marlowe, which of us can? I spend my life being polite, pedantic, all the things that go with the life of a Bursar. Surely, as I am about to slice your throat open, you will allow me a little latitude?'

'You can curse till God covers His ears,' Marlowe told him. 'I wasn't criticizing, simply remarking that such language is not like you.'

'But you don't know what is like me, do you, Dominus Marlowe?' he asked, his tongue almost dripping with acid as he crept another inch forward. 'No one knows what is like me, even William Allen, who has known me all my adult life. William, who travels the world, Rome, London, Canterbury – although mostly Rome lately, I confess – who dresses like a roisterer when he is away from the College. William, who has a wife somewhere. Oh, yes, you may look surprised. He wasn't always as you see him now. And often, about three times a year, he hears her siren call and off he goes. He comes back like the cat that has had the cream.'

'And yet, you didn't kill the Master, Dr Skelton.'

'Ah, Dominus Marlowe. You misspoke. You mean, I haven't killed him *yet*.'

Marlowe edged towards the door, just by the thickness of a hair, but Skelton saw and moved forward twice as far.

'Don't hurry to get to the door, Dominus Marlowe. I have promised myself a little indulgence, if you will excuse the word. Because I am going to kill you soon, I am going to tell you everything I have done. A confession, if you will. I can't say that my soul hangs heavy, but it is good for a man sometimes to do a little stocktaking, a little balance sheet of the good and evil he has done. We have until you reach the door. So if you want to know everything before you die, move slowly.'

'Your balance sheet is rather heavy on one side,' Marlowe said, mildly. 'I know mine is a very patchy sort of thing and sometimes it is hard to tell whether things are white or black.'

'I have never done an evil thing,' Skelton announced proudly.

Marlowe gestured with his head towards the room beyond the curtain. 'You stabbed at what you thought was Sylvie quite frenziedly,' he said.

'Yes,' Skelton replied, with the air of an injured schoolboy found with his hand in the sugar jar, 'but it wasn't her, was it? It was her pillows.'

'You meant it to be her, though,' the projectioner pointed out. 'It might not have been her, even. It could have been some poor, innocent . . .'

Skelton waved the blade at him and stepped half a pace closer. 'An innocent customer, were you about to say? An innocent customer? Coming here with lust in his heart, spending money that should have been putting bread into the mouths of his children? Innocent! I think not.' He spat on the floor, spittle trailing from his mouth to his shoulder. He wiped it away with his free hand.

'So, no one is innocent.'

'Of course not. We are born in sin.' Skelton looked infinitely smug and took a step forward, matched by Marlowe by a backwards pace.

'You decided to clean sin from the English College?' It was a simple question, but Skelton laughed when he heard it.

'Yes, let's just say I decided to clean sin from the English College, shall we?' he said. 'That's all we have time for before you reach the door. In fact –' he glanced around him – 'this room is very small. I'm not sure we have time for all of the English College, even. So, we'll leave out my mother, my tutors – technically only three of them, the fourth was an accident on the stairs, these things happen – and the first few at the College. Let's go straight to Leonard Skirrell. You have met him, in a manner of speaking.'

'Stabbed in the heart.' Marlowe remembered the dark stain on the priest's chest.

'Well done. Not my subtlest job, possibly, but effective. He was in the habit of prostrating himself in front of the altar, for hours at a time. He had lost his faith, you see. Not just the faith that we all share here in the English College – all save you, Dominus Marlowe, I fear – but faith in God altogether. He wanted it back, I will grant him that. He missed it, it was driving him mad. But he said that, when he listened for God's voice, there was no one there.'

Marlowe raised an eyebrow and Skelton took a step nearer.

'So, I blew out the sanctuary light in the chapel. He was in the habit of going there when it was empty, by the light of that one flame. He groped his way in the dark, bared his breast and threw himself onto the floor.'

'Onto a dagger.'

'Not quite,' Skelton said. 'Onto a fine blade I had secured there, by scraping a little mortar from between the flags. It wasn't a pretty sight, by all accounts. He had . . . flopped around quite a bit. Not as neat as I had hoped, but . . . well, there it is.'

Marlowe saw him prepare for another step and stopped him with a question. 'Charles Russell?'

'A filthy sodomite. No one was safe.'

'Just a lonely boy, far from home, is what I heard.'

Skelton sneered and took another step. 'Gossip can cut both ways. Laurenticus?' he said, mimicking Marlowe's voice with its precise university vowels. 'Fornicator. Brooke? Thief. And now, you. What label can I conveniently place you under in my book of my soul's accounting?'

Marlowe laughed. 'I have done so much, you may find it hard to find me a place.'

'I don't like to repeat myself,' Skelton said, his eyes blazing. 'But I think I will have to take advantage of our location. So, fornicator it is.' He stepped forward.

'Don't rush things,' Marlowe said. 'Everyone in the English College knows I never attend church services unless I have to. Why don't you list me under unbeliever, and then you have filled that niche.'

'You tempt me, Dominus Marlowe. But how can I label you as unbeliever, here in a whore's room?'

'Why don't we walk down the hill to the cathedral?' Marlowe suggested, as though planning a picnic. 'You could do something interesting to my body on the altar. That would drive the point home.' He winced as he saw a good line fly into the air – if he died, no one would ever hear that line again, and it was a shame. Once a University wit, always a University wit, even with death at the door.

'I could kill you here and carry you.' Skelton was advancing now, spittle flying from his lips.

'Surely, even in Rheims, even in this quarter, that would attract attention,' said Marlowe, desperate to keep the man talking.

'No one has seen me yet,' Skelton said. 'God shields my acts as I do His work.'

Oh, God, Marlowe thought, *if you're listening to him you must be able to hear me as well. We are only a cloth yard apart. He is as mad as any man I have ever met, and I have met some mad men in my time. He means to cleanse this College of evil in Your Name, for Your greater glory. Is that what You want?*

'Can we pray before you kill me?' Marlowe said.

'Pray? An unbeliever like you?' Skelton's eyes had lost their madness and now he was just a cold and logical Bursar. 'I think not. But you are right, the cathedral is the right place for you to meet your end.' Suddenly and before Marlowe could react, he grabbed him by the hair and pulled him to him, the projectioner's back against his chest. 'Walk with me and don't struggle,' he hissed in his ear, 'and I will make sure your death is quick and painless.'

'I'm in pain now, since you mention it,' Marlowe said, tears springing to his eyes. He leaned his head back, to try to reduce the strain on the roots of his hair near the temple. 'Can you release me just a little?'

They stepped through the door, one behind the other and Marlowe felt the cold breath of frost on his face. With luck, it would be slippery underfoot and he would be able to make his move then. Each step could bring a new plan, but for now the important thing was to keep him talking.

'Can you just release me for a minute?' he said. 'Just to let me get more comfortable? We will draw a lot of attention if we walk down the hill like this.'

The pressure on his hair stopped, to be replaced by an iron hand on his shoulder. It seemed to weigh a ton. Then, the hand clawed down his back and he was pushed forward onto his hands and knees as the weight hit his thighs. He lay there, pinned to the ground by a dead weight across one leg and both feet, twisted round uncomfortably on the ground. He had felt no pain, but thought this must be how it feels when a sharp blade has severed the spine. This is how it feels in the moment before all feeling stops. He let his head drop to the greasy cobbles and waited.

'Get up and stop behaving like such a girl,' a voice came from above his head. Twisting round to look up, he had a worm's eye view of Peregrine Salter, a dripping dagger in one hand. With the other, he leaned down and hauled Marlowe to his feet. They looked down at the man lying sprawled on the ground.

'Is he dead?' Marlowe asked.

'I don't know,' Salter said, giving him a prod with his foot. 'I hope so, for his sake. He would have spent what remained of his life chained up somewhere, for what he has done.'

'The English College is powerful,' Marlowe said. 'They would probably have taken him in and nursed him.'

'Hmm. I doubt it. But, wait a minute.' Salter knelt by the dead man and bowed his head, '*Subveníte, Sancti Dei, occúrrite, Angeli Dómini,*' he began.

Marlowe frowned. 'You just killed him. And you're praying over him?'

Salter looked up at him, a sweet smile on his face. 'Oh, Dominus Marlowe,' he said, shaking his head. 'You'll never understand us Catholics if you live with us until your dying day.' He paused. 'Which you almost did, of course. Please, let me continue.'

'I really think we ought to get away from here. The Watch is not that bright but they are not so stupid that they will ignore two fit young men, with daggers at their backs, saying prayers over a man who is still warm.'

'He is still warm, my point exactly,' Salter said, bending his head again. He whispered the rest of the prayer under his breath. 'I feel better now,' he said. 'It would have been a mortal sin to let him die without the prayer for the dying being said over him.'

'But we can go now?' Marlowe asked, pulling on Salter's arm. Windows and doors were beginning to open around the courtyard and it was time they were gone.

After a while, as they walked down the hill, Salter spoke. 'May I ask you a question, Kit, if I may call you that?'

'Is that the question? In that case, the answer is yes, of course you may.'

'No.' Salter laughed. 'That isn't the question. The question is: who are you? Who are you really?'

'I always find this really annoying when it happens to me,'

Marlowe said. 'I am going to answer your question with one of my own. Are you Matthew Baxter?'

Salter stopped in his tracks and faced Marlowe, his hand going to the wiped blade at his back. 'What a strange question,' he said.

'Does it have an answer?'

'Yes. Yes, it does have an answer.' The tension beat like a drum in Salter's throat.

'Which is?'

'Yes, I am Matthew Baxter. So, now you can answer my question. Who are you? Really.'

'I'm someone you have never met.' Marlowe said. 'I am also someone who knows the word "chunter", as anyone from Yorkshire would. My guess is, you've never been further north than the Thames in your life.'

'Damn,' Baxter said, smiling, 'and I thought I'd been so convincing.'

Marlowe extended his hand. 'It was good to meet you, Matthew Baxter. I owe you my life. Now go and live the rest of yours. And please, for your sake, no more conspiracies.'

EIGHTEEN

I t was a disgruntled Solomon Aldred who trudged home past the cathedral that night. He told himself that it was luck of the draw. There was no guarantee of course, that Marlowe's ruse would work in the first place, draw the killer out of the shadows. As it was, he, Aldred, had chosen the wrong gate. He couldn't be blamed for that. He hoped Marlowe had had better luck. But still, he felt a little silly and not looking forward to breaking the news to Veronique that one of her most treasured customers was on the verge of penury. He needed to take stock, he needed to regroup. And above all, he needed a drink.

He was just helping himself to one in a dark corner of the shop when he heard the trill of Veronique's laughter from a back room. He steadied the rattling of bottle on glass and padded down the passageway. The woman who doubled as his lover and his landlady was sitting on the lap of a large Englishman Aldred recognized vaguely by sight. At the little man's entrance, Veronique instantly became a nurse, a sister of mercy, kneeling beside the Englishman and dabbing at a nasty gash on his forehead.

'Look, Solomon,' she said, in English so that everybody understood, 'Monsieur Abbott; I have found him. The poor darling has been through such a terrible time.'

'Has he?' Aldred grunted, swigging from his beaker. 'I've had people out all over Rheims looking for you, Abbott,' he said. 'Where the Hell have you been?'

'Hell indeed!' the Londoner bellowed and winced as the effort hurt his head. 'I was about to leave this damned town of yours. And the English College can go hang. I was just buying some provisions in the market when these ruffians set about me. There must have been . . . twenty of them. I sent quite a few sprawling, of course, but twenty! Well . . .'

'I found the poor baby stumbling about in the *merde* by the fish quay,' Veronique said, fondling the man's thigh. 'He had been hit on the head.'

'Anything wrong with his leg?' Aldred wanted to know.

Veronique moved the hand away.

'It's as well you were waylaid, Master Abbott,' Aldred said. 'Some of us had you down for a murderer. Marlowe . . . er . . . Greene would have cut your throat.'

'Me?' Abbott was horrified. 'How dare you? And by the way, why were *you* looking for me? You're a vintner, aren't you?'

'Yes,' a voice sighed behind Aldred. 'I'm afraid he is.'

All eyes turned to the newcomer, a tall, pale-eyed man in the flashy clothes of a roisterer.

'Nicholas!' Aldred's face had taken on a rictus grin. 'Nicholas Faunt. What brings you to Rheims?'

'You do, Solomon,' the man said and he nodded to the lady. 'Veronique.'

'Monsieur Faunt.' She blushed slightly and curtsied.

'Where's Marlowe?' Faunt asked.

'Where you'd expect me to be, Master Faunt,' a voice said. 'Right behind you.'

'Pat – and he comes,' said Faunt with a smile. He half turned. 'Kit, it's been a while.'

'Hasn't it, though?'

'Well?' Aldred ignored the presence of Abbott and crossed to Marlowe. 'How did it go?' He caught the confused look on Faunt's face. 'Kit was chasing off a murderer, Nicholas.'

Faunt's raised eyebrow said it all.

'It's a long story, Nicholas,' Marlowe said, raising a hand.

'And you must tell me all about it,' Faunt said, 'one day. In the meantime, Veronique . . .' He smiled at the woman, ushering Marlowe and Aldred out of the room. 'Sir . . .' He nodded to Abbott.

'Good God!' Thomas Phelippes, wakened by the voices downstairs, had put on his nightcap and was tottering down the stairs with the aid of a candle, Michael Johns in his wake. 'Nicholas.' He suddenly panicked, checking his hand on the banister, the stairs beneath his feet. 'This isn't one of your tricks, is it?'

'Calm yourself, Thomas,' Faunt said. 'I've only just arrived. Who's this?'

'This,' Phelippes announced, 'is Dr Michael Johns, of Corpus Christi College, Cambridge.'

'Sometime of Corpus Christi,' Johns corrected him.

'Is he sound?' Faunt wanted to know. The man looked harmless enough, but in these Godless days, it was hard to tell.

'No one sounder,' said Marlowe and for Faunt, that was good enough.

'What news, then, Kit?' Faunt turned to the man, 'Matthew Baxter. Did you find him?'

'I did,' Marlowe said. 'He was using the name Salter and claiming to come from Yorkshire.'

'And?' Walsingham's man didn't like the way this conversation was going.

'He got away.'

'Ah.'

'I did my best,' Marlowe said with a shrug and all the time he looked Faunt straight in the eye. For the briefest of moments, the two projectioners tried to take the measure of each other.

In the event it was Faunt who blinked first. 'We can do no more,' he said. 'In our business, you win some, you lose some. Now, to other business. Thomas, you'll be glad to be back to your inkwells and party games, no doubt.'

'If that means Whitehall, Nicholas,' Phelippes said, sighing, 'I'm your man.'

'You . . . Dr Johns. Back to Cambridge?'

Johns shook his head. 'Cambridge has seen the last of me,' he said. 'I thought perhaps, God help me, Oxford.'

'God help you, indeed,' Marlowe muttered.

'You, Kit, have a report to deliver. Walsingham will need to be briefed.'

'Of course,' Marlowe said. 'Do I have some leave owing?'

'Leave?' Faunt gave him an old-fashioned look. 'We never leave this business, Kit, you know that. Take a week or two. Let your hair down. Why not stay in London for a while? Take in a show?'

Marlowe smiled. 'I might just do that.'

'And last – and probably least . . .' Faunt turned to Aldred. 'Solomon, my little . . . vintner.' He clapped an icy arm around the man. 'Sir Francis feels you've been in Rheims too long. Time for a rest, perhaps, a bit of relaxation.'

'A rest?' Aldred chuckled. 'That would be nice. I haven't seen England for a while.'

'England?' Faunt frowned. 'No, no, Solomon. Your . . . especial talents would be wasted there. Sir Francis thought . . . Rome.'

'Rome?' Aldred mouthed the word because he had all but lost the power of speech. He cleared his throat. 'No, no, Nicholas, really. I have too much to do here . . . commitments . . .'

There was suddenly a shriek of female laughter from the next room and a scuffling sound. They all heard Veronique say, 'Very nice, Monsieur, but do you know anything about the wine trade?'

'Or perhaps not.' Aldred sighed. 'I'll pack, shall I?'

The mists were curling along the Cam that Thursday morning and the town of Cambridge was struggling awake. Dr Gabriel Harvey was striding along the High Ward with an even jauntier spring in his step than usual, his robes billowing out like the sail of a carrack on a neap tide.

Only the night before he had received the news that old Dr Norgate, Master of Corpus Christi, was no more. He had gone to meet that great Chancellor in the sky and that left the world for Harvey to bustle in. Today, Corpus Christi. Tomorrow? Who knew, but his imagination soared as he reached the college steps.

The Proctors, Lomas and Darryl, stood by the wicket gate as they always did at this time of the morning. The college bell would soon toll the call to prayer and then to breakfast. It had been so for ever and would no doubt continue. Harvey had other ideas. All this endless prayer ritual – too Roman, surely? God had His place, of course, and it was a useful means of keeping the scholars quiet for a moment in readiness for his daily address. But no, Corpus Christi had been founded in the days of the Old Religion. Time for a new broom to sweep those dusty corners of any lingering traces of Popery. And then, there was the name. Corpus Christi. The body of Christ. All a bit visceral, wasn't it? What about . . . and he felt his lips moving as he climbed the steps, trying it out for size in his head . . . what about Harvey College? Yes, he liked the sound of that.

'Good morning, Dr Harvey,' Lomas said. He saluted. Darryl did too. Then both men clasped their hands in front of them again and looked straight ahead, like stone angels on the parapets of King's up the road.

Dr Harvey? Harvey mentally assessed the greeting. He looked

at Lomas. The man was clearly a vegetable. He had spent the last three weeks explaining what his new title was. 'Master Designate, Lomas,' he said, tapping the man on the shoulder as he swept past. 'But –' he paused in mid-stride and beamed at the man – 'designate no longer.' And he winked at him.

When he had disappeared into the Court, Lomas muttered, 'I'm very sorry to hear that, Dr Harvey.'

Darryl let his eyes swivel to his colleague. 'You're an evil man, Walter,' he said.

'Me, James?' Lomas looked askance. 'You can't mean it!'

And the two of them collapsed in laughter.

The sound of that laughter carried faintly up the Master's staircase into the Master's Lodge. Harvey heard it but dismissed it. Frivolous scholars. He'd compose a sermon later on the need for solemnity and sobriety in the college precincts of . . . and he found himself almost sniggering . . . Harvey College.

So he wasn't really prepared for what he saw in the Master's study. Not at all. Behind *his* desk, in *his* chair sat Dr John Copcott, the Vice-Chancellor of the University. He seemed horribly at home.

'Ah, 'morning, Gabriel.' Copcott's habitual bonhomie nauseated Harvey but he wouldn't let it show.

'Tragic about Dr Norgate.' Harvey's Puritan solemnity filled the room.

'Indeed.' Copcott nodded. 'I heard last night. We'll have the usual, of course. Funeral. Service of remembrance. All the Colleges. All the town's bells. He was a nice old boy, if a little . . . asleep for the last term or so.'

'Er . . . of course,' Harvey said, unfastening his robe and crossing to the hooks by the window. 'Just as soon as I can.'

'No, no.' Copcott leaned back in his chair. 'You must have enough to do. I'll take it on.'

'But, Vice-Chancellor?' Harvey smiled. 'Surely you haven't the time to worry yourself about one college among so many?'

'Oh, it's the least I can do,' Copcott said. 'After all, Norgate had been a faithful servant of the University for so long . . .' He paused, then looked up at Harvey with a small smile. 'And it is my college now.'

Harvey had never been poleaxed, though there were many who

would have volunteered for that particular task. He had however once seen the corpse of a man who had been and he certainly exhibited many of the symptoms that morning. He was rooted to the spot, his mouth open, his eyes wide, his brain not quite registering what he had just heard.

'*Your* college, Vice-Chancellor?' His voice was barely audible.

'Yes.' Copcott broadened his smile. 'Surely, you knew? Convocation ratified it at a special meeting I called last night.'

'Last night?' Harvey's legalistic hindbrain was kicking in now. 'But Norgate didn't die until . . .'

'Eight of the clock, when the poor man breathed his last,' Copcott said, finishing Harvey's sentence for him, 'give or take. May God rest his soul, of course. It was a bit of a rush. And perhaps a *little* unconventional, but clearly we couldn't have a hiatus. No one at the helm, that sort of thing.'

'But, I—' Harvey began.

'Have done a splendid job as caretaker.' Copcott finished Harvey's sentence for him and wiped a finger along the edge of his desk and nodded, smiling at Harvey in a way calculated to set every one of his nerves on edge. 'Splendid.'

'I understood . . .'

'What, Gabriel?' Copcott humoured him, but leaned forward ready for the next move nevertheless. 'What did you understand?'

Harvey would galliard no more with this man. 'I understood that I was to be Master of Ha . . . Corpus Christi,' he said.

'*You*, Gabriel?' Copcott frowned. 'My dear fellow . . .'

'Convocation won't do it,' Harvey snapped. 'You know as well as I do, Vice-Chancellor, the writ of Her Majesty's Chief Secretary of State is necessary for University appointments.'

Copcott rose slowly from his chair and flipped open a leather satchel on his desk. He whipped out a folded piece of parchment. 'Do you mean this?' he asked. 'I assume you are familiar with Lord Burghley's seal?'

Harvey stared at it, beside himself with fury.

'I *do* hope you'll stay on, Gabriel,' Copcott gushed. '*Seconds-in-command* like you are *so* difficult to come by.'

But Harvey had already spun on his heel. At the door he half turned. 'I'd rather eat my own shit!' he growled, his Essex vowels breaking through.

And the new Master of Corpus Christi smiled.

As he left the Court where knots of scholars were making their way to chapel at the tolling of the bell, he thought he heard again that trill of laughter borne on the wind that cut through Cambridge like a knife.

Kit Marlowe prowled Father Laurenticus' room for one last time. He'd packed up his books and left any he'd borrowed from Dr Shaw on the bedside table. He'd said his goodbyes to Antoinette and had blessed her as she had wanted. He reached into the cupboard for his sword and suddenly felt a presence behind him.

'Dr Allen,' he said, turning his head. 'This is a surprise. I was on my way to see you.'

'You're leaving,' the Master said. He was leaning against Marlowe's doorframe, his arms folded.

'It's time.' Marlowe smiled.

'It is.' Allen nodded and held out his hand. 'I wanted to thank you.'

'Thank me?' He shook it.

'You solved our little problem,' the Master said. 'You found the devil in our midst, as you said you would.'

'I'm sorry,' Marlowe said and he meant it. 'I know you and Dr Skelton were close.'

'I thought we were,' Allen said. 'It just goes to show we never really know anybody, do we? You, for instance, have never been to the Curia in your life.'

'Ah,' Marlowe still had his sword in his left hand. He may have to use it yet. 'What let me down? The paperwork?'

'Best forgeries I've ever seen,' Allen said, smiling. 'And I had no idea that Thomas Phelippes was in town. No, it was the Gran Cardinale you claimed to have written it. Alessandro Castel Giovanni.'

'No daughter?' Marlowe asked.

'Oh, yes.' The Master laughed. 'A very pretty one. Unfortunately, she was blessed with a clubbed foot. You claimed to have danced with her in Rome. And I happen to know she has never danced in her life.'

A bell tolled for chapel.

'Lauds,' said Allen. 'I must be away. And . . . Dominus

Marlowe – or whatever your name really is – make sure you are gone by the time that bell stops tolling, or I'll hand you over to the Inquisition and it will toll for you.'

'That's the best offer I've had all day, Master,' Marlowe said. 'May your God be with you.'

'What have you done?' a voice bellowed out of the darkness.

Robert Greene peered over the flickering footlights. 'Er . . . nothing. I've only just arrived.'

'No,' the voice rang back. 'I mean, what have you been in? What plays? Would I have seen you in anything?'

'No.' Greene chuckled. 'There must be some mistake. I'm a playwright. I'm looking for Philip Henslowe.'

'Well, why didn't you say so?' The voice emerged into the pool of light on the edge of the stage. 'I must say, it's probably as well, with those calves. They couldn't carry off most parts, I have to tell you.' The man looked into the darkness. 'Thomas, do we have to have this perpetual gloom? Draw the curtains, there's a good stage manager.'

Thomas obliged with much grunting and cursing and hauling on ropes. The canvas roof suddenly slid back and Robert Greene found himself standing on a little O in broad daylight, much of the magic of his entrance gone.

'I'm Henslowe.' The voice's owner came up the steps to shake Greene's hand. 'And you are?'

'Robert Greene,' Greene told him. 'I sent you a letter.'

'*Tamburlaine!*' Henslowe roared. 'Thomas, it's *Tamburlaine*.' Nothing.

'The Scythian Shepherd.'

Still nothing.

'I told you about him. This is Master Greene. The writer.'

There was a muffled shouting off stage, punctuated by a high-pitched scream.

'Sorry,' said Henslowe, putting a theatrical arm around Greene. 'Thomas,' he tutted, as if that said it all. 'He's a bit . . . well, highly strung for a glorified stagehand. And he's never at his best on audition days. I didn't expect you until tomorrow.'

'I made good time through the Essex marshes,' Greene explained.

'Yes, of course. You're from Cambridge, aren't you?'

'That's right,' Greene told him.

'Well . . . oh, dear, this is all a bit embarrassing, really. Because I wasn't expecting you . . . they're all coming over tomorrow.'

'They?' Greene was confused.

'Well, of course.' Henslowe led the man down the steps, past newly painted flats and rows of costumes, 'Ned Alleyn . . .'

'Alleyn?' Greene's eyes widened.

'Of course,' Henslowe said. 'As soon as he knew *you* had written the play he insisted on Tamburlaine for himself.'

'He did?' Greene could scarcely conceal his delight. 'He is a little young, of course.'

'Ah, but he'll grow into the part. You just watch. Tillney will be here, of course.'

'The Master of the Queen's Revels?' Greene had almost lost the use of speech and the words tumbled out in a series of squeaks.

'That's the chappie. He was *very* excited. Positively clapped his hands, in fact. And, as you know – or perhaps you don't – Edmund Tillney doesn't clap his hands for any old rubbish.'

'He can stop plays, can't he?' Greene worried. 'Official censor, and all.'

'Dead in their tracks.' Henslowe nodded. 'But don't worry.' He leaned in closer to Greene. 'Can you keep a secret?' he whispered. 'Oh, of course you can, you're a University wit.' He mouthed the next words so that Greene wasn't quite sure he'd caught it. 'The Queen herself is interested . . .' He checked the tiring room to make sure they were alone.

'The Qu—' but Greene could get no further before Henslowe's hand clapped over his mouth.

'We don't want to tempt fate, now, do we?' he said through clenched teeth, patting Greene's arm. 'But let's just say I am quietly confident that the odd honour will come our way . . . *Sir* Robert.'

'*Sir* Philip.' Greene gave his best theatrical bow.

'Shall we say eleven of the clock tomorrow, then?' Henslowe asked him. 'You'll have the script with you?'

'Indubitably,' Greene said.

'And, Master Greene?' The Rose man held him for a moment. 'May I say how very much I am looking forward to this?'

'Oh, so am I.' Greene shook the man's hand with both of his. 'So am I.'

Robert Greene splashed out a little later that day. He invested in a new doublet and Venetians, a Colleyweston cloak, second quality, and made sure his ruff was starched just so. All right, so there were sumptuary laws and you had to be careful not to dress too far above your station, but then, after tomorrow, what *was* his station? He was already Dominus Greene, graduate of St John's College in the finest university in the world. He was widely travelled – the opal earring hinted at his esoteric wanderings. And once *Tamburlaine* was the toast of the London literati, he would have to visit his tailors again. *And* spend some time at the College of Heralds advising them on exactly how his coat of arms should go. He didn't really know anybody in London, but a man dressed as he was throwing money around made friends quickly and before he knew it he was picking up the tab for a dinner for eighteen at the Black Boy in the Vintry. He had to sit down when he saw the size of the reckoning. Still, it was all in a good cause and by the end of the evening all seventeen of his guests knew a play was toward and they all promised faithfully they'd be there to see it.

So it was a poorer but no less happy Robert Greene who ambled past the bear gardens in Maiden Lane the next morning, the theatrical work that would change his life clutched under his arm. He was not alone. In the Cheap, he had hired two members of the Watch at their extortionate day rates, just to make sure he got safely to his destination. This was London, the fastest-growing city in the world and you couldn't be too careful. There were some dishonest people out there, and he should know.

A beaming Philip Henslowe met him at The Rose's gate, shaking his hand and ushering him inside. He dispensed with the Watch and followed The Rose's manager up a flight of wooden stairs. All the way, Henslowe was babbling about his plans for the rest of the new building, including a huge turret that would stand out over all the roofs of Southwark. He led Greene along a gallery, their pattens pounding the boards until they reached a door. Inside was a large, low-ceilinged room, lit by the chill sky that lowered over the river.

A handsome young man sat in a chair, one knee hooked over the other, in a nonchalant pose.

'Robert Greene, playwright,' Henslowe announced in his best theatrical manner. 'Allow me to introduce Edward Alleyn, actor.'

Alleyn got up and both men bowed, Greene going so far as to remove his hat. 'An honour, sir,' he smarmed.

'No, no!' Alleyn could not only gush for England, he got paid for it. 'The pleasure is all mine.'

A second figure was standing at the back of the room, far away from the windows in the half light.

'I'm afraid Sir Edmund Tillney couldn't make it this morning,' Henslowe apologized.

'So he sent me instead.' The figured emerged into the full light to stand beside Alleyn and in front of Greene.

'Kit!' Greene squeaked, unconsciously clutching his satchel to him. 'Kit Marlowe.'

'Hello, Robin.' Marlowe's smile was pure ice. 'I understand you have a play to show us. We're *very* excited, are we not, Ned?'

'Beside ourselves, Kit,' Alleyn enthused.

'Er . . . now, look.' Greene had never met Alleyn, he may be able to pull the wool over his eyes. Henslowe, even, might buy his Cambridge bullshit. But Marlowe? Never. He and Greene went too far back for that.

From nowhere, Alleyn hooked a cane under Greene's satchel and flicked it up so that it sailed through the air to be caught neatly by Marlowe who wrenched it open. Greene tried to snatch it back but he found his way blocked by the shoulders of Alleyn and Henslowe and gave up. Marlowe riffled through the close-written pages inside.

'"From jigging vein of rhyming mother-wits"' he read, '"And such conceits as clownage keeps in pay, We'll lead you to the stately tent of war, Where you shall hear the Scythian Tamburlaine Threatening the world with high astounding terms, And scourging kingdoms with his conquering sword . . ." Yes,' he said. 'It certainly sounds like me.'

'Kit . . .' Greene grinned, helpless now and desperately looking for a way out. 'There must be some mistake. I was doing you a favour. Bringing it to Henslowe here to be put on for you, as a surprise.'

'Surprise, indeed,' Henslowe grunted. 'You told me it was written by Robert Greene.'

'Tell me, Robin,' Marlowe said, closing the satchel again. 'What did you intend to do about Part Two?'

'Part Two?' Greene repeated.

'Well, of course. "The Second Part of the Bloody Conquests of Mighty Tamburlaine. With his impassionate fury, for the death of his lady and love . . ." Yes –' he shrugged a shoulder at Alleyn, who was looking dubious – 'I know that needs work.'

Greene looked astonished.

Marlowe closed to him. 'Robin, Robin,' he murmured. 'You didn't really think I'd leave the *whole* play for your grubby little fingers to find, did you?'

'I find there is evidence of a crime here, Master Marlowe,' Henslowe said, putting on his official voice.

'So do I,' echoed Alleyn.

'I think we need a couple of Constables of the Watch,' Henslowe said as he crossed to the window. 'Didn't I see a couple outside a minute ago . . .?'

But Robert Greene had already vanished, clattering away along the passageway to roll and tumble down The Rose's steps.

'Quite an exit,' mused Alleyn. 'I may have to pinch that!'

Henslowe sidled up to Marlowe as they left the room. 'I assume that we *can* put on *Tamburlaine*, Master Marlowe? Ned has learned the part already.' He glanced across at his biggest draw, currently adjusting his cloak in his reflection in the window. 'Or as good as.'

Marlowe let the entrepreneur sweat for a moment, then turned to him with a smile. 'Of course you may, Master Henslowe,' he said. 'And I may even offer you Part Two if I don't get a better offer elsewhere.' He slapped the man on the shoulder and ran lightly down the stairs to emerge at the back of the stage. He drank in the smell of cheap paint, wood shavings and glue and felt his blood stir. There was certainly something about a theatre that made a man feel he could do anything.

There was a scuffle of feet away in the shadows and he stepped to the edge of the stage, peering into the dark that wasn't totally dark.

'Is there anyone out there?' he called, his hand on the hilt of his dagger. 'Show yourself.'

The scuffling came closer, but still he couldn't quite make out the shape, ducking and diving across the space where soon the groundlings would cluster.

The voice when it came was very close and very familiar.

'Master Marlowe,' it said, from the level of his buskins on the stage's apron, 'Kit?'

He stepped back, saw who it was and crouched down to put his arm around the boy's shoulders. 'Tom,' he said, kneeling up and looking at him. 'Still playing girls?'

'No, Kit,' the boy said, laughing. 'Ned Sledd was right to sack me from that role. I live with a nice girl just down the road, we've got a room all to ourselves, use of pump. I'm stage manager here now, and it's a great life.'

Marlowe looked up, to where the cold winter sky filled the magic of the O. 'A great life, Tom?'

'It really is a great life, Kit. Will you not join us?'